Peach Passion
Publications

A
Dangerous
Love

Addicted To Him

JPeach

A Dangerous Love: *Addicted To Him*

JPeach

Contact Information

Email: j.peach0509@hotmail.com, peachpassionpublications@hotmail.com

Instagram: authorjpeach

Facebook: Peach Johnson

Facebook Group: JPeach's Spot

Facebook Like Page: JPeach1088

Twitter: JPeach1088

JPeach

Dedications:

To my two amazing kids, DaJah & Da'Vion if it wasn't for wanting to be better for you guys, I wouldn't have had the drive or determination to finish this story!

Acknowledgments:

I want to thank my mother for her constant support towards my writing. To my amazing niece, Tay, who's the only person in my family that read my story and loved it. Tay, I love you so much, you don't even understand. Just the faith you had in me when it came to my nervousness with putting this story out, and the fact that you read it gave me that extra push I needed to go through with publishing. If it wasn't for that and for my kids, I truly don't think I would have had the courage to do this, which I was nervous as hell about doing. I love you for giving that extra push to put my work out!

To all my followers on Wattpad, God, I love you guys as well for the nonstop support and love each and every one of you has shown me since I started writing on that site! My God, you guys will never understand how much y'all honestly mean to me! With sticking with me through the drama that site brought, it's just so much. For that I love you guys!

A Dangerous Love: *Addicted To Him*

Chapter 1

Peaches

"Fuck, baby, right there." My fingertips dug into the man's head as I moaned out loudly. The heels of my feet pressed into his shoulder blades as I leaned further into the mirror, grinding against his face. Spreading my legs wider, I gave him complete access as his tongue flicked over my clit before latching on the little pearl, sucking hard. "Ah fuck! Ah baby, right there!" I panted as my thighs started to shake.

"Cum for me, baby." The man said as his hand came down on my clit once, then twice before sucking the swollen nub back into his mouth. Licking to my opening, his tongue went into my throbbing pussy, which my walls easily caught, trying to pull it further inside me. Once his thumb came to my swollen clit, toying with it, I was done. My muscles tightened, my body shook, and I came hard into his waiting mouth.

Holding dude's head to my pussy, I made sure he tasted every drop, savoring the flavor of my sweet nectar. There was no telling if he would see me after tonight, then again, with the head I just got I needed to save that niggas number.

Dude sucked on my still sensitive clit once more before kissing my inner thigh. Fixing my panties, he helped me off the counter then pulled my dress down. To see him do that had a smile coming to my lips as well as a small laugh slipping from my mouth.

"What's funny, little mama?" He stared at me questioningly.

"Nothing really." I shrugged. "I mean you're fixing my clothes and shit. You're about the first dude who's done it without me having to get violent with, you know." I chuckled while giving him a smile. "Shit, most niggas act like they don't understand what just a taste means." I said, making him laugh. *Cute.* "So, what's your name?" I asked as he washed his hands. *He's clean, I like that.* I mentally rolled my eyes at myself I would think that *after* I let him eat my pussy.

"Chase, but that's all I asked for was a taste. You're sweet, tho', I wouldn't mind having another." He boldly admitted as he smiled at me, giving a full view of his pretty white teeth.

I laughed at his words. He didn't know how much I was going to hold him to that offer. Chase knew how to work those full lips *and* that tongue of his.

"How about I buy you a drink?" I offered as I grabbed his hand and walked us out the bathroom.

"I can buy my own drink." He shut down my offer with no hesitation.

I waved him off. "I can see that." I took in his six feet, two frame, black button down shirt, black Rolex, 501 Levi's, and a pair of black leather Timberland's, I could tell he wasn't a broke nigga. Even though I did care if he was. Material things didn't matter to me. Besides, he wasn't my man, just a dude that gave me head. Good head at that. So buying him a drink was the least I could do, *and* get his number.

Once we made it to the bar, I called Leon, the bartender, over.

"What's up, Peaches? What you drinking?" He asked while wiping the countertop off in front of me.

"Hey, Leon, let me get a Red Berry Ciroc. What you drinking, baby?" I glanced over at Chase and Leon did the same. Chase licked his full lips and once again I took in his light skin, faded haircut, chin strap beard and his bedroom light brown eyes. *I just love a man with light brown eyes. A very handsome man Chase is.*

"Don Julio, straight." Chase ordered for himself.

"Another one, Peaches? Damn, yo brother gon' beat that ass." Leon whispered so only I could hear.

"I'm a grown ass woman, quit playing. My brother ain't got shit to do with what I do, last, I checked. Now can we please get our drinks? I don't want to sit here looking at yo face all damn night." I snapped, but I knew damn well that if my brother was there and saw me coming out the bathroom with a dude, he would have, without a doubt, beat his ass. Hell, he probably would have tried to kill him and me for that matter.

You could say my brother was a bit overprotective when it came to me. Especially since I was all he had family wise and vice versa. Our mom and dad died in a car accident when I was sixteen and King was twenty-two. That was eight years ago and that nigga still treated me like I was twelve. But I didn't complain even though he failed to realize I could take care of myself.

My daddy made sure we both knew how to take care of ourselves before he died, especially with him being stuck in the drug game. Nigga's tended to get grimy and go after your family just to hurt you. But anyone who knew Dmitri could trust and believe he wasn't having any of that, which was why no one knew he had a daughter.

Once he died, King took over everything our Daddy owned which also included playing the role as father to me. But that was nothing new, King had always been there for me since our dad worked so much. Plus, with him wanting to keep me from his lifestyle, he rarely went out in public with me. King always made a point to be there for me publicly, even, though, folks around thought we were just friends. He really was the active father in my life so how could I complain?

Once we got our drinks, I took him back to the table where my girls and a few dudes they picked up sat.

"Damn Peaches, this how you doing it? Fuck you too then." Mike picked as he flipped me off.

A laugh left my mouth and I waved him off. I didn't take what he said serious. Mike was one of King's friends, he was sexy, no doubt about it, but he was also my girls,

Kim's man and was conceited as fuck. It was cute to a point but sometimes I couldn't stop myself from telling him to get off his own dick, but he was cool as hell though.

"Mike, don't nobody have time for yo conceited ass. Plus, King, gon' beat that ass if he finds out you're tryna sneak into his little sister's room. With yo creepy ass." Kim joked while muffing his head to the side. Kim and Mike had been dating heavily for a few years. Mike was a dog ass nigga, but he loved him some Kim and wasn't trying to let her go. Even with his flaws, Kim didn't seem like she was in any hurry of going anywhere either.

I laughed at them as I pulled Chase closer to me. "Y'all stupid, but this Chase. Chase, that red head is Kim, my bitch. That's Mike conceited ass. Ebony, Angel, and Missy." That was my group of friends, my only friends. Talk about some crazy bitches, hell, I didn't think crazy could even describe my girls.

Ebony, was King's girl, she had been since she was sixteen. Angel, was my black, preppy, white girl, but don't let that fool you. Tiny or not, baby girl had them hands. Missy, was my mixed Puerto Rican and black, bitch. Hell, no description could ever do her justice, just the race alone told people enough about her. And folks always wanted to talk about how black folks were crazy. Kimmy, was the laid back type. She pretended to be the quiet one at times but she was far from that. Then you had me. I was the calm, cool one who kept shit in check and occasionally liked to get head from time to time.

"Bitch, yo ass was gone for a long time. What kept you?" Kim asked, glancing over at Chase, making me laugh.

"Kimmy, don't play with me. I was talking, nothing more." Ignoring their stupidity, I turned back to Chase. "You aren't from around here, are you? I've never seen you here before, especially in this shit hole of a place. So you must be the new boy in town, huh?" I said, gesturing around the medium sized club.

"I've been here for about a month or so. How you figure I'm not from here? Gary ain't particularly small." he said with a raised brow and a sexy, crooked smile.

"Because I know this city and this club. Trust and believe, if you're from here I would know. I would remember seeing someone as sexy and handsome as yourself. You have a non-forgettable face and besides, if you were from here, we would've *been* friends." I told him and again, he laughed.

"So, we're friends now?" A questioning brow rose as he smiled down at me

"I would like to be…" Trailing off, I bit into my bottom lip as I returned his smile.

Chase fingers brushed the hair out my face. "Is that so?"

Hell yeah, if his head game continued to be as good as it was. "Yeah, if you're interested in being my friend you can give me your number." I pulled my phone from my bra and handed it to him.

Chase looked at the phone, then back to me. "What if I said no?"

"Baby, that's your choice. I don't have no gun to yo head. I'm trying to be your friend, not your woman." I told him honestly. I wasn't looking for a committed relationship at that time. I was twenty-four and I just wanted to have fun.

"I like you. We can be friends most definitely." he said, chuckling as he put his number in my phone. As soon as he was done it started ringing.

"I'll be right back. Hold on." I answered the phone as I made my way towards the bathroom where it was quiet. "What's up, King?"

"Where you at?" My brother asked.

My brows furrowed as I wondered what he wanted. "I'm at Voodoo's with the girls, why?"

"Yo, get up outda there. Yo ass got school in the morning—" He started to say until I cut him off.

"Boy, don't be callin' me with that shit, King. I'm grown last I checked." My lips popped as my eyes rolled hard. He got on my nerves so bad at times.

"Who the hell you callin' *boy*? Don't get yo grown ass whooped. My dude just got out and we about to come through. Peaches, don't be there when I get there or that's yo ass. I'll be pulling up in two minutes." With that, he hung up on me.

How the hell he going to tell me I need to leave when his ass two minutes away? What the fuck type of shit is that? A two-minute warning, it's going to take me that long to get to our table.

Letting out a frustrated sigh, I left the bathroom and headed back to the table. As I got closer, I saw this chick by the name of Trina. She was leaning close to Chase, whispering something to him. I had nothing against the girl, hell, we never talked, but her name got around. Trina being so close and secretive with him didn't bother me for the simple fact Chase wasn't my man. He was free to do as he pleased.

I knew I had a class in the morning but I felt that there was more to King's call. "Y'all." I got their attention once I made it to the table. "We got to go. King's dumbass on his way here with some of his boys. Y'all know how that nigga is if he's callin' for me to leave." The only way King would tell me to leave a place he's coming to was if the dudes he's with were unpredictable and kind of off. That was the only reason I could think of if he was telling me to leave. Hell, it was still early, it wasn't even eleven-thirty yet.

Ebony let out a groan before moving away from dude she was with. I chuckled to myself at her action. She knew if King saw that shit, he was gon' beat that man's ass, then hers.

"Why the fuck he got to bring that shit here? I'mma murk yo brother one day, watch, real talk." Kimmy said, making me laugh.

"Right, but he ain't worried about it. Plus. I got a class at eight so I need to get my ass in somebody's bed." I told her while grabbing my black leather jacket and my clutch bag. I then turned my attention to Chase, who was still talking to Trina. "Hey, Chase, I'm about to head out. It was nice meeting you, papi, don't be surprised if you get a text from me as early as tomorrow."

"Oh, I'll be expecting it. Thanks for the drink ma. You better use that number too." he said, making me laugh. *I was so calling him.*

"I will, don't trip." Kissing his cheek, I walked away from him. As I headed towards the door, I opened my clutch and took out my small baby (Ruger LCP). I put her in my pocket before pulling the knife out. Opening it, I put that in my other pocket while gripping the handle tightly. Living in Gary, you never know when a nigga might pop stupid. And Like I said, daddy taught me how to protect myself.

"Kim, you coming home with me tonight? Or you going to the crib? Shid, I don't see why the fuck you gotda leave because Peaches tack headed ass got to go." Mike said as he wrapped his arms around Kim's waist.

I glared at his back and rolled my eyes at them laughing. "Whatever." If Kim wasn't in front of him I would've pushed his ass.

"I was going to your place anyways. I just figured since King was on his way, you were going to stay up here with him." Kim said kissing him.

"King, ain't my damn girl, shid, I'll see that nigga tomorrow." He told her before he placed his mouth to her ear.

"Get y'all cake ass out the damn way." Laughing, I pushed passed them. As we were walking out the door, I went stumbling back from someone knocking into me hard, making the knife poke through my jacket.

"Damn, bitch! Watch where you going."

"Bitch?" I mumbled to myself confusedly.

"Damn, dude, what the fuck?" Angel snapped as she caught me. "You okay, Peaches?"

I didn't even answer Angel back. I pulled myself from her as I glared at the dread head dude hard. "You the only *bitch* out here, and the word you were looking for was excuse me." I snapped at him.

"Bitch—" Before he could finish his sentence, I socked his ass in the mouth before pulling my gun out, cocking it, and pointing it at him. The guy he was with made a move towards me. Quickly, I pulled my knife from my pocket, holding it to his boy's dick.

"N'all, pretty boy, this ain't what you want. Baby, I'm about that life, fuck with me if you wanna." I pressed my knife harder into his boy's dick as I felt him move. "Daddy, don't think for a second I won't cut yo dick off." I snapped, mugging him hard.

"Peaches, they ain't even worth it. Come on before K—" Angel was saying, but it was too late, King was there.

"Peaches, what the fuck you doing? Didn't I tell yo ass to go home?" My brother yelled from afar, but I wasn't trying to hear shit he was saying.

"Little mama, if I were you, I'd listen to my friends." his boy said to me.

"Good thing you're not me because I'm not moving my knife from yo dick or my gun from his face until he apologize." I told him as simple as that with a shrug of my shoulders. Wasn't no nigga gon' disrespect me when he was in the wrong, fuck that.

"Bitch, you better get that fuckin gun out my face if you ain't planning on using it." Shrugging, I shot at the same time I was yanked back, causing the gun to jerk sideways, barely missing his ear. "What the fuck! You tried to shoot me!" Dude yelled, the look of shock was written all over his face.

"Peaches, what the fuck is wrong with you? Yo ass know better." King snapped, holding onto me.

"King, don't come yelling at me. Dude bumped into me and called me a bitch." My finger jabbed in the direction of the dread headed dude. "He got me fucked up. I'm none of these little dumbass bitches that's just gon' let a nigga come at me sideways, baby, I handle mine. Fuck with me, pretty boy on boss, I'll put a hot one in yo chest. Fuckin' bitch nigga done pissed me off, punk ass mothafucka." I snapped before I made a jump for him. I was far from a killer but nowadays you never knew who you were dealing with. A nigga would kill you for just looking at them. So I was prepared and ready to go for any situation.

King held onto me tight, trying not to let me go. "Peaches, shut the fuck up and calm yo ass down."

I snatched away from King, then pushed him away from me. "Fuck you, King! Don't bring yo ass over here yelling when you don't know what the hell happened."

"Who the fuck you think you're talkin' to, Peaches?" His loud baritone voice barked at me. My eyes rolled at him, but I didn't say anything else to him. I knew how my brother, King could get when he thought I was being disrespectful. Talk about an ass whoopin, twenty-four or not, King would literally try to beat my ass in front of everybody. And I just didn't have time to be embarrassed. "That's what I thought. Now who called you a bitch?" He asked.

I pointed to the dude with the dreads, "Him, I don't know his name, but he rude as fuck. *And* his dude stepped to me too." Using my knife, I pointed to the dude's friend. "He was about to get his shit cut off." Ol' dude, I held my knife to was staring at me pretty hard. I didn't like that. "What the fuck are you looking at?" I snapped at him.

11

"Make me tell yo ass to shut up again." King snapped at me. Smacking my lips, I looked the other way before I said something else and got my ass slapped.

"King, who that, yo girl?" Dude that was staring at me asked.

"N'all B, that's my sister." King answered so freely. My brows rose at him in confusion. King was never uncaring or too opened with telling folks that I was his sister. It was always, *she's my friend*, that was it. Even with my confusion, I knew King must have trusted the two dudes for him to tell them who I really was to him.

It also raised the question in my head, *who were they?* King had a couple of friends that he trusted and I knew them all very well. Those two dudes, I've never saw before in my life. Even with my confusion and questions, I kept my mouth shut and my thoughts to myself.

King turned his attention to the dude with the dreads. "Sam, make this the last time I hear you came at her wrong. I'mma body yo ass myself, nigga, real talk." He threatened him in a tone that let us all know he was serious. King pointed to me. "From the sound of it, you owe baby girl an apology." He told him.

Dreads, or as I now knew his name, Sam, spit a wad of blood from his mouth while staring from me to King. "Damn King, I didn't know she was yo sister. I'm sorry, sweetheart, I ain't mean no disrespect." Sam said.

I chose not to say anything because I didn't want to get my ass kicked for saying, *fuck him and his apology.*

"Sam, what happened to yo mouth? That shit looks nasty as hell right now." King laughed before he pulled me into his side, causing my eyes to roll.

King's friend, B, pointed to me as a chuckle left his mouth. "Lil' mama socked his ass for calling her a bitch. But check this Lil' Bit, yo ass hold another knife to my shit I'mma put yo itty bitty ass on your head." B threatened me.

My brow rose at the words, *itty bitty*. Those niggas were all types of disrespectful. Everybody knew you didn't call a short person *itty bitty*, that was just rude and mean.

"Don't ever call me that." I glared at him before I looked him over. B, was sexy as hell, I had to admit to myself. *Damn*, I thought as my eyes roamed all over him. He was a sexy brown skinned man. He stood about six-three or six-four, cocky, maybe two hundred, fifty pounds of pure muscle. I mean his shoulder muscles had *muscles*. He had a clean low cut fade with deep ocean waves. His arms were tatted and he had a set of full sexy pink lips. He was *fine* as fuck.

I bit into my bottom lip as I smiled at him shyly. "Then again keep talkin' that shit, daddy. Because I'll love to put those lips of yours to work." I told him, and he licked his lips, making me laugh. He had a nice set of lips on him. I decided that I just might have to see what those felt like.

"Blaze, you my dude, but I'll fuck you up. I know you just got out and all, but don't come looking this way. She's off limits to all you niggas." He warned them before his attention was turned back to me. "Peaches, I don't know what the fuck you looking at. This ain't that, get yo stuff and get out of here. Yo ass got school tomorrow." He fussed at me.

13

Blaze continued to stare at me like he didn't give a damn what King had to say. He didn't even respond. His eyes just roamed over me as a sexy smirk came to his lips.

I felt my cheeks go hot and I looked away from him. I pushed myself out of King's arms then picked up my handbag off the ground. I glanced at Blaze again and let out a small laugh as I closed my knife, putting it into my pocket. Looking back to King, I held out my hand.

"What?" He asked confused.

"Dude, give me my baby and stop playing so I can go." He gave me my gun back. "Thank you." I stood on my tiptoes and kissed his cheek. "I'll call you when I get home, love you."

"I'ight, you too." He gave me a hug.

"We're gone. We have work in the morning." Ebony said with her arms linked with Angel and Missy's. "See y'all."

"Y'all call me in the morning." Angel and Missy spoke then waved to us at the same time, making us laugh.

"Alright, babes." I waved to them as they started to walk off.

"Ebony, where yo ass think you going? I can't get no hug or nothing?" King said to Ebony.

"Fuck you, Ha'Keem." Ebony middle finger went up as she continued on walking. I knew she wasn't playing with King because she called him by his first name.

"Ebony, bring yo ass here!" King jogged off after her when he saw she wasn't going to stop. "Peaches, get up out of here." He yelled back to me as he caught up to Ebony.

My head shook at King's foolishness as I walked off to my car. Once I opened my door, I looked over to see that, Mike had Kim hemmed up against his car, kissing her. "Bye Kimmy, I see yo hot ass!" I yelled at her.

"Close yo damn eyes, you don't see shit!" She yelled back, making me laugh.

I hopped in my candy lavender purple Camaro Coupe, with the matching twenty-two inch Asanti rims. I started my car up, then rode up on my brother. I let the window down and blew the horn twice. I waved at him then drove off, headed home.

Chapter 2

Peaches

My apartment was thirty minutes away from the club, so it wouldn't take me long to get there. Even so, I was speeding. It was almost one in the morning and I had to be up at six to make it to class on time. Not going to school didn't even cross my mind for the simple fact that I knew King's ol' baldheaded ass would be at my place around six-thirty asking for breakfast. Plus, if I wasn't dying, he wasn't gon' let me miss school.

I said, *let me miss*, like I was not grown and couldn't make my own decisions.

King used to always say, he wasn't going to have a dumb sister. And that, *living in the hood didn't mean I had to be stupid.* He always made a point to tell me that. And even though the statement was true, I sometimes felt that it shouldn't apply to me. For the simple fact, we didn't even live in the hood. More like middle class right up the street from the projects. But I got what he meant which is why I didn't bitch at him when he was down my neck. King was basically a father who wanted the best for his girl.

Once inside, the first thing I did was strip. After that, I went into the bathroom, turned on my shower and then sent King a text telling him I made it home.

After I finished with my shower, I grabbed a pair of hot pink boy shorts and a lime green sports bra with a pair of rainbow socks to sleep in. As soon as I climbed in my king sized bed I pulled the covers over my head and fell asleep instantly.

***

I was passed out, sleeping good, until the sudden loud banging on my door caused me to jump awake. My body jerked hard as the sound scared the hell out of me and I got pissed off. I grabbed my 9mm from under my mattress then left out my room. A yawn left my mouth, and I wiped the sleep from my eyes while I made my way to the door.

The banging suddenly got louder as if the arrogant ass person decided to kick the fuckin' door instead. I was about to pistol whoop the fuck out of whoever it was that decided to act like a freaking lunatic early in the morning. I threw the door open and when I saw who it was a loud irritable groan left my mouth and I put my gun down.

"Why the fuck are you beatin' on my door like that when you got a key?" I snapped at King's dumb ass. I wanted to slap the hell out of his ignorant ass so badly. *He's too old for this shit.*

"Because I figured this was the best way to wake yo ass up. What you cookin'?" He asked, pushing past me. It was then I noticed that he had Blaze and Sam with him.

"I'm not cookin' and yo rude ass friends ain't comin' into my apartment." I told him as I childishly blocked the front door. It was too damn early in the morning and I just didn't have time to deal with no rude ass niggas. Hell, it was bad enough I had to deal with King's irritating ass.

"Peaches, don't start that shit, it's too early for all that." King had the nerve to say.

My eyes slanted and I put my hands on my hips as I glared hard at him. "Says the nigga that was beating on my fuckin' door at six in the morning."

"Come on, Peaches. Man, I'm hungry as hell." King grunted out as he rubbed his stomach.

He was so damn lucky I loved his ugly ass. I let out a heavy sigh, then I opened the door wider. "Y'all might as well come in." I told his friends. Using my gun, I waved them in.

"Lil Bit, you better watch that gun." Blaze warned as he walked in.

"There you go with that mouth of yours. If I was gon' shoot yo ass I would've done so by now." I replied as I walked into the living room. I sat my gun on the side table then grabbed the remote and handed it to King.

When he took it from me, I held my hand out.

"What?" King asked.

"King, don't play stupid, give me my money for making breakfast or leave. I only have enough food to feed myself." I told him while rubbing my fingers together.

His head tilted and he glared at me. "Yo ass be hustling me. I give yo ass twenty dollars every day."

My hand waved off his point. My eyes rolled at King and I laughed at him. "That's because yo ass over here every day eating my damn food. Now give me my money or you don't eat, simple as that." *How he sound?* If he expected to eat, then he was going to pay me. I knew my brother all to well. And when the food was gone, King wasn't going to take his ass to nobody's damn store to replace a thing.

"I can't stand yo black ass. Here." He reached into his pocket and pulled out his money. King then pulled out a twenty and slapped it into my hand.

A huge smile came to my lips as I held the bill up into the light, as if I was checking to make sure it was real.

"Thanks, bubba." I put the money in my sports bra then looked at his friends. "Are y'all eating here too?" I asked, but before anyone could answer King was out his seat.

"Peaches, what the fuck do you have on?" He seemed to just notice I was half dressed. It was also then that I realized I was still in my boy shorts and sports bra. "Take yo ass in the room and put on some fuckin' clothes." King snapped as he pushed me towards the back.

I jerked away from him, feeling embarrassed. "Okay, damn!" I glared at him hard, before I turned and walked off. Once I was inside my room, I went to my drawer and grabbed a pair of red sweat shorts and a white tank top. After

I put them on, I went back into the living room. "Is this better?"

King looked at me with a nod. "Yup! Much better."

My eyes went into my head as I rolled them hard at him. "Are you two hungry?" I repeated my question.

"Hell yeah, I'm starving." Sam answered as he patted his stomach.

I looked towards Blaze. "What about you?" I asked him. Damn, that man knew he was sexy as hell.

His only response was a *hum,* as he licked his lips.

Blaze gaze was intense as his eyes held a sexy slant to them. I didn't know if his stare was in anticipation of breakfast or if he simply wanted to eat my ass up. Hell, which ever it could have been, I was ready to give it to him. My teeth gripped at my bottom lip as I let my eyes roam over his muscular frame.

But since he was King's friend, I knew nothing could happen between us. Even so, that didn't mean I couldn't fantasize or flirt.

I looked away from Blaze, then stared at Sam. My eyes rolled hard at him. Even, though, they did, I had to admit that he was also a sexy, brown skinned guy. He had a little less muscle than Blaze, but he was still cocky with his dreads.

Sam smiled at me, I smacked my lips and held my hand out towards him. "Dude, I'm not feeding you for free." I told Sam before my gaze slid back to Blaze. "Same thing goes for you, daddy. You wanna eat, then pay me." Our eyes locked for a short second before I looked away from him.

Mentally, I let out a groan as I began feeling that sexual tightness form in the pit of my stomach. Regardless of how King felt, I was most definitely going to see how Blaze's lips worked.

"Damn you mean as hell." Sam head shook at me.

My lips pursed together and again I rolled my eyes at him. "And you rude as hell but you don't see me complaining. So do you want to eat or not?" I asked him. "I mean I don't have to cook for you, I got a box of Lucky Charms on top of the fridge and that'll be two-fifty, milk included." My tone was as serious as it could be. I wasn't about to play with them or feed their asses for free.

They all suddenly burst out laughing at me.

Sam dug into his pocket and pulled out a twenty. He held it out and gave it to me, which I gladly accepted and put with King's money. "You better know how to cook too, or I want a refund."

My head shook and I let out a chuckle. I turned my attention back to Blaze who had stood up. His fingers traced across the lining of my sweats before tucking his money into my waist band.

His action caught me off guard, leaving me stuck for a second. I quickly got myself together and mugged his ass hard. I opened my mouth to check him, but King beat me to it.

King hopped up from his seat and pushed Blaze away from me, causing him to fall back on the couch. "Nigga, what the fuck I tell you?" He snapped at him. "B, don't fuckin' play with me, fall back my nigga."

Blaze gave King a slight smirk, he didn't seem fazed by King's hostility whatsoever.

I had to admit, I was hella impressed.

"Can I use your bathroom?" Blaze asked with a wink, completely ignoring King's warnings.

I was most definitely fascinated by him at that moment. I had never, ever witnessed someone who didn't cower away from King before.

"Um, it's the second door on the left." I stuttered as he stood once more. He towered over my five-foot-three self. Being so close to him had heat rushing through my body, making me feel flushed.

I diverted my eyes from his and looked at King. His face was contorted into a mean glare. "King, chill out, damn. It's not even that serious." My eyes rolled at him and I pushed him back before I looked at Blaze. "I wouldn't go there with him. Now, sit down." With a slight shove, he moved back, but grabbed and tucked me under his arm. I had to resist the urge to cover my face, as I felt every bit of twelve years old.

"I'm just letting his ass know, stay the fuck away from my baby girl." *He was so fuckin' embarrassing.* "Gon' get ready for school."

Ignoring his last sentence, I set my sights on the other two in the room. "Let me get showered and I'll start on breakfast. Blaze, come on, I'll show you to the restroom." I wiggled myself out of King's arm, grabbed my gun off the table, then quietly led Blaze to the hallway bathroom.

Once he was inside, I went into my room, closing the door. I stripped out of my clothes then walked into my ensuite and hopped in the shower.

After fifteen minutes I was done. I slipped on my black lace boy-shorts with the matching bra. I then went to my closet and got a pair of grey ripped jeans and my lavender Ed Hardy *Love Kills Slowly* tank top.

Once I was dressed, I slid on my lavender flats then began to comb my hair down, letting it fall over my right shoulder. I then grabbed the money the boys gave me, my wallet, cellphone and book-bag, then left out my room.

I went straight into the kitchen and started on breakfast. I got the pancakes, bacon, eggs, sausage, and biscuits started. I then cut up some potatoes and seasoned them before I put them into a frying pan. The food began to cook, and I made a pot of coffee. That was one thing I needed in the morning to get my day going.

I went to the cabinet and grabbed the plates then I started to set the table.

"Damn, Lil Bit, you got it smelling good as hell in here. I ain't smelt nothing like this in over two years." Blaze walked into the kitchen and went to the stove. He looked over the food and rubbed his stomach.

My lips twisted so I wouldn't laugh at his hungry looking ass. I cleared my throat, trying to get rid of my laughter. "Thanks." I gave him a friendly smile then pointed towards the living room. "The food will be done in a minute, so you can go back in there and sit down." I told him as I finished setting the table.

"Why you wanna get rid of me? I'm just trying to make conversation." Blaze stated as he leaned against the counter.

Turning the stove down, I moved to the counter and leaned against it before I looked up at him. "Okay, sweetie, you got my attention. What's this conversation you're tryna have?"

He pushed off the counter and walked closer to where I stood. He didn't say anything he just stared down at me before his thick pink tongue swiped across his full bottom lip.

A laughed left my mouth and I smiled at him. "If your tongue looking for something to lick besides your lips, I can think of something else and put it to work."

Blaze brow rose and he rubbed his bottom lip. "You got jokes knowing a nigga just got out?" His head shook and he laughed.

My laughter immediately stopped at the word, *jokes,* and I gave him a serious look. "Oh baby, I wasn't joking. It was actually a serious suggestion." I pointed out to him.

His head nodded and he hummed. "I'll take that in consideration." He then pointed to my book bag. "What you going to school for?" He asked, changing the subject.

I don't know why, but his question caused a smile to come to my lips. I turned away from him and focused back on the stove. "Nursing." I shrugged as I stirred up the potatoes.

"That's what's up, Lil—" He started saying until I cut his words short.

"It's Peaches." I corrected him.

24

"What?" He asked as his brows furrowed in confusion.

With a roll of my eyes, I looked at him. "My name is Peaches, not Lil Mama or Lil Bit. It's just Peaches." I snapped at him. It irritated me when a nigga I barely knew tried to give a dumbass pet name. Especially one that started with, *Lil*. "This was a nice conversation by the way. We should do this more often." I spoke sarcastically, basically ending our talk. I was hella offended by the word, *Lil*. "King, the food's ready!" I yelled while making his plate.

"It's about time, a nigga about to die waiting on yo ass." I had just finished with his plate when he walked into the kitchen. "This looks good, Peach. Thanks." He took his plate and sat down at the table.

"Do either of y'all drink coffee?" I asked while giving King his cup of coffee. Once my brother was straight, I made the other two their plates.

"You don't have anything else to drink besides coffee?" Sam asked.

You can never be nice to niggas, but that's okay because I'm charging for everything. "Orange juice gon' run you a dollar-fifty. Heineken, two-fifty. Bud Light, two dollars. So, what you want?" I asked while putting the coffee pot back.

"Peaches, sit yo ass down somewhere and leave him alone, damn." King fussed at me before he started to laugh. "Yo ass would squeeze a nigga pocket until he gave you his last damn penny. Yo ass might as well open up a damn restaurant with yo expensive ass." He shook his head.

King always had to jump in something.

"Fuck you, King, you get on my nerves." I sat next to him and blessed my food then began eating.

As we were silently eating our food, one of their phone's went off. And immediately the three of them started to check their cellphones.

"I don't know why y'all grabbing your phones like you're going to answer them." I glanced at the three of them as I waved my fork in their direction. "There's a no phone at the table rule, I even made a sign." I pointed to the sign that was taped on the wall behind them. "King, you know better." With a grunt, King put his phones away before continuing to eat.

Blaze was the only one who turned around to look at the sign. When he saw it, his head shook with a laugh. He then looked between me and my brother. "King, why you ain't never tell me yo ass had a sister?" Blaze asked.

"You know how niggas is out here. Shid, I got to protect what's mine." He shrugged nonchalantly. "Mothafuckas will be quick to come for her if word got out." The two men nodded their heads in understanding.

"What changed that you told them who I really am to you, though? You usually just say I'm a friend." I asked him.

"Hell, y'all never crossed paths so there was no need to really tell them. But shid, I trust B, I know he wouldn't do no slick shit like that. Especially not with me knowing his folks." King replied.

Blaze agreed with a hum and a nod of his head. "I feel you. But, aye, Lil Bit look like she could handle herself if some heat came her way. She ain't scared to pop a nigga off, that's for sho. If you ain't grab her when you did she would've shot Sam's dumbass." Blaze said laughing.

"That shit ain't funny, her crazy ass almost took off my damn ear." He glared at them before he looked at me. "If she wasn't yo sister I would've beat her ass, then once I was done, I would have asked her to marry me." Sam gave me a flirty little smile as he stroked the hair on his chin. My head shook as I laughed at him. "Shid, you laughing, I'm serious as fuck. What you say baby girl?"

"Get fuck'd up." King warned him.

I, on the other hand, smiled. Sam had some sexy lips. "That depends on what your lips and tongue feel like." I told him seriously, causing both King and Blaze to choke off their food. "Y'all okay?" I asked, beating King on the back because he was choking real hard.

Once he calmed down, he brought his hand up and slapped me hard in the back of my head.

"What the hell is wrong with you, hittin' me like you fuckin' stupid?" I snapped, jumping out of my seat.

He grabbed my forearm and yanked me right back down. "Sit yo ass down, don't act stupid, Peaches. Get yo little ass fuck'd up because you wanna act grown."

I didn't even respond back to his ignorant ass. I simply rolled my eyes at him as I lost my damn appetite. *I swear I can't stand his black ass sometimes.*

"What's this I hear about you and some dude at Voodoo's last night?" He questioned me.

Shaking my head, I pretended not to hear him, so I didn't say anything. He was not about to try and have that conversation in front of his friends. I thought about lying and saying I didn't know what he was talking about. But what was the damn point in lying when he already knew because of Leon's funky ass?

Leon had known King since they were in elementary school. There was only about a handful of people who knew King and I were related and that was my group of friends, Mike, Leon, his brother, Jerron, and my employer, Sly. Mike and Sly, were the only two people that never went back to King, running their mouths about what they may have saw me doing.

"Peaches, you don't hear me talking to you?" King asked as his fork clanged against the plate from him dropping it. I felt every bit of a kid getting scowled by her pissed off father.

"It wasn't even like that, King." I lied knowing damn well it was exactly like that, but I wasn't trying to get embarrassed even more.

"Bullshit, it's always like that. I know yo ass." He accused as he glared at me.

My head went back as a loud, irritated groan left my mouth. "King, it was only head, God! Don't nobody say shit when you have them ol' nasty mouth, ass bitches suckin' yo dick. So I don't know why you trippin'. It's not like I'm fuckin' none of these dudes. It's just them doing me. What's wrong with that? Head is head." I pointed out to him.

"Most definitely." Sam agreed, smiling at me.

"See." Pointing to Sam, I returned his smile.

There was no shame in my game, call me what you want, but in the end, I was just a female who liked to get her pussy ate more than a little bit. My hymen was still intact, so I was no hoe.

If men could get head without being labeled, why couldn't I? I was twenty-four and still a virgin in all three of my holes, so I didn't understand why King's ass was tripping when he already knew that. I wasn't out there fuckin' random ass niggas. I was just getting head from them.

"Peaches." Blaze called my name, getting my attention.

He made my damn name sound so good. "Hm?"

He placed his elbows on the table. I could tell from the twitch of his lips that he was trying hard not to laugh. "That's why you keep making comments on my lips? You want me to eat yo pussy?" Blaze's words had my eyes going wide in disbelief.

Is this nigga tryna get me killed? What the fuck is wrong with him? He was sitting there hearing our conversation, so why would he say some shit like that in front of my already pissed off brother?

That nigga was stupid.

"Damn, I'mma be late. Clean up this mess or don't, I don't care. Bye King, love you." With a kiss to his cheek, I ran out the kitchen to the front door where I grabbed my Ruger, my book-bag, and my keys before leaving out.

"How old is she?" I heard Blaze ask as the door was closing behind me.

I didn't try to hear what was said afterwards. I closed the door and headed straight out to my car.

***

After school I went home to see they'd left my kitchen a total mess, half my beers were gone and they asses ate all my damn Scott Petersen's hot, polish sausages. I couldn't wait until I saw them.

After cleaning up the kitchen, I lounged around my apartment until two o'clock, then met up with my girls at the mall.

We all sat at the food court talking.

"Y'all bitches are crazy." I said, laughing while hitting the table.

"Us, bitch? Yo ass was on one last night, pulling out guns and shit. On what though, dude eyes didn't get big as fuck when she pulled out that gun?" Kim said and we hollered out laughing. "I'm not saying he was scared, but he was surprised as hell. As soon as Mike and I got in the car we just broke out laughing. That shit was too funny." Her head shook and her laughter died down. "But check this, though, ain't them dudes from Marshall Town'?" Kimmy said, making my brows furrow.

"What were their names?" Missy asked.

"The one with dreads is Sam, the other one, Blaze." I told her, causing Ebony, Angel, Missy and Kimmy to look at me. "What?" I asked dumbly.

"How the hell you know?" They asked in unison before laughing.

"Blaze?" Missy asked and I nodded with a shrug.

"Yeah, they're cool with King, but I don't know where they're from. I've never seen them before last night." I told them truthfully.

"You don't know who Blaze is?" Missy asked, looking at me like I was crazy.

"Bitch, you don't either. If you had, you wouldn't be asking his name." I told her, causing Missy to roll her eyes at me.

"Hoe, I was drunk off my ass last night. I didn't even remember this happening *or* the dude I woke up to this morning. All I remember is Ebony droppin' my ass off." Missy confessed as she groaned.

Laughing, I threw a piece of meat from my rice at her. "Bitch, you stupid. Now who is Blaze and why is he important that I should know him?" I asked seriously.

"Dude runs a lot of areas in Gary." She told me. "Like, Marshall Town, Tarry Town as well as the Bronx. That nigga crazy, I heard. Besides King, he the only other nigga I know in that line of business that's smart as hell." Of course, Missy's ass would know, she lived out that way. What she said about him being smart, I wasn't the least bit convinced.

"Nigga ain't too smart, he just did two years." I replied back to what Missy said, pointing my fork at her.

"Bitch, two years ain't shit when that nigga is supposed to have twenty-five to life. And to only do two, baby boy can't be that dumb. Remember Blue from Tarry Town? Rumor is Blaze ass did that shit." Kimmy finished for Missy.

Blue was a cool ass white boy that I had the pleasure of meeting a few times. I heard he'd hit a trap out in Tarry Town and the dude's spot he hit killed him, hell, killed everybody in the house. It was about six other people in there, but I didn't know if Blaze did that. He didn't seem like a killer to me, but I really couldn't say, for the simple fact I didn't know him.

If it was true my brother knew that and brought that nigga around me, to my crib. King's ass must really trust Blaze with his life. That was the only explanation I could think of for him to bring dude around me, period.

If his ass did do that, I was cool on tryin' to find out what his head game was like.

"Okay, enough about that. What are we doing tonight? It's Saturday and I don't have to go back to work until Monday and school on Tuesday. I don't want to be home alone." I hated to be by myself on the weekends.

"I'm with you on that. I'm cool on Voodoo for a while after last night." Angel stated before her eyes lit up. "Ooh, Joe's having a barbeque at the Rex. I think it starts at five." She said, looking at her phone.

The *Rex* was a recreational hall on the beach that King bought about a year or so prior. He had it open for the kids Monday thru Thursday so they could play basketball, volleyball, or whatnot. But as soon as Friday hit, it was a different story. That's when all those ratchet ass hoes came out and you'd find out who was fuckin' who's baby daddy or momma and what bitch burnt whose nigga. Shit got crazy Friday through Sunday.

"That's cool, I got this purple, black, and silver two piece I could wear with a purple wrap." I said more to myself then them.

Ebony laughed before nudging me. "Your purple ass, I need to find me something, though."

"Bitch, you're in a mall with hundreds of stores—" I started, but Ebony cut me off.

"I said find, not buy. Unless you want to buy me something to wear…" Ebony trailed off, batting her lashes. I looked behind me for a split second before turning back to her.

"Do I look like King to you?" I asked her.

"Kind of, you both have the same nose, eyes and mouth… Mmm." She hummed as she continued to look me over.

I looked at her like she was crazy. I swear I couldn't stand her ass sometimes.

"What?" She stared at me with her head tilted sideways, making us laugh.

"Damn, you've been studying that man hard, huh?" Angel asked with a laugh. "I don't blame you, that man is just nasty sexy. If he wasn't with you, I'd ride his ass, no lie."

My head shook at Angel's stupid ass, and I laughed. I stood up, then went to throw my food away. When I returned back to the table, I pointed to Ebony. "E, I got you, though, I need to find some black bangles to go with my swimsuit. Y'all ready to go?" I asked them.

"Go ahead, we'll just meet up later. I got to take my black ass back to work." Kimmy stated getting up.

"Yeah, I got a class in about thirty minutes." Angel replied before she went to throw her trash away.

I turned to look at Missy who wasn't even paying attention because she was too busy eye fuckin' some dude across the food court.

"That's a damn shame, I swear." My eyes rolled at her hot ass before we all laughed at her. "Well, Missy, we'll leave you to that." I told her as the dude started to walk over to us.

"Okay, I'll call y'all at four-thirty to see what's the plan." She told us as she got up. "Bye, ladies." She waved us off as the guy reached the table. "Hey, papi." We heard Missy saying.

I turned my attention back to the other girls. "Kim, when you get off and Ang, when you finish school, call us and we'll meet up. Okay?" I told them.

"Alright, we might just meet up at my house and just leave from there. Y'all just figure out a time." Kim said.

"We always meet up at yo crib anyways. So, it doesn't matter." Angel linked her arm through Kim's and started pulling her towards the escalators.

"I'ight, y'all." I waved them off. I could see that they both were in a rush to go so they wouldn't be late.

"Let's go find me something to wear." Ebony said excited as she pulled me to the first clothing store she saw.

***

Ebony and I walked around the mall for another hour before finding her a red and blue swimsuit along with my bangles from Carson's.

We went to Sassi Soles to find some shoes to go with our swimsuits. Ebony found a pair of blue and red wedges whereas I just went with a pair of simple, black, tie up the leg wedges. By the time we finished shopping it was four-thirty.

"Thanks Peaches, I'll text the girls and let them know we're meeting up at Kimmy's at six-thirty, then we'll go to the Rex from her place." Ebony said.

"Okay..." My words trailed off at her glaring face. "What?"

"Peaches, don't just be saying that shit and show up an hour later." Ebony warned as she mugged me hard.

I waved her off while opening my car door. "I promise I'mma be there on time, seven-thirty, right?" My serious expression had her eyes slanting.

Her eyes rolled at me. "I'mma beat yo ass if you're late." Ebony fussed as she pointed a threatening finger at me.

"I won't, damn, E. Did King not give you some today?" I asked her playfully.

"Fuck you, hoe. Bye!" She gave me the finger before getting in her Honda Civic Sedan.

Still laughing, I hopped in my car that was parked right in front of Ebony's. Turning on the air, I pulled out and went straight home.

Chapter 3

Peaches

I got out of the shower, then dried myself off. Once I was dry, I tucked the towel tight above my chest as I left out of the bathroom. I headed to my closet where I grabbed my swimsuit from its hanger, then laid it on the bed.

After I laid my shorts out, I then grabbed the lotion from my dresser and put some on. Just as I got done, my phone started ringing.

King's name flashed across the screen, so I answered it. "What's up, King?"

"Shit. What you doing?" He asked.

I shrugged even though he couldn't see me. "I'm getting ready to go to Joe's barbeque at the Rex with the girls. Why?" I replied while putting the phone on speaker. I grabbed my swimsuit and began to get dressed.

"Oh, okay. Peaches, don't be up there on that bullshit either. Yo ass gon' fuck around and get one of these mothafuckin' niggas hurt, no lie." He warned in a serious tone of voice. My eyes rolled and I let out a heavy sigh. "No need for that damn noise."

"King, it's not like that. As I said before, it's just head. Nothing more, nothing less, period. So, let it go. Dang, you irritating as hell sometimes." I mumbled that last bit to myself while I tied my top around my neck and back. Before King could catch on to the ending of my statement, I started talking again. "Oh yeah, y'all mothafuckas were wrong as hell for leaving my kitchen like that and for drinking my damn beers. Y'all was bogus as fuck, I promise and you niggas better have my money too." I told him, making him laugh. "Don't laugh because that shit ain't funny, King." I snapped at him.

"Man, chill, we'll pay for yo damn beers." He continued to laugh at me.

"Just my beers? Bullshit, don't play with me Ha'Keem. Y'all replacing my damn hot polish sausages too, and at my prices." King ass had life all messed up if he thought he was only going to pay for the beers and not the rest of the shit they ate.

"I'ight, Peaches, whatever." He chuckled before he got serious. "So, you and yo girl's, huh?" King questioned.

My head shook at him. His ass was so damn hopeless. "Yes, including Ebony." I laughed as I answered his unasked question.

He hummed into the line. "I'ight, I might come through and see what's up." He said. Ebony must have had him in the doghouse and he was only coming up there to make sure her ass wasn't trying to be on no slick shit. "Y'all ass be safe, Peaches. And remember what the fuck I said. Real shit, I don't mind bodying none of these fuck ass niggas." He reminded me.

Again, another sigh left my mouth, it was never ending with him. "I know. Bye, King." I was ready to hang up the phone.

"Peaches, I ain't fuckin' playin' with yo ass, man. I'm deadass serious, yo!" His deep voice raised as he yelled at me.

He was so fuckin' irritating. I swear if it was up to him, I wouldn't have a damn personal life. Hell, I barely had one as it was. "Okay, damn!" I snapped into the phone.

"Yo, check that attitude. Peach, don't get fuck'd up." He laughed into the line. "But I'll see you later. Bye, Peaches."

I think he purposely piss me off at times.

"Love you, King. Bye." Not waiting on his reply, I hung up then tossed my phone to the side. I swear that man get on my damn nerves sometimes. But no matter what, I was going to do me regardless of what King said. I wasn't down his throat when he had hoes on his dick. Besides, it wasn't like I was fuckin' those niggas. It was just oral sex, them doing me.

I pulled on my black shorts, then grabbed my black wedges, putting them on.

After spraying myself with Victoria Secret's Love Spell, I grabbed my black necklace. A pair of purple spiked brass knuckles hung from the chain, which laid right at the center of my breast. I gave myself a once over, not seeing anything that needed to be added or changed, I was ready to go.

I picked up my phone to check the time, "Shit!" I cussed out loud. Seeing that it was six-twenty, I quickly grabbed my wrap and wallet, then left my room.

I swiftly walked into the living room and snatched my keys from the table by the door, then left out of my apartment. I didn't bother to answer my ringing phone because I already knew it was one of my girls trying to see if I had left out. I threw my stuff in the passenger seat, jumped in, then started the car before I pulled off.

***

I parked in front of Kimmy's house to see the other girl's cars already there. *Ebony's ass better not start talking shit.* Going to the front door, I rung the bell and waited for someone to answer. I didn't have to wait long as the door was thrown open. Kimmy's older sister, Mya, stood at the threshold, staring at me.

"Where Kim at?" I asked, not wanting to play with her at that moment.

Kimmy lived with her older sister, Mya, since she was sixteen. That's when the guy her mom was dating tried to rape her. King had taken me over to her house one night. I had just gotten to the door when I heard her screaming. We had gotten there just in time and King almost killed him. He damn near did but Kim was crying so hard and begging him not to. All she wanted to do was get as far away from that house as possible. Once Kim told Mya what happened, they'd been living together ever since.

Mya was five years older than us, but with the way her ass acted, you'd think she was five years younger. Hell, ten.

"Damn, you can't speak, Peaches?" Mya asked, leaning against the door frame with her arms folded over her chest.

"You the one looking at me like you have a problem." I told her as she looked me over, smiling. "Go on, Mya. Don't nobody have time for you today, move." Pushing past her, I walked in the house. "Kimmy!" I yelled.

"Damn, Peach, you looking good. When we gon' get together?" She flirted, jokingly.

Laughing, I shook my head at her. Mya was beautiful hands down and any guy would have loved to be with her, but she preferred women. Mya was a straight fem and that's how she liked her women. Baby girl had hoes. Bitches would straight fight over her like they fought over dudes. Shit would be crazy. Even so, she still pulled chicks. That was a dangerous game if you asked me. Hell, fatal attraction even. Bitches were crazy, possessive at times, especially when you messed with something they considered theirs.

Mya and her women were a disaster waiting to happen.

"Mya, don't even. I don't have time for none of yo ratchet ass hoes to be coming after me because you can't keep that tongue in yo mouth or that strap in your pants." Mya glared at me hard as we walked to the backyard.

"So, you got jokes, huh? Fuck you too, Peaches. Bald headed bitch." She snapped, muffing me from behind.

I turned around and punched her in the chest. "Mya, keep your hands to yourself before I beat yo ass."

Mya let out a cough as she rubbed her chest. "I got you, Peaches."

Ignoring her, I walked fully into the yard. "Bitches!" I yelled to my girls before pushing Mya away as she tried to wrap her arms around me. "Girl, go on, Kimmy, get yo damn sister." I laughed.

"You late, trick. We were about to start without you." Ebony said, holding up a bottle of Tequila in one hand and a shot glass in another. "Yo black ass shouldn't even be involved in this, seeing as yo ass can't ever be on time for shit."

My eyes rolled at Ebony as I snatched the shot glass out of her hand. "Hoe, but I'm here now. So lose the bitchy attitude and give me kisses." My lips puckered up, causing her to laugh and push me away from her. "So what time are we leaving anyway? Because I do plan on swimming."

They all looked at me then rolled their eyes. "Bitch, you can't swim." They said in unison before they looked at each other, then they burst into a fit of laughter.

"Yes, I can! King taught me how to swim when I was eight. Don't play me." I let out a small laugh while filling my shot glass. "Okay, ladies, on three." After counting, we all tossed our glasses back.

***

Ten shots and two cups of pineapple juice and Tequila later, we were tipsy as hell and the sun was killing us.

"We need to go. King's supposed to be at the Rex—" I started saying, but Ebony cut me off.

"I'm ready, oops." Ebony quickly jumped out of her seat only to fall right back down. Which caused her to knock the half empty bottle of Don off the table. She hurriedly fixed herself up, then she stood once again. Ebony fluffed her straight hair. "Okay, now I'm ready." She said, almost tripping over her feet.

Looking at the other girls, we burst out laughing.

Okay, so maybe we were a little more than tipsy.

"Look at her, and she be acting stank when he around. Ebony don't be using my brother because you drunk and need some." I laughed while grabbing my bottle of water.

"That man is fine. I'll be fucking him if it wasn't for Ebony." Missy joked with her as she sighed dreamingly.

"Bitch, don't even think about it. That's mine—" Ebony started until Angel cut her off.

"E, sit yo ass down, y'all ain't together. If he wants to share that dick of his, I'll gladly take it, front, back, side to side, it don't even matter. We can even sixty-nine it." Angel joked, smacking her lips before laughing as Ebony threw a cup of water at her. "Bitch!" Angel yelled with a laugh.

"Hoe, we got back together last night so talk what you know." Ebony told her in a matter of fact tone. Even, though, the girls were joking around with her. Ebony drunk ass couldn't hide her slight attitude, which no one clearly cared about.

To hear Ebony say they got back together had me rolling my eyes. That was typical of her and King. He'd get caught cheating, she'd leave him for a few days, a week top's before they'd be right back together again.

What was the point of the breakup if she was going to take him right back knowing he wasn't going to change? I couldn't do that or be with someone that cheated.

"Come on, y'all, let's go. I wanna dance." Kim pulled Angel up and started dancing with her.

"And I need some head." I added only half joking about that. I seriously just wanted to hang with my girls and dance the night away.

"I can help you with that." Mya licked her lips as she looked me over.

My eyes rolled hard before I waved her off. "Whatever."

"That's yo damn problem, always got that damn tongue out like a thirsty ass dog." Missy told Mya, causing us to burst out laughing once again.

"Missy, shut yo jealous ass the fuck up. If you want me to play with that pussy again all you had to do was ask." Mya winked at her before her tongue ran across her lips.

I think all our mouths dropped watching Missy's face go red.

"I knew it! I fuckin' knew it!" Kimmy yelled loudly, causing all of us to look at her. "Yo ass was coming over here way too much and half the time I wasn't even here, talkin' about, *I was waiting on you*. Oh, my God, Missy. Ugh, why? Have you been to the clinic yet?" Kim's mouth hung opened as a look of shock covered her features.

We fell out laughing so hard, Kimmy's ass was stupid.

"Fuck y'all. It was a one-time thing and bitch I'm always over here." Missy defended herself.

"Missy, yo ass lying but it's okay babe." Angel kissed Missy on the corner of her mouth. "I knew y'all were a little to close up in that kitchen. It's okay, Missy. I got yo back when her hoes come for that ass." Angel said laughing.

We all agreed with Angel because Mya's hoes were sure to come.

"Y'all get on my nerves, I'm gone." Missy fussed getting up from her seat. She walked past Mya who grabbed a handful of her ass. She squeezed it first, then slapped Missy's booty hard. That caused her to receive a punch to the shoulder. "Ain't nobody playing with yo ass, Mya, make me knock yo ass out." Missy snapped.

"Trick, we grown. If you like to play with cat, so what bitch, do you. Just don't play with Mya's kitty." I told Missy while wrapping my arm around her shoulder as we made our way through the house, to the front door.

"She does give some good head, better than most these niggas." Missy sighed before her teeth gripped her bottom lip and she smiled.

I pushed away from her, laughing. "Yo ass just nasty, ugh!" I looked back to see the other girls behind us. Smiling, I hurriedly ran to my car and opened the door. "Last one there buys lunch for the week!" I yelled out to them before I quickly hopped into my car. I started it up, then pulled off fast. I broke out laughing as I went.

***

A loud groan left my mouth and I hit my head against the steering wheel.

Ain't this bout a bitch, here I am thinking I'm about to win this race. When my good dumbass gets caught by a freaking train!

Once the train went passed, I took off over the tracks, then jumped over a curb as I rounded a corner. I was so glad there were no kids around.

After running at least three stop signs, I made it to the Rex at the same time Angel did, but she parked before me. *Hopefully none of the other girls saw that.*

I was quickly trying to beat Angel, that I jumped out of the car, forgetting all about putting it in park. And I ended up hitting the yellow pole in front of me.

Oh, my God!

I threw my baby in park, then I quickly jumped out, running to the front of my car to look at the damage.

Oh, my God!

Maybe I was drunker than I realized because next thing I knew I burst out crying, bawling my eyes out. Seeing that had the girls running over to me.

"Peaches, stop crying, sweetie. It's not that bad." Kimmy said, looking at my car.

"Not bad? Kim, look at that! Oh, my God!" I fussed at her as I cried. "I can't believe this!" I grabbed my phone, then called my brother.

"Yo, Peach, what's up?" King's voice came through the line.

Immediately, I started to bawl harder. "King, I was just in an accident. Oh, my God! I can't breathe, King." I sobbed into the phone.

"What? Peaches, calm down. Are you hurt? Where you at?" King's questions flew from his mouth as concern filled his voice.

"Yeah, my head hurts! I'm at the Rex. Oh, my God! My baby. King, she's messed up, this can't be fixed. I can't believe this." I cried, sitting in front of my car as I heard laughter. I turned to see all four of my girls on the ground laughing their asses off at me. I cried harder as I tried to glare at them but my feelings were so hurt. "Y'all laughing, when I could've died!" I yelled at them before I looked back to my car. "Look at my baby!" My forehead pressed against the front of the car and I just cried.

"Peaches, calm down, I'll be pulling up in a minute. Did you see who hit you?" King asked and I shook my head.

"King, I can't talk, just hurry, *please*." With that, I hung up, falling to the ground sobbing.

"Peaches, get up and clean yo face. It's not even that serious, boo." Kimmy said, trying to pull me up.

"Not that serious? Look at her, I can't believe I was in an accident. Dude, I saw my life flash before my eyes—" I was cut off as they started laughing again. "That's not even funny!" I sniffled, wiping my tears from my cheeks.

I heard the sound of tires as they came to a screeching halt before it was followed by doors slamming shut.

"Peaches!" King called before coming to me. "What happened? Where you hurt at? Do you need to go to the hospital?" He looked me over, slowly his brows started to furrow when he didn't see any marks on me. King pulled me to my feet.

"I'm fine, look at *her*." I cried as I pointed to my car. "How am I going to fix that? This is unfixable! Oh, my God!" I cried once more, falling into King.

"Let me look at the car, i'ight?" He pulled me from him.

"Okay." I said sniffling. I then moved back.

He turned around and looked at the front of the car. King glanced my way then walked around the car looking at it once more. "Where was you hit at?" He asked dumbly.

"Right there." I pointed to my front grill.

"Where?" His face scrunched up, showing his confusion.

I let out a heavy breath then walked to the damage, I pointed again. "Look right there. Now tell me you don't see that." It was then I noticed Sam and Blaze because they started laughing.

"Peaches, I'm about to slap the shit outda you. You called me crying over a damn scratch that you can barely even see!" He snapped. "This shit ain't funny. Peaches, get yo ass out my face before you make me put my hands on you, real talk." King snapped before looking at his friends. "Can you believe this shit? From the way her dumbass was crying, I thought she was fuckin' dying. Not over a fucking scratch you can barely see. Man, her ass almost gave me a fucking heart attack."

Having the accident sobered me up and my shock was fading. I looked at the damage, realizing it wasn't that bad. The scratch wasn't bigger than a pinky nail. "I need a drink." I said. King turned towards me and slapped the shit out of me in the back of my head. "King —"

"If you fix yo mouth to ask why I hit you, I'mma do it again. N'all, fuck that, I should take off my damn belt and put it to yo ass. In fact, let me see you with another drink and I'mma do just that. Dramatic ass, give me yo damn keys. I need to smoke behind this shit, let's go." After King snatched my keys from my hands he hopped in his truck. He quickly parked next to me, then pulled out a blunt.

"Fuck you, King." I mumbled to myself, I was about to turn around when I saw his passenger side window roll down.

"What the fuck you say?" He yelled out to me.

I turned away from the window and walked off, pretending that I didn't hear him.

"N'all bitch, don't run now. She said, "Fuck You!'" Ebony's drunk ass yelled, while sticking up her middle finger at him. "So, we're not speaking now, King?" She asked with an attitude before she walked to his truck.

"I'm hungry and I wanna swim." I told them while pushing what just happened to the back of my mind.

"Yo drunk ass gon' drown, but I'll get in if you really want to swim." Missy said, pulling off her shirt, revealing a cute hot pink one piece.

"Sexy, aren't we? Where you get that from?" I asked as I admired the diamond shaped material that covered from her pelvis to her chest, then it formed into a thin bikini top with diamond shaped patches only covering her nipples. The sides were cut out in the shape of diamonds, and she had the strings around her back and neck tied into a cute bow.

"Mya— I mean my Aunt. Yeah, my Aunt saw this and got it." Missy quickly caught her word slip. My brow rose at her explanation, causing her face to go red. She cleared her throat, then waved me off as if it was nothing. "Anyway, it's *Piink La La* by this new designer, Piink. You know them underground workers got that hot shit. I can give you her number if you want, she makes all type of stuff." She told me with a shrug of her shoulders. Even, though, she did that, I could still tell she was a bit embarrassed with letting Mya's name slip.

My eyes rolled at her before I laughed. I didn't understand why she would be embarrassed about messing with Mya, "Well whoever bought you the swimsuit, it's sexy as hell." I told her before I looked at the other girls. "Hey, we're about to go swimming. Y'all coming?"

"Hell n'all!" They yelled in unisons. "Y'all drunk bitches gon' drown!" They hollered at us again, laughing.

I grabbed Missy's hand and we walked to the beach. Once there, I took off my shorts and shoes, then looked over to Missy. I pushed her down, then took off running into the water while laughing loudly.

"I'm gon' kick yo ass, Peaches. You *better* run!" She yelled from behind me. A few seconds later my head went under the water. I took in a gush of water as I went down. Quickly, jumping back up, I began choking as I heard Missy's booming laughter come from behind me.

"Miss, that shit ain't funny. Hoe, I could've drowned." I fussed at her once I regained my breathing.

"Shut yo crybaby ass up." She continued to laugh as she threw water into my face.

"You bitch!" I laughed yelling at her. I made a dumb dramatic jump for her and missed completely. Maybe I wasn't as sober as I thought.

Missy pulled me up and we started laughing all over again. "Let's get out before you drown us both." Missy laughed, but I stopped her from moving once I noticed Mya looking our way.

"Miss, are you really feeling Mya? Like, for real?" I asked and immediately her face went red.

"No, it was only once—" She tried to lie.

My hands wave as I cut her off. "Don't lie to me. You're one of my best friends so you can be real with me. If you like Mya then you do, but you know how she is." Looking over her shoulder, she stared at Mya before looking back at me.

"I guess we've been kicking it a lot these past three months, but she still be fuckin' with these bitches, though, and when we're around folks she be acting like I'm just her little sister's friend, nothing more." Her eyes rolled and she shrugged. "That's why I'm still doing me by seeing other people. But it's messed up because my dumbass done caught feelings for that hoe." She let out a heavy sigh then groaned. "Am I that obvious, Peach?"

My head nodded and I laughed. "Kind of, yeah." Noticing Mya staring at us hard, my arms went around her waist and I pulled Missy to me. I didn't think Missy was the only one who caught feelings. "Because you're my bitch I'm going to help you out."

"What you mean, help? Peaches, stop pulling me." Missy wiggled herself out of my hold.

Sighing, I grabbed her arms and brought them around my neck. "Shut up and just kiss me before I change my damn mind." I told her. Missy's head reared back fast, and she stared at me like I had lost my mind. I bust out laughing at the look she was giving me.

"Just because I like Mya doesn't mean I like all girls. It's just her." Missy serious expression had me rolling my eyes.

"I think she shares your feelings, so why not make her jealous? Plus, Sam, Blaze and some other dudes is looking over here, staring pretty damn hard. Why not give them a show? I could use some good head and I'm thinking some random with sexy lips is just what I need. You know getting my kitty ate is my only source of sex." I explained truthfully as I glanced around and noticed quite a few dudes looking our way.

I could've used Blaze for the same thing, but after hearing what the girls said earlier, I was cool on him. Even though he was fine as hell, it wasn't worth it, the same with Sam. I knew there was a reason King hadn't introduced us before that night. And if we hadn't bumped into each other, I still wouldn't had known they existed.

"Are we going to kiss or not?" I outright asked.

Missy started laughing as she looked over her shoulder once more. "Fine, but you didn't have to ask like that. Okay." She leaned in and pecked my lips, then pulled away.

"Who the hell are we going to make jealous with that? Bitch, kiss me like you would Mya." I told her while giving a wide smile with a laugh. I was trying hard to put on a show for anyone who was watching. I had to sell our performance and make it look real as possible.

"Fine, Peach. Damn, this nasty, man, you like my sister." Missy groaned, laughing as she tried to stall.

"Bitch, shut up and kiss m—" My words got cut off as her lips came crashing on mine. After a few seconds Missy's hand tangled in my hair as she tilted my head to the side.

"Open your mouth." She mumbled between pecks.

"Bitch, no. This is fine." I replied moving my head from one side to the other, making it look good. Apparently, though, it wasn't good enough for Missy as one of her arms left my neck and she suddenly grasped my ass, squeezing it.

The action caused me to gasp in a breath. She took that as her chance to thrust her tongue into my mouth.

I'm going to beat her ass. I mentally thought to myself

We were pulled apart moments later by the water that was splashed all over us, causing squeaks to leave our mouths.

"You bitch!" I yelled out automatically as Missy started laughing.

"Sorry about that. Can you throw it back, please?" Some chick asked, pointing at the volleyball that caused the splash.

I grabbed the ball, then took Missy's hand and we walked back toward the sand. Once we made it close to the chick, I stared at her. *To me*, she didn't look sorry if that smile on her face was anything to go by.

"I don't think you are, so if you want your ball, go get it." I said before throwing the ball back into the water. "Let's go." I snatched up my shorts and shoes, then took Missy's hand once again. We started walking towards our group of friends.

"Bitch, you got me fuck'd up if you think I'm getting that ball. You better get yo ass over there and go get it." The chick had the nerve to yell at me.

"Bitch, fuck you!" I stuck my middle finger up at her and kept on walking. "Yo dumbass shouldn't have thrown it, ignorant ass hoe."

"You stupid, Peaches, she gon get you." Missy said, laughing as we spotted the others sitting on the beach.

"You better be worried about Mya, she looking mad as hell— oh!" I stopped midsentence as I remembered what she did. My hand slapped the back of her head.

Missy looked at me like I was crazy. "What the hell, Peaches?"

I glared at her. "That's for sticking your damn tongue in my mouth, you hoe." I whisper/yelled, making her laugh. "It was only for pretend. Bitch, you've been kissing Mya. Ugh, that's Mya's tongue. Ugh!" I gagged, joking with her.

Missy broke out laughing and pushed me away from her. "You loved it and probably dying to do it again."

"No, I'm not for real." I wrapped my arms around her shoulders then kissed her cheek. I then pushed away from her. We walked over to the others, laughing.

Once we made it to them, I sat down next to King, leaning my head against his arm.

"I'm sorry I scared you." I whispered to him; I knew he was pissed even though I didn't mean it as a joke. But I understood the seriousness he took behind it because it was how our parents died. *In a car accident.* When he didn't say anything, I let out a sigh. "King—"

"Don't do no shit like that again or I'mma kill yo ass myself." He said while glancing down at me. "I still can't believe you did that, Peach. You were crying hard as hell because of a scratch you can barely see. *I can't breathe, King, how I'mma fix this?*" He tried to mimic my voice, causing everybody around us to laugh.

"Stop!" I whined as my hands covered my face. "I was over my limit tipsy and overreacted okay. It'll never happen again." Blaming the alcohol was my only explanation.

"It better not." King muffed my head to the side, making me fall down.

"Stop! With yo stupid ass." I snapped at his playful ass.

"No, y'all asses should've seen her fall to the ground when she seen the scratch, that shit was too funny." Angel laughed out while clapping her hands. "So, you're buying lunch tomorrow?" She asked me smiling hard. "I'm thinking I want some Joe's Crab Shack. Their snow crab legs be the shit." She moaned, rubbing her stomach.

I rolled my eyes at her. "I guess so, why yo ass can't want a damn buffet or some shit? Oh, wait, speaking of food." I turned to King and punched him in the arm. "Give me my damn money for my hot polish sausages and beers y'all asses ate and drank." I snapped while holding my hand out.

"Missy, let me talk to you for a minute." I heard Mya say from behind us. A small smile came to my lips as my eyes locked with Missy's. She winked at me, then got up from the sand and walked off with Mya.

"Man, gon' with that. Yo ass always got yo hand out." King slapped my palm then pushed my hand away.

Muffing him, I got up and stood in front of Sam and Blaze. "Y'all know that was wrong, especially after I made breakfast for y'all. Come on now." At the mention of breakfast, King shook his head at me.

"I've only known you for a couple of hours and you done managed to get forty bucks out of me. My main lady can't even get that." Sam chuckled before he handed me a twenty.

"You got me feeling special. Just for that, I may make you breakfast without charge." My lips twisted to the side and my eyes rolled at him basically saying, *yeah right*.

I looked at Blaze. "You…" My voice trailed off as I stared at him. I became distracted quick, from the small action of his tongue slithering across his pink lips.

Blaze licked those sexy lips of his, *damn*. His light brown eyes were sucking me in, and I was finding it hard to focus on what he was saying. Hell, my mind went blank as I watched his lips move. I bit into my bottom lip and my eyes roamed over his body as I mentally undressed him. My stomach tightened and I groaned inwardly.

Damn, I needed to get myself right before I lost all rational thoughts and jumped on that damn man.

Why do he have to be crazy, though?

"Peaches!" King's hard voice had me jumping out of my thoughts.

I cleared my throat as I tore my eyes from the tempting sex on legs in front of me. "So, yeah, let's go dance." I told my girls while pulling King and Ebony up.

"You don't want my money?" Blaze asked, holding his money up.

With a shake of my head at Blaze, I began to pull them towards the group of folks who were dancing. "Keep it for a rainy day." Blaze laughed at me, but I didn't care. I just wanted to get far away from him.

But that thought was short lived. As I danced with my girls, I could literally feel Blaze eyes on me the entire time.

***

After five long songs I was thirsty and went to the little table, grabbing a bottle of water. Only to turn around and bump into Blaze.

My teeth gripped my bottom lip as I stopped myself from laughing. "So, you're following me now?" I asked him.

"Damn, why you got to be so harsh? A nigga can't get a drink without being accused of stalkin'?" He asked while grabbing a beer from the cooler.

56

A smile came to my lips and I gave a little nod. "Okay, my bad. Well, I'll be going, nice talkin' to you Blaze." I replied, about to walk away, but he caught my wrist.

"Why you rushing, Lil Bit, you can't talk to me?"

"It's Peaches and we *were* talkin', now we're done unless you have something else to say." I stated pulling my wrist from his grip.

"Man, chill with that fuck ass attitude. I ain't done shit to yo ass but try and talk to you." He snapped at me.

A sigh left my mouth because he was right. It *was* me, and maybe I shouldn't have been judging him off of a rumor.

"I don't have an attitude. And you right, you've done nothing to me. I just try not to associate myself with King's friends, you know. But if you want to talk, then we can. I mean, I'm still standing here, aren't I?" I said, leaning against a table.

Blaze arms crossed over his chest and he laughed at me. "You a mean little thing, ain't you?"

Here I am trying to be nice and he insults me.

"What I tell you about that mouth of yours? Keep on, I'm going to put your lips to work, no lie." I couldn't help myself with that comment, but did he really have to keep referring to me as *little* something?

Blaze let out a deep laugh. "I just got out, ain't had none in two years, don't tease me, sweetheart." He bit into his bottom lip as his eyes roamed over me.

"Daddy, it ain't even like that. I don't tease, if I feel that yo lips can give me a good nut, of course I'm going to offer you a taste. And that'll be the only thing happening. And that's me letting you get a taste. Nothing more, nothing less. Meaning there's no sucking, fucking, or whacking of any kind on my part. But as I just told you. I don't mess with King's friends, so ignore everything I just said." With that I gave him a smile, then walked away and went back to my group.

While dancing with Kimmy, I could feel eyes on me. Discreetly, I looked around, but didn't see anyone. Even so, the nagging of someone's stare was heavy. I glanced around once more, and my eyes locked with his.

He was standing in the same spot I'd left him in a few moments prior. With a smile and a slight wave, I turned away from him.

I felt Blaze's eyes on me, but I simply ignored him as I enjoyed the rest of my night with my bitches.

Chapter 4

Peaches

One Week Later

"Today's Mike's birthday and he's having a party. Are y'all going to come?" Kim came back into the living room and sat on the couch with a cup of water in her hand. "I do not wanna be there like some damn stalker watching over his dirty ass."

We hardly went to parties unless it was a friend or family thing because folks were crazy and there was a ninety percent chance some ignorant ass person would be shooting. Even though Mike was a friend, he didn't live in the safest neighborhood. So, hearing he was having a party, I was kind of sketchy about going.

"How the hell is you gon' be considered a stalker when that's yo nigga? That's an automatic invite." Angel stated, rolling her eyes before she started dancing like the fool she was. "But you know I'm in that thang. Conceited and all, that nigga can throw a party. Plus, I'm man hunting, so I'm there." Angel said way too excitedly, making us laugh.

"Right, you man hunting and you're choosing one of Mike's parties to hunt at?" I asked with a laugh. "That's disastrous, Angel, for real. Half the niggas there probably already have girlfriends they didn't bring and/or they married trying to be on some low shit. We're talking about Mike; he don't associate himself with nobody good. Shid, half his friends probably burning too, you never know. Mike ass probably burning—" Kimmy hit me as I said that.

"Bitch, no, he's not. I take that ass to the clinic every other week. That's my bae and all, but I know his ass triflin'. So, if he wants to keep fuckin' with me it's a must, which he knows." She rolled her eyes and moved her fingers as she stated matter of fact. "Mike ain't fuckin' these hoes raw, he knows better. I'd kill his mothafuckin' ass if he brings me some shit back." Kimmy said seriously. There was a hint of an attitude in her voice, which I paid no attention to. Mike was a hoe, we all knew that, but Kimmy was crazy about him for some strange reason.

Yeah, he was sexy with his six-foot frame, light brown skin complexion. His green eyes had speckles of brown in them. He had a fade with deep waves, that chinstrap beard and penciled mustache, complimented his muscular facial features. Mike was cute, no doubt about it. But he still was a hoe. What Kimmy really saw in him was beyond me.

"Bitch, no need for the attitude. You know if yo coochie burning or smelling or not—" I burst out laughing, as Kim jumped on me and started whacking me with a pillow.

"Fuck you, my pussy not burning nor does it stank. Wanna smell it?" She asked still hitting me.

"Bitch, get up." I pushed her ass off of me as I continued to laugh. "I was just playing, then again, Missy, smell her."

Missy threw a pillow at me, rolling her eyes, making me laugh more. "See, this why I didn't want to tell y'all ass about Mya." Missy rolled her eyes with an attitude, making us all laugh.

"Now you know I was just playing. If you like to play with kitty, then you do. So what? If you thought a joke or three wasn't going to come then that's your fault, hoe. You know us, well me. So, lose the attitude and come smell Kim's pussy to see if it stank." Angel and Ebony started laughing as both Missy and Kimmy jumped on me, whacking me with the couch pillows.

"I can't stand yo ass, you get on my damn nerves. I don't know why you trying to make me smell that funky shit—" Missy started saying until Kim gasped out loud, making us burst into a fit of laughter.

"Oh, bitch. No, the fuck you didn't just go there when yo ass probably done tasted every lesbian's pussy in Gary." Kim pointed to Missy. "I mean, seeing as you're fuckin' with Mya's hoe ass. Who I know done tongued every bitch pussy around this city. I also know her triflin' ass done fuck'd these hoes with the same damn strap she fuckin' you with." Her hand went to her mouth as she stopped herself from laughing. "Bitch you should be the last one saying shit. In fact, is that a sore on your gums?" Kimmy asked, getting in Missy's face.

We all just started gagging at that, me more so than them. "Ugh, I kissed her! I knew my gums were hurting."

Missy hit Kim before muffing me. "See, that's where you're wrong. I bring my own toys and I don't suck the strap I only fuck it." Laughing at Missy's relaxed demeanor as she said all that, hell, I believed her.

"Okay, enough about the pussy and dicks y'all getting and about Peaches obvious none dick or pussy getting ass. Are we going to this party?" Ebony asked, looking directly at me. I didn't mind going to Mike's party, but it really wasn't worth the drama I thought it might bring.

"I'm with Angel, I'm hunting tonight too, so I'm going." Missy said, dancing in her spot on the couch.

"See, these bitches going to be hoes. Which means, I'm going to be left alone. Kimmy gon' be in Mike's ass the whole time." Ebony popped her lips and whined. "Peaches, please come, you don't never do shit. You can't keep letting King control your every move, damn. You got to live your life just like he does. Bitch, yo ass is grown and it's about time you start acting like it." Ebony snapped.

That was easier said than done. I didn't mind going to Mike's party, but it wasn't worth the fight between King and I. "Bitch how you gon be alone when King's going to be there?"

Ebony rolled her eyes at my question before replying. "That's not the point, though." She said making us laugh. She was so damn ignorant at times. "You're going, I don't give a fuck if I have to drag yo ass out this apartment naked, you're coming." She fussed at me.

I didn't even reply back to her. What was the point when I knew King wasn't gon' let me go to that damn party? It's funny saying, *let*, when I was grown.

"Yeah, Peach, you got to stand up to King sooner or later. Yo ass gon be thirty and lonely singing the same damn song." Angel said shaking her head at me. "Look, all of us going to be there, so if he tries to start some shit with you, we can jump his ass." She shrugged. "Plus, I've always wanted to lay hands to him anyways. So, you might as well take yo yellow ass in the room and start looking for something to wear." Angel added, tossing a pillow at me.

She was right, it was about time I started standing up to King. But I knew that even doing that he would still end up winning.

"Okay, I'll come, but y'all ass better help me." Of course, King would be at the party because him and Mike were cool.

"King ain't gon be on nothing, I promise—" Ebony started saying, making me roll my eyes.

"Don't even. Bitch, you know damn well his ass gon' try some shit. What are you doing?" I asked as she held her phone to her ear.

"I'm calling King, now shut up." Ebony waved me quiet.

"Put it on speaker." The girls said in unison.

"Yo?" King answered, making me roll my eyes.

"Hey bae, what are you doin'?" Ebony asked while leaning back on the couch.

"Shit, out, why what's up?" He replied nonchalantly.

She rolled her eyes at his reply. "Nothing, bored, thinking about you." She told him.

King laughed at that before humming. "What about me got you thinkin'? Huh?" He asked in a low tone of voice.

Ebony suddenly got this big smile on her face. "Um... us last night—"

There I was thinking she was tryna play shit off, but her whole damn body language changed. "Hell n'all, bitch, go in the room." I pointed towards the bedrooms. I was not about to listen to them talk nasty to each other.

King let out a chuckle. "Tell Peaches to shut her hatin' ass up."

Ebony laughed as I stuck up my middle finger. "Hey, bae, are you going to Mike's party?" She asked, getting straight to the point.

"Mhm, yeah I'mma be there and hell n'all she can't come." King snapped into the phone.

"Nigga, she *is* comin'. How the fuck you sound? All of us are going and so is she." Ebony stated, returning his hostile tone of voice. "She's a grown ass woman, nigga, if she can't go yo ass ain't goin' either."

I rolled my eyes at that. Since she said something to him about me going to the party. I knew damn well he was gon' make sure I really didn't go. That was one thing I loved, but also hated about King, he took overprotective to a whole new level.

"Shut the fuck up, yo ass ain't even going. Boss, you walk yo ass in that house I'm fuckin' you up—" King's loud pissed tone was quickly shut off as she took him off speaker.

"Hold the fuck up, if yo ass think you goin' to this party and I ain't goin' you done lost yo damn mind. King, yo triflin ass ain't slick—" Ebony stomped to the guestroom and slammed the door behind her.

Looking at the girls, we started laughing.

"Here I'm thinkin' that bitch got pull, only to hear her ass get told she can't go. Yeah, she a grown ass woman, though." Kimmy said, laughing.

"King just be running his mouth when it comes to Ebony. He knows damn well she's goin' to that party." I told them and they all hummed their agreements. King was a punk when it came to that damn girl. She could talk her way in and out of everything.

"So, you're not going now, huh?" Kimmy asked with a shake of her head as if she already knew the answer.

I had to agree, though, it was about time I started doing what I wanted to do. I had to stop worrying about how King's overprotective ass was going to react. They were right, it was my life. I was a twenty-four-year old who was still getting treated like I was sixteen.

Fuck it!

"I'm going, but if he tries something y'all's asses better be there to help me." After I said that, Ebony came back in the living room.

"Yeah she can go, but I don't want no shit outda y'all damn girls, man." King's voice came from the speaker.

Ebony smiled at me before mouthing the words, *we in that bitch*. "Daddy, ain't gon' be no shit, I promise." She replied back while flopping down next to me.

"I'm on my way over there, you gon' blow a nigga when I get there." King had no shame.

Ebony took him off speaker, looking slightly embarrassed, which we paid no mind too. We knew what their nasty asses did in private. Hell, I had walked in on them many-of-times before.

"No, bye King. No, I'll think about it. Man, bye, get off my phone. Mhm, if you do that, then yeah—"

I tuned out their conversation and turned my attention to Kim. "What time this thing starts?"

"Shid, I don't know. Late, when night hits. We gotda get there early tho', otherwise there ain't gon' be nowhere to park. I hope Mike's baby momma don't pop up." Kimmy said, letting out a heavy breath. "Y'all I don't want to have to drag that triflin' ass hoe again." She said with a roll of her eyes.

We all knew how stressful it was to her just being with Mike, but to add a stupid ass baby momma in the mix was bullshit. His baby momma was crazy over Mike's triflin' ass. If it was me, I would've stopped fuckin' with him, especially when he had a baby on my ass.

"If she does, then we'll just beat her ass." Angel shrugged. "It's as simple as that. She can get it just like any other bitch in there that wanna start some shit." Leave it to Angel ol' violent ass to say some shit like that, but she wasn't lying. We never started anything, but we damn sure would finish it.

"Missy, where you going?" I asked as she got up, grabbing her purse.

"About to see what you got that I can wear before you go looking." She told me as if it was nothing.

"Oh yeah, I need to see if you got some shoes that'll match my outfit." Kimmy added to Missy's reply.

"No, the fuck y'all not. See this why I don't like you two bitches coming over here." Ignoring me, they both laughed and kept going. "I can't stand those two hoes." Getting comfortable on the couch, I turned on the TV.

"Peach, what you got to eat, I'm starving?" Angel asked, rubbing her stomach.

"Leftovers from last night if you want. It's some meatloaf, corn, green beans, and mash potatoes left. I don't know how much really left though, King came over with that Sam dude and that nigga can eat. Got forty dollas out that ass though."

Laughing, Angel walked into the kitchen. "I'mma be pissed if he did, I'm hungry as hell." She yelled from the kitchen.

The loud knock on the front door had me looking over towards it. The door opened and King, Sam, Blaze, and Mike walked into my apartment.

"Kim, Mike's here!" I yelled from the couch. "Happy birthday." Sitting up, I gave Mike a hug.

"Thanks, you coming to the party, right?" He asked as he sat on the recliner.

Nodding my head, I sat back down and stretched out on the couch. "Yeah, I'll be there— Damn!" Snapping, I looked at Sam like he was crazy. "Yo big ass gon' flop on my damn feet. You see me stretched out and you come over here to sit down." I pointed to the other couches and chairs that surrounded my living room. "Yo ass could sit anywhere. Move!" My feet pushed at his thigh, urging him to get up but he didn't.

Ever since that Blaze dude got out him and King's ass seemed to be joined at the hip. To me it was crazy because before last week I'd never even heard of a Blaze or Sam. Suddenly those niggas were like the best of fuckin' friends.

"Damn, I'm sorry. I didn't even see yo legs right there." He apologized, then grabbed my legs and put them on his lap. "Hey Peaches, how's your day going?" He asked smiling at me.

I stared at Sam, then shook my head with a laugh. Since that night we met his ass had been none stop flirting. King had already gone off on his ass, but that nigga still hadn't quit.

I must admit, though, it was hella attractive to me. Most niggas King snapped at ran away like a scared dog with its tail tucked between its legs.

"It's been alright." I replied before turning to Mike. "Can you go get yo bitch out my room? She in there stealing my damn shoes."

Mike laughed, shaking his head. "Kimmy, get yo ass out her room, you got yo own damn shoes." He yelled, looking towards the back. "That babe got a shoe fetish, you should see my damn room, fuckin' heels everywhere. Fuck'd up thing about that is, her ass don't even stay there."

I laughed at what he said and shook my head. I knew he wasn't lying because her room was the same damn way. It was funny because Kimmy's ass was always the first to say she didn't have no shoes to wear.

"Hey bae, don't be in here talkin' 'bout me. I do stay at your house when I want to, so my shoes can be at your place too." Kimmy told him as she stood between his legs with her arms around his neck. Mike pulled her into his lap and kissed her.

I found myself awing to myself. I had to silently admit that even though Mike was a triflin' ass nigga, he and Kim were cute together. His tall, muscular build with her short, but shapely chubby figure was cute.

Chubby or not, it didn't take away from her beautiful light brown skin complexion, pretty dimpled smile, or glowing dark brown eyes. Even with the extra weight Kim was beyond beautiful, better looking than most small bitches who thought a size two made them the shit. With Kimmy's personality, looks, and the fact my bitch could throw down in a kitchen, the bitch was the total package.

That's probably why Mike's ass didn't want to let her go.

Realizing I was just staring at them, I quickly looked away only too catch the ending of King's sentence.

"...I'm not fuckin' playin', you hear me?" *Was he talking to me?*

"King, chill, damn. It's a party, she can do what the fuck she wants. Last we checked she was grown." Angel said, walking into the room with a plate of food.

"What's that you eating?" Mike asked, trying to make a grab for Angel's plate.

"Boy, get on now, shit. It's some more left in the kitchen." Angel pulled her plate out of his reach.

"Shut yo black ass up, I wasn't talkin' to yo stank ass." King stated, causing Angel to stop mid bite to look at him.

"King, don't make me beat yo ass then make you kiss my stank, round, black ass." We laughed at them, those two forever stayed into it.

"Bitch, I ain't kissing shit. You can suck my dick, though." King said, undoing his jeans. As he was doing that, Ebony hit him.

Angel broke out laughing. "King, don't tease me." She said, then started back eating her food.

"Leave her alone before we have to whoop yo ass." Ebony joked, which made King muff her.

"Dreads, don't be staring, baby, you can get it too." Kim added, staring at Sam who had been quiet, both he and Blaze.

I glanced over to Blaze, he stood, leaned against the living room wall. He didn't say anything, just looked around. He must have felt my eyes on him because his soon jumped to mine.

With a slight laugh, I looked away from his intense stare. Blaze gaze on me had the pit of my stomach tightening as well as a giddy feeling stirring up. I felt a smile trying to come to my lips and I wiped my mouth, laughing again.

"Kimmy, shut the fuck up, he ain't said shit to you." Mike snapped at her. Leave it to his ass to blow shit outda proportion.

"You shut the fuck up, he didn't have to, he was lookin', though. Peaches, he looks like he's about to jump on you." Kimmy said, making me as well as Sam laugh.

"I was thinkin' about it. But she probably got a gun under that pillow." Sam had the room going quiet. The girls and I made eye contact before we all burst into a fit of laughter. "What's funny?"

Laughing, I leaned up, then reached between the couch cushions and pulled out my Ruger. "You can never be too careful, so come on pretty boy. Go on, jump yo ass over here." I pointed my gun towards him and waved him over with my free hand.

Sam scooted away from me, then looked at King., "I ain't fuckin' with you. King, what's up with baby girl and guns?"

Before King could reply Ebony hauled off and slapped the shit outda him. The impact of the sound was so loud I felt that shit.

My hand went to my cheek and my mouth dropped opened from shock. King's facial expression—I'm pretty sure—mirrored mine.

"Damn!" I heard Blaze say as Ebony started going off, jerking on King's shirt.

"What bitch was you just with? And I dare yo ass to fuckin' lie!" She yelled, slapping him again. That second slap brought King from his shocked haze and he quickly jumped up. I did the same because I already knew shit was about to get ugly.

"This bitch leaving marks, huh, for real. Go on' lie, Ha'Keem, you triflin' ass mothafucka! And you gon' bring yo ass over here after being with some bitch!" Ebony snapped, muffing King in the head as she waited on him to say something.

His hand went to her neck and King pushed her back hard as hell, making her fall to the floor. "Yo stupid ass hit me like that again, I'mma beat yo ass! I wasn't with no bitch—" Ebony jumped up from the floor and slapped the shit outda him again. "Bitch! What the fuck I just tell yo stupid ass?" King snatched her ass up by the neck, slammed Ebony on the couch and slapped the fuck out of her. "I wasn't with no bitch."

From the way he said that I already knew his ass was lying and I shook my head.

"King, let her go!" I yanked on his shirt, tryin' to get him off of her, but she wasn't letting him go. Ebony's hips bucked with King on top of her, she held onto his shirt tight, swinging on his ass.

He pushed her hard into the couch, then hopped up. Ebony was pissed the fuck off, the mean glare her face contorted into told us that. She quickly jumped up. Her chest heaved up then down, as she failed to control herself.

"Yo, Ebony, you better chill the fuck out. I said I wasn't with no bitch, unless you're callin' these two niggas bitches." He pointed to Blaze and Sam.

"You really gon' stand here and fuckin lie? Nigga you got fuckin lipstick on yo collar. Ain't this red lipstick?

Please tell me it ain't, you lying sonofabitch. *And* yo ass smell like some funky ass corner store perfume!" Ebony yelled, punching him in his chest before slapping him hard across the face.

King hauled off and slapped the shit outda her, harder than the first time.

Ebony went crazy. Jumping on King, she started beating the shit outda him. Punching, slapping, biting, whatever she could do.

Yeah, King was a dog ass nigga. She knew it and every time she found out he cheated. It was always this same dumb shit, but in the end she never left. So, I didn't understand why she would react that way if she was going to continue taking him back. Especially when she knew how he was.

I just didn't understand it.

"Y'all need to chill the fuck out! I do stay in an apartment! Take that shit outside or to yo own house!" I yelled, grabbing the back of King's shirt, trying to pull him out of Ebony's grasp. But that bitch wasn't letting go, she was whacking the hell out of him on his back, upside his head, everywhere she could hit him. King's ass was no better, he wasn't punching her, but he was slapping the shit out of Ebony and choking her.

"You triflin' ass bitch, I'm fuckin' done! Go back to that bitch you was just with! I fuckin' hate yo triflin' ass!" Ebony yelled in King's face as he managed to grab her which wasn't smart on his part. Ebony opened her mouth and bit into his chest hard.

"Bitch, yo ass better quit fuckin' bitin' me. I told you I wasn't with no fuckin' bitch." His lying only seemed to piss her off more. It suddenly seemed like she got the strength of ten men as she got out his hold and tackled him. King lost his footing and went falling backwards towards me.

I was pulled back just in time as they both fell down with a thump.

"You think it's smart to stand that close to them?" Blaze pulled me against his chest as his arms held securely around my waist.

"I can take care of myself. If you wanna grab somebody, though, get yo boy, please." Blaze hummed just as King picked Ebony up and started carrying her to the back where the rooms were.

Chapter 5

Peaches

Everybody in the living room was quiet as we watched King carry Ebony out. The bedroom door slammed hard as their yelling continued. A sigh left my mouth, and I shook my head at them.

Blaze suddenly let out a chuckle. "Shid, from where I was standing, yo girl the one who needed to be grabbed from the look of it. She whooped that niggas ass." He laughed once again. "Plus, that ain't have shit to do with me."

I felt him shrug as he finished answering my question. Looking down at his arm that was still around my waist, I let out a small laugh. "I think it's safe to let me go now."

Blaze turned me to his front, then pulled our bodies close together. "I don't know, about that. Yo girl looked possessed as fuck. You ain't think so?" He questioned seeming serious, even, though, I knew he was joking. I bit into my lip to suppress my laughter. "So, what's up with you? Why the hell you rolling yo eyes?"

Laughing, I shook my head. "No reason, ain't nothing been up but school, work, the usual. What about you? You've been out for a good week. How's the outside world treating you?"

Blaze shrugged before he leaned against the wall. "I can't call it yet, though, I did meet this one babe, but she ain't tryna give a nigga no play." He explained as his hand rubbed up and down my side.

My lips twisted to keep my smile at bay. "Well maybe she has her reasons to not give you any play."

Blaze gave me a blank stare before he hummed. "What the fuck kind of reasons would she have?" He questioned confusedly, like I hadn't given him a reason as to why before.

I pressed myself more into him, then slowly began moving my hands up his chest to his broad shoulders. Licking my lips, I smoothed out his shirt, my eyes not once leaving his chest as I began to talk.

"There could be a lot of reasons, one of which, you hang out with King and he just so happens to surround himself around dog ass niggas. Two, you're his friend." My teeth sank into my bottom lip as I peeked up at him. "And as I said before, I don't date my brother's friends." Grabbing his arm from my waist, I stepped away from him. "You thirsty? I got beer, juice, and water." My smile was still intact as I walked backwards.

Our eyes never broke contact.

He laughed. "Is it free or you gon' charge me for it?" That was his question.

I didn't answer him. Instead I let out a laugh of my own, then turned away from him. My eyes were trained on the floor as I smiled. I was about to walk into the kitchen only halfway hoping he would follow. I looked up and glance into the living room.

I stopped walking. "What?" I asked the prying eyes of my friends and Sam, as I noticed them staring at us.

"Shid, I been around this dude for damn near a week and this is the most I've heard him say. I thought prison made him lose his voice." Mike exclaimed while looking at Blaze as my other friends just sat there cheesing.

"Nothing, nothing at all baby, we about to head out, we'll be back before the party because Missy and I are riding with you." Angel said as she and Missy grabbed their stuff. Missy tried to hide the grey, strapless, tunic mini dress in her purse, but it was sticking out.

"Okay Ang, try to be here around nine o'clock." I told her before I pointed to Missy. "Missy, I got some black, rhinestone platform shoes to go with that dress."

Missy raised a brow then opened up her bag and pulled out some silver red bottoms. "I got the wrong shoes?"

Shaking my head at her, I turned to Blaze. "You can go in the kitchen. I'll be there in a minute." I didn't wait on his reply as I quickly ran to my room. I went to my closet, then grabbed the right shoes and the black leather jacket I bought to go with the dress.

As I was leaving my room, I could still hear Ebony and King in the guest room arguing. Letting out a sigh, I went back into the living room. "Here, I want my shit back Miss, I'm not bullshittin'."

Missy's eyes rolled up in her head before she looked at me smiling. "I promise I'll bring it back. You're giving me the jacket too?"

Nodding, I handed it to her. "Yeah, I bought it to go with the dress. I want all this back, bitch." I told her seriously.

Laughing, she hugged and thanked me. "Thanks, mami. Come on, Ang, before she changes her mind. Bye Kim, babe, we'll see you at the party. Later Mikey, and happy birthday." Missy called out, while dragging Angel out of my apartment.

"I'm 'bout to head out too, Peach. You cool alone with these two sexy men?" Kimmy pointed to Sam, then towards the kitchen where Blaze was. "I can stay if you want me too, just let me get rid of him." She tried to whisper as her head jerked in Mike's direction.

"Get fuck'd up, Kim." Mike got up and walked up behind her.

"Bae, you know I was playing." She looked back at me, then she shook her head, *no*, while mouthing, *no I'm not.*

Laughing at her, I just smiled. "I think I can manage. I mean, what can really happen with King in the next room?" I asked her seriously. "Not a damn thing."

She hummed to that as her lips pursed together with a head nod. "You got a point. Alright babe. I'll see you later. Peach, don't make me have to come back here to drag yo ass out this damn apartment. You better be there. Bitch, you know I will." I knew she was telling the truth.

"I'll be there, promise." I waved her off.

"King, I'm out!" Mike yelled towards the back rooms as he grabbed Kimmy from behind, then whispered in her ear. *Probably* something sexual because her yellow ass turned red in the face.

Mike let Kim go, then gave me a hug and a kiss on my cheek. "You better show up, otherwise I'm with Kim on beatin' yo ass." He playfully threatened.

My mouth twisted to the side and I pushed him away from me. "I'm coming, I promise. Now get out." With a final wave, I watched them start down the stairs before I closed and locked the door.

"You want something to drink? Here's the remote if you wanna change the channel." I told Sam while handing it to him.

"Yeah, a beer's cool." Sam said as he leaned back on the couch, making himself comfortable.

Nodding, I walked in the kitchen where Blaze stood leaning against the counter. With a slight smile in his direction, I went to the fridge. "Mr. Blaze, what do you want to drink?"

"I already got my beer." He said, holding up his bottle. "But you can grab me another one." He stated before he finished off his beer.

Grabbing two Heineken's, I slid him one then took the other one to Sam. After giving Sam his beer, I went back into the kitchen and poured myself a cup of orange juice. "Yo shit always this full?" Blaze asked.

"Full? You call this full? I'd hate to see what your meaning of small look like." Blaze let out a chuckle as he opened his second beer. "It's probably like a person, no, I'll give it two people. Anything above is a full house, huh?" I asked while sitting on the stool opposite him.

"Something like that. So, where you work?" He asked as he took a sip of my juice. My brows rose at him before I nodded my head. "What kind of work you do?" He continued to question me.

"I'm a medical assistant and I work at a clinic downtown." I replied bluntly while shrugging. I didn't give him the name of the office I work at. Just in case he did turn out to be crazy. "I know you're just getting out, but what's yo profession? And are you planning on going straight or…" I let the sentence hang out there for him to fill in the blank for me. I knew whatever Blaze was into, was illegal, I just wanted to see if he would be straight up with me.

Blaze picked up his beer then came around to my side, sitting on the stool next to me. Grabbing my orange juice, he took a long drink, only leaving a swallow once he finished.

Looking at the cup, I picked it up. "Oh, you just getting beside yo damn self. I offer you a drink and you just taking full advantage, huh?" I asked with a laugh.

He took the cup from me and drunk the rest of the juice. "You can finish that." He gave me his beer and watched me.

He was probably trying to see if I would drink it or not. Grabbing the bottle, I wrapped my lips around it then took a swig. "Now answer my question." I licked my lips and smiled at him. Blaze made a grab for the beer bottle, but

I pulled it from his reach, then finished it off. "You were saying?"

That caused a chuckle to leave his mouth and he nodded at me. "What make you think I ain't already straight?"

Giving him a blank look, I rolled my eyes. "My brother doesn't surround himself with straight dudes. Plus, if you were straight, I'm pretty sure we would've met before now. How long have you known King?" I twisted the stool around so that I was facing him. I sat up straight, then crossed my legs, waiting on his response.

Blaze's eyes followed the movement, then continued to move up my bare thighs as he started talking. "About sixteen years—"

I cut him off with a shake of my head in total disbelief. "Yo ass most definitely ain't straight. Sixteen years, really? Damn." That was a long time, it puzzled me how we hadn't crossed paths until that point. Something most definitely wasn't right about him. Even so, for some odd reason, it didn't bother me. I was attracted to him, learning that bit only added to what I felt. Strangely enough, it made me want to know more about Blaze.

Blaze had a dangerous streak.

"So now that you're free, what are your plans?" I asked.

"I'm a straight dude. My plans, though? Shid, a little of this and that, you know." He stated vaguely with a shrug.

I shook my head no, letting him know I didn't understand. "Not really, but whatever it is can't be good, which means my time will be wasted. Number three as to why you can't get no play." Licking my lips, I held up three wiggling fingers.

Blaze laughed and stood up. He took hold of my legs, then he uncrossed them. His hands moved up and down my thighs before he gripped my waist. He then lifted me off of my stool and place me onto the counter.

My breath got caught in my throat from a small, unexpected gasp.

"That's what yo mouth saying, I could always change yo mind." His thick, pink tongue slid out then swiped across his full bottom lip before pulling the top one into his mouth.

This unrecognizable grunt came from the back of my throat as I fought with myself not to jump on him.

Letting out a shaky breath, my hands slid up the back of his shirt. I pulled him closer to me, then dug my nails into his lower back as my tongue swiped over my parted lips.

"You probably could, and I'd probably let you." Dragging my nails up his back, I moved even closer to him, bringing my face to the side of his, then slowly rubbing against him. "I believe we could possibly have hella fun together." I whispered in his ear before I bit, then sucked on the lobe. Pulling back slightly, my lips trace along his jaw, until they were a few inches from his, as I scratched across his back once again.

Hearing him groan, I smiled while staring into his light brown eyes. "Mmm, we most definitely could have fun together…" My words trailed off as I stared at his lips. "Only, if it wasn't for the fact, you're King's friend."

My tongue flicked over his bottom then top lip, making his mouth part. Our eyes tore apart for a second so I could glance down at his full lips. My eyes came back to his and my smile grew wider as I felt him become hard.

My mouth moved to the corner of his. "And as I said, I don't mess with my brother's friends." Removing my hands from under his shirt, I slid down off the counter, forcing him back. "It was nice talking to you again, Blaze." I squeezed past him, then I walked out of the kitchen with a little more sway to my hips, I didn't give a second look back as I left out. Even so, I could feel his eyes on me.

I walked into the hallway and immediately I could hear Ebony and King fuckin'. Going to the guest room, I started banging on the door hard.

"Y'all asses should've took that shit somewhere else!" I yelled, hitting the door once again, but harder. "Turn on some damn music or gag that fuckin cat, damn!" I hated when they had sex in my house. Ebony's ass always made these loud weird noises, sounding like a wailing banshee as well as a choking cat. I lived in a damn apartment, these old folks probably thought somebody was getting murdered.

I went into my room and slammed the door, then plugged the iPod onto its dock and turned up Trey Songs as loud as possible. Once I tuned them out, I walked into my closet and began to search for something to wear.

***

Standing in the full length mirror, I took in my five foot, three, one hundred thirty-five-pound self. My eyes roamed over my short royal blue, flower cut, lace dress. The royal blue complimented my light brown skin and long straight sandy brown hair perfectly. I turned to the side and smooth down my dress as I stuck my butt out.

I didn't have a huge, ghetto booty, but a nice plump little something going on.

"What the hell are you doing? And what the fuck you got on?" King asked as he walked into my room without knocking.

"Damn, I'm glad I had clothes on. Don't yo ass know how to knock?" I snapped at King.

King looked me over and I rolled my eyes at him. I quickly caught an attitude because I knew he was about to start talking shit.

"I did knock, and you know yo ass not wearing that. Put on some jeans or something." King started to fuss, making me groan.

"King, for real? Ain't nothing wrong with what I have on, so gon' on somewhere with that shit, damn." That was the bullshit I had to deal with, and I was honestly tired of it. I was too damn old to have him telling me what I could or couldn't wear or do for that matter. I was so tired of it.

He got up off the bed and stared at me like I was crazy, causing a laugh to slip through my lips. King stood there with his face contorted into a hard glare. His eyes were slanted, and a wrinkle was in the middle of his forehead. He looked exactly like our dad whenever he was pissed off.

"You look just like Dmitri's ass standing there. King, I don't want to argue with you, there's nothing wrong with what I'm wearing. I think I look good. I'm thinking about getting butt implants, get my Nicki Minaj on. What you think?" I joked as I pushed my butt out once again.

King started laughing before getting serious again. "Peaches, don't bring yo ass to this party on that bullshit. I don't wanna have to kill a mothafucka because you out there actin' hot and shit." He warned as he snapped at me.

"Okay King." I let out an irritated breath, then rolled my eyes as I combed through my long, sandy brown hair.

"Peaches, I'm serious as fuck, yo. Don't bring yo ass to this party doing that shit you be on. I don't wanna have to beat yo ass, but I will. You understand me?" He asked.

I didn't respond to him right away, instead, I finished putting on my lip liner, then put on some clear lip gloss. I rubbed my lips together then puckered them up.

"Peaches! Don't make me slap the fuck outda yo ass." He yelled at me. "You don't hear me talkin' to you?"

"I hear you, damn. No getting head from a random at this party, check. Anything else, Dad?" I rolled my eyes at him while sliding the big black oval shape ring on my index finger. I then grabbed my black chain with the royal blue spike brass knuckles and clamped it around my neck.

"Baby girl, I ain't tryna run yo life, I'm just lookin' out for you, is all. I know how niggas out here are. They'll see a pretty, educated female like you and see dollar signs. They either gon' try leeching off you or try to bring you down and I don't want that, you understand? So if I gotda be the dick of a father to make sho' yo head straight, then so be it. I don't want this life for you." He explained and I knew it was true because King had always told me that. So I knew his intentions were truly coming from a good place. But it didn't change the fact that, he was still hard as hell and it felt like he was suffocating me at times.

Sighing, I sat on the bed, then slipped on my royal blue pumps. I glanced at King and rolled my eyes at him before laughing. "I know, but you should know that I wouldn't let that happen. I know what my priorities are and what I have to do to see them through. You just have to trust me, Ha'Keem. If I make a mistake so be it, let me make it and learn from it. Plus, I wouldn't trust any nigga's mouth that showed up at Mike's party, ugh."

Laughing, King grabbed my black, leather jacket and helped me put it on. "I'ight, Peaches, I'mma fall back a bit, but the first time you step outda line, I'm beatin' yo ass." He zipped up my jacket and I once again rolled my eyes at him.

"You do know I'm twenty-four and not fourteen, right?" My brows raised as I stared at him.

King waved me off and shrugged. "It don't matter how old you are, you gon always be my baby girl." King was such a sucker when it came to me it didn't make any sense. And he was supposed to be this rough, tough nigga. *Tough dude my ass.*

"Hey, what's Blaze's story?"

He stopped in his tracks before blocking my way out of my room door. "Stay the fuck away from him! He's crazy, Peaches. He my nigga, but he crazy as fuck."

The seriousness in his voice and eyes had me laughing out of pure humor. "For you to say some shit like that about somebody is like Lucifer calling Abaddon a saint." King muffed my head back and I punched him in the stomach.

"Peach, I'm serious. Stay away from Blaze, I done already told him the same thing. You don't want to date me. If I had to name anybody in comparison to me, it's Blaze." From the serious look that came to his face, once again I knew he wasn't joking.

"So, he's a dog ass nigga, with hella bitches, baby momma's and all that?" A disappointed feeling settled in the pit of my stomach as I asked my questions.

"N'all, he ain't got no kids or hoes. B, don't really chase after chicks—" King was in the middle of saying.

My hands waved and I cut him off. "Wait, if he's not a hoe then why can't I talk to him?" King looked like he wanted to slap the shit out of me.

"You're making this hard, Peach. Blaze is the type of nigga I don't want you to fuck with, that's my point. I told him not to fuck with you, but knowing that nigga, he ain't gon' listen. He been askin' about you since that night at Voodoo's." King explained. "I can't control shit that nigga does, but since you my sister. I know outda respect for me, you not gon' take it there with that nigga." He sounded as if he was certain of that fact.

Even, though, my head nodded in understanding of what he was saying, on the inside I was kind of *giddy*. I was glad Blaze didn't keep hoes around or had hella baby mommas. Hell, he was too damn sexy for all that drama anyways.

"Okay, stay away from Blaze, check. What about Sam?" I asked smiling at him.

King shook his head before turning off my room light. "Stay away from him too, that's Blaze's dude. He a cool cat, but Blaze is already askin' questions about you, it'll only cause problems between those two." King explained, making me sigh.

"Crazy or not, Blaze is sexy. Well, can I play with him?" Once I said that he slapped me in the back of my head hard. "Ow, you son of a bitch! I was just playing, damn!" I snapped at him.

"Well don't fuckin' play..." He said, trailing off as he grabbed his ringing phone. "Yeah, I'm at Peaches crib, I'll be there in a minute, just be ready."

I already knew it was Ebony on the phone. I laughed, shaking my head. After their apparent make up sex and King's triflin' ass spittin' whatever lies he told her, Ebony forgave him. Which I knew was going to happen. It was a never ending cycle with them, one I just didn't understand. After doing all the cussin' and fighting she still takes him back when she knows he's a cheater, who's going to do it all over again once the drama cools down.

Once he hung up the phone, I stared at him as I went to open the front door. "Didn't you just leave her ass?" I asked him.

"Shut the fuck up. I was supposed to go pick her ass up, but I came here first. But shid, knowing her dumbass, she 'bout think I'm with a bitch." King shook his head as he put his phone away.

I knew my brother all too well, it was no telling what he did after he dropped her off at home. My hand paused on the doorknob as I looked at him like he was stupid. My mouth opened and then closed, trying to form the right words to say to him, but the knocking on the door stopped me.

I chose not to reply to his ending sentence because I knew he would get pissed off at me for bringing up the reason he had the fight with Ebony. So, I opened the door instead.

"Why you bitches banging on my door like y'all the laws? When the both of you have keys?" Angel and Missy just laughed, following behind me. Walking back into the living room, I grabbed my handbag then my Ruger off the table, putting it in my purse.

"What the fuck did I just say? I'm at Peaches crib. Man, shut the fuck up and be standing at the fuckin' door, I'm on my way." King snapped before hanging up the phone once more. "Peaches, I'm out. I'll see you at the party, don't forget what I said."

"King, get out my damn house before I call Ebony and ask her have she seen you." Missy and Angel laughed while King mugged me. "You gone keep on and one day she going to get tired of all yo shit and leave. Given she's the best thing that's happened to you, I don't want that to happen." I told him truthfully. "But seeing as she's my best friend, I don't want her to be treated like shit either. I hope she comes to her senses soon and be done with yo triflin' ass." My head shook at him. "King, you're not right at all for how you do her, she can do so much better than you." I told him as I locked my apartment door.

"She sure in the fuck can. I mean if you gon' cheat then let her go. She can do bad by her damn self or find a man that's gon' treat her right." Angel agreed, bumping into King as she bypassed him.

"Shut the fuck up, ain't nobody ask none of y'all shit. Ebony ass ain't going nowhere because I don't cheat." He snapped at us.

"Lies, you tell!" Missy slapped the shit out of King on his neck from what he just said.

"Missy, bitch, make me beat yo ass." He threatened her, but she wasn't fazed, she simply rolled her eyes.

"You don't cheat? Get that bullshit outda here. Don't worry about it though, keep doing you. I got my bitch set up, fuck you triflin' ass hoods." Missy quickly hopped in my car, closing and locking the door.

"You got her set up? What the fuck you mean?" King snapped, jerking on my car door, trying to get to Missy. "You hook her up with anybody, boss, I'm beatin' the fuck outda you and I put that on my life, don't play with me." King was really pissed at the thought of Ebony being with somebody else.

"King, stop snatching on my damn door like you stupid. Go get Ebony and we'll see y'all at Mike's." Not waiting on his reply, I got in after Angel. Once inside, we started laughing.

"Missy, he gon' kill yo ass. You know he don't play when it comes to Ebony trying to cheat." Angel said, laughing. "Peach, roll yo window down."

I did as she asked and let my window down. Once I did, I smelled it. "Damn, Ang, you couldn't do that shit before you got here?" I wasn't pissed or anything, I just didn't care too much for weed smoke.

"Sorry, Peach, but I have to get right on the way, otherwise I'd be lazy as hell." Angel replied. "Here, Miss." She held the blunt out for Missy.

Missy grabbed the swisher, then leaned across the seat and kissed me on the cheek. "Sorry, babe."

I laughed at her stupid self. They started smoking, the two of them passed the blunt back and forth as I started driving. I turned up the radio and drove us to the party.

Chapter 6

Peaches

I parked in front of an empty house across the street from Mike's. We got out as I popped the trunk, putting our purses inside of it, I closed it back. I hit the alarm button then we headed to the two-story brick house.

"Look at this shit, it ain't even ten yet and niggas out here dirty." I commented, looking at the group of niggas pissy drunk in the front yard with a few bitches in the middle of them groping and grinding.

"Train! Three niggas to a bitch." Angel's high ass spoke loudly, making us laugh. From the looks of it she was 'bout right. Those niggas/bitches had no shame to their shit.

"Oh, hell n'all, look at this shit." Missy stopped in her tracks, as a glare covered her face. She pointed to Mya who was leaning against a silver Nissan Altima. She was in some bitch face whispering something, before she kissed her. Mya was so busy in ol' girl's face that she didn't even see or hear Missy.

"That lying ass bitch told me she wasn't even gon' be here. So, this is why she didn't want me to come? I'm done, fuck that hoe. Y'all hurry up in the house before she sees me." Missy rushed us and we quickly walked to the front door and opened it. Missy stopped once again. "Can I have this?" She asked some random dude for his beer. She didn't even wait on his reply; she simply took it. Missy then threw the glass bottle towards Mya and ol' girl. The bottle didn't even reach them, but it got their attention no less.

"What the fuck?" Some dude yelled as the bottle landed a few inches from him.

Missy's mouth formed into an *O* as she pushed us the rest of the way in the house, closing the door behind us. Both Angel and I looked at her like she was crazy.

"I'm high, I don't know." She explained for her actions with a whine.

Glancing at Angel, she wore the same expression I did. We bust out laughing at Missy's serious excuse.

"Y'all, don't laugh at me." She groaned out. "I can't stand that bitch for real, though. She was just at my crib a few hours ago. And her lying ass talkin' about how she wanted to spend the night with me, layup, watch movies and just cuddle." Her eyes rolled hard as she relayed to us what Mya had said. "I'm glad I didn't stay my stupid ass at home like I told her I was. Dumbass hoe, I'm so fuckin' done with that bitch." Missy wasn't one to really show her feelings, but when she did, you knew she was hurt.

That pissed me off. "Hold this." I handed Angel my wrist bag that had my gun in it. I twisted my necklace around to unclamp it so I could get the brass knuckles off. Oh, I was about to beat Mya's ass. That hoe had my bitch in there looking like she was about to cry. Nuh uh, that shit wasn't even cool.

"N'all, Peach, don't even go out there. I promise it's good." Missy grabbed my arms, stopping me from taking off my chain. "That bitch ain't even worth it." She assured me before laughing.

My mouth opened and I was about to start reasoning with her about letting me beat Mya's ass. A scream left my mouth instead as someone grabbed me from behind, picking me up. I was caught completely off guard.

"Damn, I didn't expect to see you here."

The voice, I recognized immediately and laughed. "Leon, put me down you damn fool." Once I was back on my feet I turned around and hit him. "I should kick yo ass, I thought you was one of these drunk fools tryna get on my booty."

He laughed as he spoke to Angel and Missy. "Y'all looking good as usual. Am I gon' get a dance from you two?" Angel pursed her lips together, acting as if she didn't hear him as Missy looked him over.

"Leon, no, my friends are off limits to yo triflin' ass. What's up though, baby? So we snitchin' on each other now, huh?" I referred to him telling King about me and Chase the week before.

"Shid, I don't know what you talkin' about." He lied like it was nothing. Leon smiled down at me and shrugged.

"Aye, you talked to my brother? He was askin' about you. He told me to tell you to hit his line." He quickly changed the subject.

My eyes rolled at the mention of his brother, Jerron. "No, I haven't." Truth be told, I didn't even want to think about his younger brother at that moment.

Leon laughed at my attitude. "Y'all don't mind if I steal her?" He asked my girls.

Angel waved us off. "Nope, gon' head and take her. Make sure you loosen her ass up some." Angel told him while linking arms with Missy. "We're about to get a drink." She threw up two fingers and pulled Missy along with her.

"Come on, let's dance." He grabbed my hand, and I didn't protest.

I let Leon drag me in the living room where it was hot as fuck and musty from the multiple gyrating bodies. If there was one thing Mike could do, it was throw a house party. Whether it brought in ratchet bitches, hoes, triflin' niggas or not, the shit was always hyped as ever.

Gucci Mane blared through the DJ speakers as I danced with Leon. It was nothing but innocent grinding, hell, we were barely touching. We stayed on the floor dancing through a few songs until I got hot and thirsty.

I grabbed Leon's hand and pulled him with me to the kitchen. So we could get a much needed drink. Hell, and to take off that hot leather jacket I still had on.

"Damn, Peach, you looking good in that dress. King let you come out like that?" Leon complimented as well as joked.

Opening the bottle of water, I took a long drink then let out a heavy breath. "King can't tell me what to wear, I'm grown the last time I checked." I waved him off before I drunk more of my water.

Leon laughed as he nodded his head. "I see yo grown ass. So why you dodging Ron? He asks about you every time we talk."

I twisted the top on my water and shrugged. "I'm not dodging him; I've just been crazy busy with work and school. I planned to call him sometime during the week." Again, I shrugged, lying. That was a big fat lie.

Things between Leon's brother, Jerron and I were complicated as hell. Even, though, I never had a boyfriend because of King, Jerron was the closest it got. I hid my feelings from him for a long time and they were deep. But then he moved away to go to school and I never got to tell him the truth. After he left, things between us was just crazy. And with us being in two different states, it seemed like a lot of back and forth, then the lack of communicating, which I got tired of. So, for the past few years, other than a few calls every other six or seven months, I'd been avoiding him.

"Yeah, right. Don't be playing my brother like he one of yo little head buddies. The least you can do is call him and say what's up." Leon saw right through my bullshit.

Taking another sip of my water, I hummed. "I will, promise." I gave him an innocent smile.

He shook his head and looked away from me, into the living room. "Look at that mothafucka right there. Man, I don't know what's up with yo girl, but you need to watch her ass. She be on some reckless shit with those niggas she be finding." Leon said. The attitude in his voice didn't go unnoticed.

Following his gaze, I found Angel grinding on some big, bulky, killer looking dude. That nigga was big as fuck and looked mean as hell. He had to be around six foot three, maybe four, weighing about two hundred sixty pounds give or take, of straight muscle. I never knew what was up with my girl and big niggas. But she loved her some big dudes, and it was so funny, given how small she was.

"That mothafucka look scary." I commented, looking on as Angel's little ass grinded and winded herself on dude. She looked like she was really enjoying herself. So, who was I to knock her type?

"The other day her ass was in Voodoo about to leave with some nigga who looked just as crazy as that mothafucka." Leon's head shook and he seemed really pissed off.

We watched Angel turn around to face dude. She grabbed the side of his face and pulled his head down; she began to whisper something in his ear.

Without another word, Leon left me in the kitchen, and he made his way to the dance floor where she was. After saying something to ol' boy who was on Angel, dude walked off, not looking too happy about it. Neither did Angel as she slapped Leon in the back. Leon didn't seem fazed by Angel's attitude as he grabbed her. Of course she tried to fight him off her. Even, though, she was, I could tell she wasn't serious.

Leon arms went around her waist and he held her to him before he whispered something into her ear. She started laughing at what he said then began to dance with him.

I understood that Leon was just trying to look out for her. So how could anyone really be mad in the end? As I stood there watching my two friends dance, a hand suddenly covered my mouth. I was then lifted off of my feet and pulled into a dark corner in the kitchen.

"Estás tratando de meterme en problemas esta noche?" (You're trying to get me in trouble tonight?) Hearing that had me laughing as I pushed myself more into him. "Por qué te pones ese vestido?" (Why you wear that dress?) He asked while dipping his head into the side of my neck, kissing and sucking on the skin.

My arm hooked around the back of his neck and held him to me. I tilted my head further to the side, giving him more room. "Papi, King's, en su camino aquí. Y si él nos ve…" (Daddy, King's, on his way here. And if he sees us…) I trailed off.

He let out a breath as he began mumbling in my neck. "I know. I just saw him pull up." His arms still held onto me as he continued to kiss my neck. He turned me around to face him, then he pressed me into the wall.

"Sly, you just said King's here, so stop before he walks in or somebody sees." I mumbled as I pecked his lips twice. I began to move away only to have Sly pull me right back.

"Let's get out of here." His Spanish accent was thicker as he continued to kiss me.

As tempting as the idea was. I couldn't just up and leave. That would raise suspicion and King would flip the fuck out thinking I had ducked off with some random ass nigga. And that was a fight I wasn't ready for.

98

"I can't, King has to at least see me. But you can come home with me tonight." I offered smiling at him.

Humming, Sly leaned down and kissed me again. His hand slid down to my ass and he squeezed it. His hand then slapped my booty before he let go and pulled away.

Sly was an associate of King's, who he did business with on the side. I didn't know the full history of their business, but I did know Sly had certain connections in Puerto Rico that King benefitted from. I also knew my brother made a lot of money doing business with him.

Sly was older than King by five years, which made him thirty-five. It wasn't until one drunk night when I was fifteen and I let Sly eat my pussy for the first time. After it happened, I freaked out and told him my brother was going to kill him. That was when he found out that King was my brother. Hell, he was just as scared, so much so that I didn't see him for about two years.

It wasn't until I turned seventeen when we met back up again, and we'd been going hard ever since. No one knew besides my girls. He was the only associate of King's that I messed with.

I was a virgin and Sly knew it. He never pressured me into sex because he knew I wasn't ready. For that reason alone, I liked him.

"I'm tired of us sneaking around, Peaches." He complained.

Leaning up, I kissed Sly again to shut him up. He knew King would flip the fuck out if he found out that we'd been semi-dating for the past few years. Given that Sly's eleven years older than me, King wasn't going to take that news good at all. For that reason, I was going to stall for as long as I could.

"Sliverio…" I used his full name to let him know how serious I was. "Bae, I know, but can we please not do this here?" I asked with a sigh before deciding to change the subject. "What are you doing out here anyway? You sure you should be seen at such a hood party?" I joked with him. I was trying to lighten the mood because I honestly didn't want to argue with him at all.

A smile came to his lips as he caught on to what I was doing. But I didn't care, for the simple fact, I knew my brother. He wouldn't hesitate to beat the shit outda of Sly or me for that matter if he saw us together.

"I have to let loose sometimes, that's why we need to get out of here." He couldn't stay mad at me for too long because deep down, he knew, just like I did, King would try to kill him.

Recently, he'd been pressuring me a lot about telling King about us. Maybe he was really ready to be out in the open with me. But the big question remained.

Was I? I knew he was getting impatient with me. But truthfully, I didn't think I was ready for a relationship. Even so, a part of me felt I owed him that.

"And Mike's party is where you thought to get loose at—Sly, stop, somebody is going to see us." I laughed as he picked me up bridal style with his head tucked into the side of my neck. He started sucking on the skin. "Mr. Rodriquez, no marks." I warned him, with a chuckle. He placed a kiss on my neck, then lifted his head. Sly secured his arm under my butt and started walking towards the back door. I slid it open, then he stepped outside into the night's air.

Just like inside the house, the backyard was packed with grinding bodies surrounding the pool area, as well as niggas passed out in the grass. The music was loud and blaring from the DJ's speakers as it switched from Gucci Mane, Lil Wayne to Juvenile. The DJ was live as hell.

I spotted Mike and Kim by the pool; they were sitting together in a lounge chair. Sly made his way over to them, still carrying me.

"For real, put me down before King's sees us and get the wrong idea." The closer we got to Mike the more nervous I got.

"What's the wrong idea?" Was Sly's question. He ignored my request to be put down. Sly continued to carry me over towards them. "Now you're mad?" He asked as his pace slowed.

My eyes rolled at his question. "No, I just think you're being stupid is all. I get you wanna tell him, but now isn't the time to be all hugged up in his face. It's best if I talked to him first." I felt if I talked to King first the blow out wouldn't be as bad, especially if we were alone when I told him.

"You're not talking to him by yourself. Peaches, I was serious when I said I love you and want to be with you." Sly's fingers pushed at my chin, turning my face so that I was staring at him. "If that means me having to fight your brother, then so be it. That something I'm willing to do to be with you. Peach, I'm serious about us." He confessed to me as he stared into my eyes.

My anger quickly left because I knew he was telling the truth. "I know you are." My thumb ran over his bottom lip as a sigh left my mouth. *Did I love Sly? No.* But I liked him a lot and maybe one day that *like* I felt could possibly turn into *love*.

"Look who it is, bae. I told you we weren't going to have to drag her ass out." Kimmy joked, kissing Mike.

"If King, didn't give the go ahead then we would've." Mike joined in, laughing.

Sly put me down as he stood behind me. I could feel his body slightly shaking. I looked over my shoulder at him. "Oh, that's funny? Remember that. Nuh uh, go on, don't even try to apologize." I laughed.

Sly grabbed me from behind. "Bae, you know I was playing—" Sly was saying until he was cut off.

"Bae?" King's questioning voice came from behind us.

I cussed to myself but played it cool. "Yeah, bae. Sly knows he's my baby." I joked while turning around and hugging Sly. "Ain't that right, bae?" My lips puckered up towards him. A look of confusion crossed his face before he started leaning towards me.

Mentally I glared at Sly, was he seriously thinking about kissing me? Quickly, I turned my head to the side. My eyes locked with King's. A glare covered his face as a smile plastered on my lips, once Sly kissed my cheek.

"Hahaha, hell. Get fuck'd up." He pushed me away from Sly and walked between us. He then went over to Mike and shook up with him.

I turned to face Sly and gave him a look that asked, *what the fuck*? But he didn't seem fazed by my stare one bit.

Stupid ass dude, I swear.

With King, of course, there was Sam and Blaze.

"I bet you're feeling hella uncomfortable right now, huh?" I asked Blaze before looking at Sam. I gave him a smile. "Hey—" My words were cut off as he hugged me, then kissed my cheek like he saw Mike do earlier that day.

"What's up, Peaches? Damn, you lookin' good." He said, letting his eyes roam over me.

"So, do you." I took in his baggy Gucci jeans that hung low with the matching blue shirt.

"Keep lookin' like that I'mma think you want it." Sam suddenly said with a wide smile.

I barked out a loud laugh. "Dude if you don't go somewhere…" I trailed off and bit into my bottom lip as I looked him up. "Then again, Pretty Boy, I just might wanna see what those lips of yours feel like." I smiled back at him.

Sly's hand gripped my waist tight. That action caused me to remember, he was still standing close to me. I had completely forgotten all about him.

Sam rubbed his bottom lip and laughed. "Let's dance." He offered his hands to me.

"Sam, cool the fuck out. Nigga, go get a drink." Blaze pushed him away from me, making him laugh.

"Peaches, let's go dance." Before I could respond Sly was already pulling me to the dance floor. Once we were far away from everybody else, he pulled me slightly behind a tree. Sly turned me around to face him. "What the fuck is you doing? And in front of me, Peaches? Do you know how disrespectful that is?"

"I wasn't being serious." I explained to him. "I was just playing. I've been joking with both him and Blaze every time I see them. It's nothing serious, Sly, damn. You can't be acting like the jealous boyfriend when we aren't even officially together." A heavy sigh left my mouth, and I crossed my arms over my chest.

"Then we need to change that because I don't like this shit." He fussed irritated. "Do you even wanna be with me?" He questioned staring down at me with a serious expression. My mouth opened, but no words came out. "Is that why you not rushing to tell him?" He asked.

"Sly, I do wanna see where things go between us. Believe me, I really do, but I know my brother." That was my explanation. Telling King that I wanted to date Sly, honestly scared the hell out of me.

Plus, I wasn't really ready for a relationship for a lot of reasons. Even so, I couldn't shake that part of me that felt like I at least owed it too Sly. For years he had been patient with me. He never pressured me to have sex, so for that I could at least see if there was really something between us. There had to be something if we kept us a secret for seven years.

"Alright, Peaches, if that's what you're saying." He let out a sigh and looked at me like he didn't believe me. My arms went around his neck and I stood on my tiptoes. I went to kiss him, but he pulled away from me. "Nuh uh, gon' head on, Peaches." Sly grabbed my arms, trying to pull them from his neck.

"Don't be mad at me, I promise I'll talk to him. Just give me a few days. Okay?" I turned my back towards him and pressed my body against his. I then brought his arms around to my front and began rolling my hips into him.

"So, you gon' do that?" Sly whispered in my ear.

Glancing over at him, I nodded my head with a smile. I bit into my bottom lip and started grinding into him. I leaned forward and my ass shook from side to side before I dropped down low into a crouch then came back up. My ass stuck out and rolled against him until I felt his growing erection. Pressing harder into him, I started rolling and grinding on him.

Sly held my hips as his head went into my neck once again. He then started to suck and kiss on the skin. Smiling, I continued to work my hips against his growing dick.

We had danced close together through five songs and I completely lost myself in the feel of his dick pressed into the crack of my ass. I pulled myself from my sexual haze once my pussy started to throb. That's when I knew I had to stop. It was times like that I hated being a virgin.

"You tryna make me nut in my damn jeans? That shit ain't cool, Peaches." Sly groaned out as he stopped my rolling hips. "I need a drink."

Laughing, I turned around to face him. I stood on my tiptoes, then kissed his cheek. "And a cold shower—" I whispered into his ear before I sucked on the lobe.

"Forget you, Peaches." Sly said as he muffed my head back.

I hit his arm, laughing. "Stop. I was going to say me too, so stop before I beat yo ass out here." Grabbing his hand, I pulled him towards the back doors where a few coolers sat.

"Do you want a beer or water?" I asked, while grabbing myself a bottle of water.

"You can toss me a beer." Blaze said from behind us.

At the sound of his voice, I smiled, then grabbed two beers. After handing Sly his beer I gave Blaze the other one.

"You welcome." I told him while looking him over. Blaze ass was sexy, I had to give it to him.

"Yep." He replied before looking at Sly. "What's up, Sly, this you?" He nodded towards me.

My gaze fell on Sly and I hoped like hell he didn't say anything. But as I looked at him, he seemed kind of nervous all of a sudden.

"N'all, we just cool. I work at his clinic." I answered for him. I didn't understand why Sly got choked up. When just a few moments prior he was ready to step to King and let him know about us. "I'm nobody's. What about you? I'm pretty sure you got a few bitches and baby mommas running around here." Even, though, King already told me he didn't. I still wanted to hear him say it.

Blaze shook his head as he tilted his bottle back. "N'all, sweetheart. I ain't got no bitches, baby momma's, none of that. You sure you single, tho'? I mean I don't give a fuck if you are or not, it makes me no never mind." Blaze made it obvious he didn't care who Sly was to me as he openly checked me out.

I had to admit, though, I was loving his boldness. My face went hot as his eyes roamed over me.

"Sly, you don't mind if I take her away from you for a bit?" He asked as his finger ran down my stomach.

When Sly didn't respond, I looked at him again to see that he was pissed. Regardless of how he felt, he still wasn't saying shit.

"Why should he care? As I said, I'm single. With no attachments to anyone." My eyes rolled at him and my arms crossed under my chest.

Blaze stepped closer to me with a slight mug covering his facial features. "Could've fooled me with the way you two mothafuckas were out there. I was sho' you mothafuckas were about to start fuckin'." He snapped at me. His attitude was so unexpected, but I ignored it no less.

Locking eyes with Blaze, I hummed. "You were staring pretty damn hard to see us from way over there. And if we suddenly did start fuckin', so what? As I said, I'm single, with no attachments to anybody." I shrugged at him uncaring. "Sly, I'll see you later." My eyes stayed locked with Blaze's as I spoke to Sly. With a shake of my head, I walked off the porch and over to my group of friends.

Chapter 7

Peaches

My group of girls, along with my brother and his friends sat by the pool laughing, drinking, and smoking. I walked over to them and sat on Missy's lap.

"Damn, bitch, just come and sit on momma's lap." Missy wrapped her arms around me.

Looking at her, I laughed. "Shut the hell up, so what I miss?" I asked her. My gaze soon fell on Ebony and King all hugged up like they hadn't been fighting that morning. Shaking my head at them, I leaned back on Missy.

"You and Sly being reckless." Missy whispered into my ear.

I quickly turned to face her. "I know! Like, what the fuck? This shit stressing me out and it haven't even started yet." I complained with a groan. "I already know King gon' flip the fuck out when I tell his ass and Sly know the same fuckin' thing. And he wanna play jealous, talkin' about he *don't wanna hide no more*." My eyes rolled as I thought about what he said. "Miss, what the fuck am I gon' do? King gon' go off and it don't help that it's somebody he knows who does some low shit on the side." I whispered to her as I shook my head. "This is so stressful."

"Baby, don't stress over it, we got you no matter how it plays out. Peach, you can't keep letting him run you, sweetie. This the age where you're supposed to fuck up. I get he has your best interest at heart, but babe, you have to live for you. Shid, go out, find some random nigga to pop that cherry, then have a threesome. And I swear you'll feel so much better, with no worries about King's ass." She gave me her solution to fixing my problem.

I burst out laughing at Missy. "Ugh, I do not like yo ass!" I pushed her away from me before I turned my attention to my girls. "Ang, Kim, Ebony, y'all, why the fuck this bitch tryna tell me to have a damn threesome?" I yelled loudly while cracking the hell up.

"Missy, you gon' join in to teach me?" My lips formed into a pout as I asked.

"Bitches, we can make this into a five-some gotdamn it. I wanna try it too!" Kimmy said excitedly. She then got off of Mike's lap and came to sit at the bottom of the chair with me and Missy.

"I'm with it." Ebony said holding up her cup.

"Ang, what about you?" I asked her.

Angel's face scrunched up and she shook her head. "I'm sorry, but I ain't eating nann one of you bitches pussies.

Hell n'all! Not after y'all done fuck'd with these dirty dick ass niggas. I'm cool on that shit. And Missy, after Kim said that bullshit about yo bitch, nuh uh. Peach is the only one I'll fuck." Angel said and I broke out laughing.

"Y'all, now that she said that I'm good too. Ugh!" I literally started shaking as I thought about the niggas they messed with, Mike, King, Mya, they were cause enough to run away. "I can't deal, no I can't. Sorry Missy, my cherry staying intact, ugh, though. Eating pussy after Mike, King, Mya and whoever Angel's fuckin', ugh, no. Now y'all got eating pussy stuck in my head. Y'all nasty." I covered my face, feeling it go hot. I broke out laughing all over again.

"This bitch done turned ten shades of red, hell n'all, y'all look." Missy said, pulling at my hands. "Aw, baby, it's okay. Come on, put yo face in my titties."

Pushing her away from me, I shook my head. "I can't stand yo ass." Even though I said that I hugged Missy nonetheless.

"Y'all bitches crazy, if y'all do decide on that, I wanna watch." Mike spoke up, pounding Sam's fist as he agreed with him.

"On everything, I'm there." Sam said laughing.

Taking Missy's cup, I took a few sips of her Don Julio and orange juice.

"Boss, I'mma beat all they ass if either one of them do that shit. That's some incestuous shit." King said and we all fell out laughing because it was so damn true.

"Missy already fuckin Peaches, so what you mean?" Ebony stated, cutting King off before laughing. "Missy, duck! He 'bout to start shooting." Again, we broke out laughing.

"You see why I told yo ass to stop hanging with these mothafuckas? Y'all a bad influence on her. Peaches, sex is bad." King told me and Ebony slapped the shit outda him once those words left his mouth. "Bitch, hit me again."

She did but hit him harder that time. "How the fuck is sex bad when you can't seem to keep yo little dick in yo fuckin' pants?" Ebony snapped at him.

"I plead the fifth." King said, holding up five fingers.

"That's what the fuck you better had said, shorty whooped yo ass earlier." Blaze spoke for the first time to the group.

"Fuck you, B, ain't nobody ask you shit." King snapped in response, making Mike and Sam laugh.

"Boss, she was tagging that ass, fuck'd my man up." Mike laughed shaking up with Blaze.

Covering my mouth, I looked at my girls only to find them looking around at each other as well. We then broke out laughing.

"Ebony ass went straight beast on his ass. Peaches went to pull King off of her, only to have that bitch drag his ass back down into the fight." Angel said. "She was on her back, though, whoopin' yo ass. Now King, that's just sad." Angel shook her head laughing.

"Bitch, shut the fuck up. I let her do that shit. Get the fuck outda here with that. Ebony ass knows what's up." He claimed, shrugging.

Ebony lips twisted to the side as did her eyes before she wrapped her arms around his neck. "Y'all don't tease him. Bae, we know what's up. I mean sometimes I have to put hands to you." King muffed Ebony, pushing her head back. "Stop, King, damn." She laughed. Ebony straddled his legs, then leaned forward and bit into his bottom lip. Taking his hat off, she covered their faces. King's free hand went to Ebony's ass and he pulled her up on him.

Shaking my head, I looked away from them. Even though their relationship wasn't picture-perfect, just like Mike and Kim, they were cute together and Ebony really did balance him out.

Leaning back on Missy, I crossed my legs. As I did that, she pushed me in my back slightly, making me go forward. I glanced back at her and she nodded straight ahead. Following her gaze, my eyes fell on Blaze. He was staring at my legs. My head tilted to the side and I dropped my hand in front of my legs. I then began to snap my fingers.

Once Blaze noticed my fingers, his eyes jumped to mine. He beckoned me to him with his index finger and I shook my head before looking over at King then back to him.

"Fuck King, come here." His finger still waved me forward.

My eyes widened slightly as he said that. That nigga was crazy. Shaking my head again I looked away from him to Missy. "Missy—" I started to whisper to her.

She quickly cut me off. "Don't come whispering to me. You got three options, dreads, sexy caramel over there, or Sly. Seeing as you already know what Sly's about, I'm rooting for sexy caramel. I'll distract Sly and you go sneak off with him. Ebony got King distracted, so go." Missy whispered, trying to push me off her.

"No, Missy. Stop, you damn fool." I laughed at her.

"Peaches, let me holla at you for a minute." Blaze called out to me again.

Sighing, I turned to face him, about to get up. That was until Mya suddenly came walking towards us. She roughly pushed past Blaze and stormed over like she had a purpose.

"Oh shit, Peaches, get up." Missy cussed as Mya reached us. Once I got up off her lap, Mya grabbed Missy's arm and tried to yank her up from the chair. "Mya, let me the fuck go." She snapped looking at her like she was crazy.

"Why the fuck you lie? Yo ass supposed to be at home." Mya snapped at her like she was really pissed off.

No, this bitch didn't. From what I heard she was supposed to be at home too. In fact, they were supposed to be at home together. What the fuck?

"Mya, let me the fuck go. Bitch, I been here for two hours and you just now deciding to come say something to me? Get the fuck out my face, go back to that bitch you been hugged up with all fuckin' night. Bye!" Missy snapped, muffing Mya's head back with each final word.

"Nuh uh, bitch, don't be—" the girl that was with Mya yelled as she came rushing our way. I was already standing so I was ready for that ass to try to run up. "—puttin' yo fuckin' hands on her. Ahh!" She suddenly screamed as Blaze caught her ass by that long weave ponytail she wore. He yanked her head back hard making her fall to the ground.

"N'all, bitch. Watch where the fuck you going, y'all some rude ass hoes." Blaze told her and my mouth fell to the ground in shock.

"Damn, B done snatched that bitch hair out!" Sam burst out laughing before taking the weave ponytail from Blaze. Ol' girl looked beyond embarrassed as her facial features mirrored the shock we felt. Her mouth was slightly parted as she stared at Blaze in disbelief. "Damn, baby girl, here." Sam said, helping ol' girl up while trying to push the ponytail back on her head.

"Missy, let's go!" Mya wasn't even thinking about the girl who had tried to help her out. Hell, I don't think she gave her a second glance as she tried to pull Missy away.

"Mya, let me the fuck go! Take yo ass over there and tend to the bitch that just got her weave snatched out." Missy snapped, trying to push Mya off of her.

"Missy, stop playin' and come talk to me." Mya was trying hard to get Missy to go with her.

"Mya, let's go." Ol' girl called out as she pulled away from Sam. She went over to Mya and grabbed her arm. Either she wasn't a fighter, or she was hella embarrassed because she wasn't paying Missy ass no attention. She was just trying to get Mya to leave with her. "Bae, let's just go." She stated.

"Go sit yo ass over there until I'm done with her, damn!" Mya suddenly turned around and snapped at the girl.

Once again, my mouth fell open. *No, she didn't.*

"Mya—" The girl started to whine but was cut off.

"Didn't I just say go sit the fuck down?" Mya yelled, pushing ol' girl off of her. With a sigh and a roll of her eyes, she walked over to an empty chair and sat down.

I wanted to slap the shit out of her for doing so. Ain't no way in hell I would've done no shit like that.

Missy laughed, shaking her head. "Peach, you ready to go?"

I wasn't ready to leave, but I understood she wanted to get away from Mya. "Yeah, come on. Ang, you ready?"

Angel shook her head, waving us off. "Y'all gon' head, I got a ride." She said. "I'll get my stuff tomorrow."

"Come on, Miss—" Mya wasn't letting her ass go, though.

"N'all, hold on Missy. Can we talk?" Mya asked again. Missy, realizing Mya wasn't going to let her go, she agreed.

"Peaches, give me a minute." She snatched away from Mya, then she walked off with her in tow. Ol' girl Mya was with just sat there watching the two of them walk off together.

"Damn, yo sister got these hoes in check." Mike started laughing. "I need to get some pull from her ass."

"That's what the fuck I'm thinkin'. Let me pull some shit like that, a nigga starting World War Three in this bitch." King admitted with a shake of his head, as he glanced over to ol girl. "Get up right quick." He tapped Ebony's legs and she got up. King stood up, grabbed his snapback from Ebony. He put it on his head, then walked over to the girl, where he pulled a chair close and sat down next to her.

After what he'd just said, it surprised me that he took his ass over there. I looked to Ebony and she shocked the hell out of me even more. She didn't make a move to get up, she simply sat there. A glare covered her face and she watched King.

Rubbing my forehead, I flopped back down in the chair Missy had occupied a couple of minutes ago. I scooted all the way back, then crossed my legs at the ankle. A heavy sigh left my mouth as I prepared myself for the drama I already knew was about to start.

Blaze came over to me. He lifted my legs up and sat them in his lap. "So, you gon' play me all night?" He asked.

My lips twisted as my head shook. "You was wrong for pulling ol' girl weave out like that." I responded by saying instead. I stared at him and laughed.

"Shid, she was wrong for bumping into me, her and that other bitch." He shrugged uncaring. Blaze moved closer to me as his fingers stroked along my legs. "Fuck them, though. Tell me what I gotda do to get you to spend the night with me?" His tongue swiped over his lips as he continued to look me over.

My brows rose at the seriousness in his voice. "Not be King's friend—"

"Fuck King, I told you that. He ain't got shit to do with this. I'm tryna get at you, been tryin'. Shid, I've honestly been goin' about it nicely if you ask me." Blaze moved closer to me, so close that I was practically sitting on his lap. "I'm starting to get impatient, though." That made me laugh. "Oh, that's funny?"

Nodding, I licked my lips. "Very funny actually. Don't get me wrong…" My words trailed off as I looked him over. "You're very attractive and your lips are a bonus. Sexy, full, and when you lick them." My teeth gripped my bottom lip and I let out a low moan. "Mmm, my damn." My head shook and I sighed. "Even so, you're not my type. I don't wanna mess with King and from what I hear, you're both one in the same."

Grabbing my waist, Blaze pulled me into his lap. "What's yo type? Sly, hm? That nigga ain't gold, sweetheart." He made a point to tell me.

Cutting him of with my laugh, I shrugged my shoulders. "To be honest, I don't care if he is or not. I mean he's not my dude, like I said I work at his office." What did he mean when he said Sly wasn't gold? Last I checked he was single, only dirt he had on him was involving himself with King and that wasn't often.

"So, you kiss all yo employers?" His question caught me off guard for a second, causing my mouth to open then close. "If so, I think I got a job for you. Yo ass can come work for me if that's all it takes." He smiled at me. I was shocked that he had saw me kiss Sly. I didn't know what to say. "Cat got your tongue?" He asked cockily.

Quickly, I composed myself. I bit into my bottom lip before raising a brow at him. "How hard were you watching me?"

Humming, his hand moved up my thigh. "It don't matter, but I ain't like what I saw."

"So what? A kiss is nothing to me, it's a simple, meaningless gesture for me to see how good one works his mouth and tongue." Leaning closer to him, my tongue flicked the rim of his bottom lip. "Daddy, you wanna show me how good your lips work?" Not giving him a chance to reply, or myself to think about what I was doing. I pulled his bottom lip into my mouth, sucking on it then doing his top.

"Oh, damn!"

I heard someone say and I pulled back. My mind was mentally saying the same thing. *Oh, my Damn!* I stared at Blaze before my eyes dropped to his mouth. His lips were full and so damn soft. I wanted to kiss him again. Before my mind could process what, I was doing, my arms wrapped around his neck and I began leaning into him once again…

"Peaches, what the fuck are you doing?" At the sound of King's deep, barbaric voice, I jumped off of Blaze as if fire had been set to his lap.

"Nigga, don't say shit to her. While you over there with that bitch!" Ebony snapped, jumping in front of me.

"Man, shut the fuck up? I was seeing if she was straight." King said that as if it was okay to do.

Ebony slapped his ass. "Nigga, I don't give a fuck if that bitch was bleeding to death, you ain't have to take yo triflin' ass over there. You know what, King?" Ebony started to laugh as her head shook at him. "I ain't even fuck'd up about yo dirty ass no more. I swear fuck you, it's cool, though, because just like you can slide into the next bitch, I can easily hop on another dick."

King slapped her so fuckin' hard that she stumbled into the chair. My hand went to my cheek as I felt the hit.

"You can hop on what?" He grabbed a handful of her hair, then yanked her up to his face. "I ain't hear you. What the fuck you say you can hop on? Boss, say that shit again, Ebony." He snapped at her.

He was so damn ignorant. They got on my damn nerves with that stupid shit. "King, let her go!" I yelled at him while jerking on his arm. "You act so fuckin' stupid, I swear to God! You gon' hit her when yo triflin' ass just sat over there makin' conversation with another bitch in her face!" He was beyond wrong for that shit.

"Peaches, get the fuck off me!" King pushed me so hard I stumbled back in my heels. Thanks to Blaze, I didn't fall.

"King, I said let her go!" Pulling Ebony out of his grip, I pushed him back as he'd just done me. The only difference was that he didn't stumble. Hell, he didn't budge.

"You busted my lip." Ebony said in a shocked tone. Rubbing her lips, she laughed. Reaching over me, she slapped him again. "Fuck you! I'm so done with you! I hope you have fun with that bitch!" With that she walked off and King didn't follow after her like he usually did. Instead he picked his hat up off the ground, hit it against his pants, then turned and went back over to ol' girl.

"King, you really gon' do that?" I asked him.

"Take yo ass home, Peaches!" He snapped at me.

"You stupid as fuck and she's just as dumb if she stays with yo triflin' ass after this shit. You foul as hell, King, I swear." For that reason, right there is why I don't want to be in a relationship. Niggas is just triflin' for no reason.

"Shut the fuck up and take yo ass home, don't make me tell yo ass again." He yelled at me.

To avoid getting into a fight with him, I snatched my jacket off of the chair. "Fuck you, King." With that I started walking away.

"I don't get a goodbye kiss?" Blaze called to me.

Sticking my middle finger up in the air, I kept going. He was probably no better than King's ass.

Sexy or not, I wasn't going there with him. All of my brother's friends were hoes and with Blaze just getting out of jail. His ass was more than likely to jump into anything that walked.

"Aye, this the last time yo ass walkin' away from me. I'll be seeing you again, sweetheart." Blaze yelled to my retreating back.

Ignoring him, I quickly made my way into the house to find Ebony. Once I found her, I pulled her into a hug. "E, don't be crying over his ass. Baby, you can do so much better than him, I swear." King was so fuckin' stupid and he wasn't going to be satisfied until he lost her for good.

"I'm good, let's just go." She wiped her eyes then rolled them.

"Here, go to the car while I go find Missy." After handing her my keys, I went in search of Missy. Going up the stairs, I went to the first bedroom only to find it empty. I continued looking through rooms until I came to the last one at the end of the hall. Knocking, I didn't get a reply, so I opened the door. "Oh, my—" slamming the door shut, I started laughing. Only Missy's ass.

Knocking on the door again, harder this time, I yelled. "Missy, we're about to leave, boo. You good?" That was a stupid question seeing as Missy had Mya's ass eating her pussy. I shook my head trying to shake the image from my mind.

"Here I come!" Missy yelled with a moan from the other side of the door. I didn't know if that was for me or Mya. A few minutes passed when I suddenly heard ruffling in the room followed by Mya's voice.

"You're really about to leave with her?" She asked, not sounding happy at all.

"Yeah, I told you I'm done fuckin' with you. This here was nothing. You ate my pussy because you wanted to, I didn't ask. Now let me the fuck go, that bitch somewhere around here waiting on you." The door was snatched opened and soon after, Missy emerged. Looking at me, she pointed her finger in my face. "Don't say shit." She warned.

I zipped my lips and laughed. "I won't say shit."

"Bitch, you stupid. Her ass thinks I'm playing. Peaches, I'm so done, I just can't deal with a lying ass bitch and Mya is just that. Fuck her for real." She said as we came down the stairs.

I pushed the front door open and we walked out the house. "If that's what you wanna do then fuck her." I shrugged before I smiled. "So, was she good?"

Looking at me, Missy nodded her head. "Yes, but not even that can make me stay with her ass. I'm serious as hell, Peaches." She stressed.

I believed her. At that moment her mind was made up. But who was to say that later on she wouldn't go dipping back to the bullshit that was Mya?

Seeing the shit my bitches went through made me not want to ever date.

121

Hell, at this rate I might die a virgin.

Chapter 8

Peaches

One Week Later

"**O**h, my God! Right there, ooh, fuck! Ah!" My moan rang loud as my orgasm shook my body. "Oh. God!" My chest moved tiredly up and down as I panted heavily.

"Damn, Peaches." Chase mumbled before he leaned forward, sucking my clit back into his mouth once again.

"No, no, no, no, no, don't." Pushing his shoulders away, he laughed at me. "That's not funny, Chase, stop." My eyes rolled and I chuckled as I stared down at him.

The day after Mike's party, I called Chase out of boredom and we had hung out at least four times since. Sly

123

was pissed about the fact that I kissed Blaze so he wasn't talking to me outside of work. I wasn't too messed up about it because I really wasn't ready to take things to that level with him anyway. Plus, it made it easy for me to have Chase over without the two of them running into each other.

"You set me up. I'mma stop fuckin' with you on some real shit." Chase said, sitting up.

I caught the seriousness in his voice and laughed. I sat up as he did, then pulled my shirt down over my ass. "How I set you up, Chase?" My hand rubbed over his head and he turned to look at me.

"This," he pointed to his erection. "Don't get me wrong, I don't mind eating yo pussy, but shid, I wanna get to know you on some real shit. I ain't tryna be one of yo head hoes or whatever you call these niggas. I wanna get to know you. Peaches, let me take you out?" Chase was sexy as hell and had a boyish look to him.

Even so, I wasn't looking to date him or anything. Plus, the thing I had with Sly… "At this moment I can't say yes. I'm sort of kinda seeing someone." I told him truthfully. Even, though, Sly wasn't talking to me at the moment. It wasn't going to last long at all. He was bound to show up, it was a routine we stayed going through.

"I'm not asking for a relationship just yet. I just want to take you out and get to know you on a personal level. I already know you not shy and you sick with this head thing. Hell, to be honest, yo ass worse than some of these niggas out here." He laughed with a shake of his head.

What he said didn't offend me for the simple fact I knew how I was. I liked getting my pussy eaten, which was my only form of sex. I could admit that I liked it more than a little bit, shid, I was ridiculous with the shit. So in response all I could do was shrug.

"But that don't stop me from wanting to know you. So, what you say to a movie and dinner? If we have fun then we do it again, if not then we leave it at that, no hard feelings." He seemed sincere but I just didn't know about him. My teeth sunk into my bottom lip as I watched him. "What?" He asked.

"I'm just wondering how long you gon' play good dude? What's yo game? Woo and soothe me, make me fall head over heels for you, then let you fuck before you start to dog a bitch? How long do I have until you really start to show yo ass?" I asked seriously. Until it was proven otherwise, there wasn't a faithful nigga around. All they asses were lowdown, triflin' niggas, from my prospective anyways.

"A month, give or take, and I'll show you my ass. But if you're impatient, I'll show you now." Standing up, he started undoing his belt.

Laughing, I hit him in the stomach. "You know what I'm talking about. I know too many dog ass niggas that seemed good at first. You know? So, I choose to do this instead, no feelings are involved it's just head to me." I explained honestly.

Sitting back down, he stretched out on the couch and then pulled me to him. "We can be friends for as long as you want, ain't no rush. I ain't looking to jump into anything serious right now anyway, but I do want to get to know you."

A hum left my mouth as I got comfortable on top of him. "We can be friends, ain't nothing wrong with that. Dinner and movie though, we'll talk about it some more."

Peeking up at him, I couldn't resist grabbing his bottom lip between my teeth.

Chase grabbed my ass and pulled me up his body. He lifted me so that I could put my legs on each side of him, straddling his hips. His pelvis raised as he grinded me into him.

A moan left my mouth and his tongue slid through my parted lips as he slapped my bare ass.

"Yo, Peaches!" King's loud voice rang out as well as the front door closing.

Once that door was opened, you could see directly into the living room and seeing that's where we were. I didn't have time to really do anything but lift up. And that didn't include me getting off of Chase's lap.

Oh shit!

Looking over at Mike, Leon, and King, they stood in the living room entrance. They all seemed as frozen as I was. What was he doing at my place?

I came to my senses, then quickly got off of Chase's lap and pulled my shirt down. Doing so seemed to unfreeze everybody and their eyes moved from me to Chase then back to me.

"What the fuck is y'all in here doing?" Mike asked, trying to sound like King.

Leon laughed as he walked into the living room. He bent down and picked up my black boy-shorts, dangling them from his finger. "Oh, we know what she was doing."

Snatching my panties from Leon, I punched him in his chest. "Shut the hell up. We weren't doing shit." I snapped at him.

"Then what the fuck *was* y'all doing?" King finally asked, folding his arms over his chest.

"It's not what you think." I didn't know what else to say but that.

Mike and Leon started laughing as they flopped on the couch. "It's always what we think baby girl. And what I'm thinking is—" Mike started saying.

King cut him off. "Mike, shut the fuck up." He snapped at him before he looked back to me. "Now, Peaches, tell me what the fuck it ain't?" I didn't have an answer because it was what it looked like. "Who the fuck is this nigga?" King asked, coming into the living room, stepping to Chase who stood up.

"King, wait, he's my friend." As I was saying that Leon and Mike once again started laughing. I swear I hated them sometimes. "That's it, King. Please don't." I didn't want to be embarrassed and knowing King, he was likely about to start some shit.

"Aye, ain't that's dude from the club?" Leon asked, looking at Chase who seemed kind of confused as he looked from me to King. "You the dude she was with a couple weeks ago?"

"Yeah, he is, damn, Leon. King, Chase, my friend. Chase, King, my overprotective brother." I introduced, trying to avoid any confrontations. "Chase just moved here about a month ago—"

"Damn, and he's already in?" Mike asked, grinning.

127

Grabbing the pillow, I threw it at him. "Shut the fuck up, Mike. Chase, these two idiots are King's friends. I'll be right back." I took hold of King's wrist and started to drag him with me, but he pulled away.

"N'all, go on put some damn clothes on while I talk to dude." King said, mugging Chase hard.

"King, please don't—"

"What I just say?" He snapped at me.

The glare he sent my way had me quickly leaving the living room and going into mine. I threw on some sweats and I was leaving right back out. In case King decided to do something to Chase I could at least try to fend him off while Chase ran.

Given King didn't know Chase, he was probably going to feel him out and if he didn't like the smallest thing it was a no go.

"So, what you do? Professionally I mean. You a corner hustla? Pimp? Snitch? Police?" King questioned Chase.

Is he serious right now? Rolling my eyes, I went back into the living room and sat down next to Chase. I guess that was better than King trying to fight him.

"N'all, my pops and I just opened up our shipping business out here. Express Shipping. We got one out in Illinois and one in Ohio." Chase explained.

King's brows went up and I could see the wheels turning in his head as he rubbed his chin. "No shit? What y'all got, big rigs or them little vans?" King asked.

"We got Semi's and trucks." King glanced at Mike before looking at me.

"Peaches, why don't you go start making dinner. I'm hungry as hell." He said, waving me off.

No, he wasn't.

My mouth opened to protest, but once again King gave me a hard look and I knew what he was about to do. "I hate you." I got up off the couch and went back into my room, making sure to slam the door behind me.

King was so fuckin' dirty. Maybe it wasn't intentional, but he always found seemingly straight dudes to get on his team. Finding out Chase was part owner of a shipping company was like him hitting the lottery. He was about to give Chase a proposition to ship cocaine, weed, pills, anything he needed all over the place. Once Chase took that deal, which he'd more than likely will. Because they always took the proposition he offered. Then he'd be dirty. And whatever we had going on was going to have to stop.

***

"Because he fuckin' stupid as hell, Kim. Then his ass had the nerve to tell me to go make dinner. Bitch, I wish the fuck I would've. I went my ass in the room, took a shower, got dressed and left. King got me fuck'd up, he really starting to piss me off." I ranted, walking out of the gas station a few blocks from my apartment, using the ATM in there.

"Peach, calm down. I know how he is and it's about time you started standing up to him. Yeah, a fight gon' start, but still, he's getting fuckin' ridiculous with this shit. It's like he doesn't want you to have no fuckin' life at all. Babe, you gotda do you, if messing with this Chase dude or Sly is what you want, then do it." Kim spoke the truth. I knew she was right.

Even so, that was easier said than done. I could yell, fuss, and cuss all I wanted, but in the end what King said goes. "I know, Kim, but we're talkin' about King."

She laughed and I knew she rolled her eyes. "Right. I'm so glad I don't have a brother for this reason. King's reasons for his actions are understandable, though, Peach. Mya was hella protective when I came to stay with her. Shid, she still is and after years of being with Mike, she just starting to semi like him. She isn't as possessive as King, but she has her moments. Especially, when I was going to Kaplan Community College. But I learned to ignore her ass." Kim said reminding me of how Mya used to be.

I laughed. "Remember she tried to ground you because Mike picked you up from school one day and you ended up staying the night at his place?"

Kimmy burst out laughing. "Girl, yes. I think that was the second time we actually had a fist fight. Mike was pissed, he tried to get me to move with him after that shit."

"That shit was crazy." I blew out a heavy breath. "I really need to do something about King, though." I crossed the street and headed towards Maxi's shoe store a block down. "I'll figure something out."

King trying to get Chase to become a driver was low. I just didn't understand him. He said he wanted me to have a dude that was straight. Yet all the good niggas out there, he ended up liking their job description. Then he offers them a fuckin' proposition and it's over. Hell, he was making these mothafuckas dirty.

"You will, Peach. So, don't stress over it. Where you at now?" She asked.

"I'm walking down Broadway on my way to Maxi's."

"Ooh, see if they got something cute for me, please? I'll give you yo money back, I promise. I need some new shoes…" Kimmy trailed off as Mike started yelling in the background at her. "Nigga, shut the fuck up. You ain't paying for them, therefore you don't have a say." She snapped at him.

As I was walking, my brows furrowed in confusion. I stared at the black truck that suddenly drifted into the turning lane before it quickly shot towards me. "Ahhh!" A scream left my mouth, and I dropped my phone. I jumped out the way, trying to dodge the big black truck that was driving on the sidewalk. The truck came to a complete stop in front of me. *What the fuck?* The tinted windows rolled down. "Are you fuckin' crazy? You could've hit me!"

"N'all, I wasn't gon hit you." He chuckled before he shrugged. "I am a little crazy, though." He admitted.

Laughing, I rolled my eyes at him. My head shook as I picked up my phone. "What do you want?" I stared at Blaze in the driver's seat of the truck. Yeah, that nigga was most definitely crazy.

"You, but yo ass on that bullshit. Come take a ride with me." He called out to me as I started walking backwards, towards Maxi's.

"Sorry, daddy, this is my stop. Maybe once you ditch King we'll talk. Bye, Blaze." I waved while smiling at him. I turned and walked into the store while powering my phone back on. Once it came on I called Kimmy back. After the second ring she answered.

"Bitch, what the fuck happened? One minute we're talking, the next you're screaming, then the line went dead." Kim's worried voice spoke loudly through the phone speakers.

"Girl, I'm good. But why the fuck I'm walkin' and this mothafucka pulls on the sidewalk in front of me?" I told her, finally looking behind me out the store. When I didn't see Blaze's truck, I turned back and started looking at the many pair of heels on the shelves.

"Mike, we don't have to go, she's alright." She told him with a heavy sigh.

I picked up a pair of gold glittery, red bottom heels, while laughing. "Where were y'all going?" I asked while taking off my black flats and putting on a stocking to try on the heel.

"We were on our way to Maxi's to see if you were good. I heard you scream, then the call went dead. Who the hell rolled up on you, though?" Kim asked as I found a salesclerk.

"Excuse me, do you have this in a size six?" I asked the woman who looked to be in her late twenties or early thirties.

"I think so, let me go check." She replied before walking off.

"Girl, Blaze ass. He straight drove on the sidewalk like that shit was normal." My eyes rolled as I looked at a pair of lavender, silver studded, ankle boots.

"That man want some of yo good stuff. You better stop playing and let him have some." She pointed out, joking.

Laughing, I picked up the lavender boot. "I'm not playing, he's King's friend, though."

"*And*? So is Sly's ass." Kimmy said, cutting me off, causing my eyes to roll up in my head.

"That's different though, Sly don't hang with King on a regular, it's strictly business. Plus, Sly is legit. I don't know too much about Blaze, though. Regardless of that, I can actually see King really flipping out over him more so than Sly." I explained as the woman came back with the shoes and I handed her the lavender boot, asking for the same size. "He is sexy, though, I gotda give him that. But King said he's crazy, like he actually admitted that dude was on the same level crazy as him, if not worse, so I don't know." I shrugged as I sat down and tried on the shoe.

"Well, damn, I'll sample him for you to see how the goods work." Kim grunted out. "That mothafucka is sexy. Girl I almost forgot all about Mike's ass when I saw that nigga." She told me.

I burst out laughing, I knew my best friend and her crazy ass would definitely do it. "Mike gon' fuck you up, Kim. You want a six right?" Kimmy wore a size five and a half, but sometimes she got them a half size bigger or a whole size up, it depended on the shoe.

"Yeah, get a six. If I need a smaller or bigger size, I'll take them back." Humming my response, I sat the gold shoes to the side and continued looking. "And if the dick good, the fight between Mike and I will be worth it."

Laughing, I opened my mouth to reply, but the phone was taken from my hand. I quickly turned around about to go off on whoever, but my words got caught in my throat.

"She gon' have to call you back." With that said, Blaze hung up the phone before pocketing it. "I know you didn't think I was gon' let you walk away like that, right?"

My mouth opened, then closed as I stared at him in disbelief. "You did not just—"

"I did." Blaze said, walking by me. He purposely bumped into me, then sat down. "What's the rest of yo day lookin' like?"

Rolling my eyes, I turned away from him. "The rest of my day consists of pointless shopping, then treating myself to dinner before going home, hopefully to an empty apartment." Once I finished talking the sales lady returned with the boots.

"They were hard to find, but I found them. They're the last pair, actually." she said while handing me the box.

"Thanks." I sat down next to Blaze, then took off my shoes to try on the lavender boots. "I can't believe you hung up my phone." I stated while glancing at him with a look of disbelief on my face.

"Talking about me to yo girl wasn't all that important." My eyes widened slightly as my mouth parted. *He heard me?* He must have caught the look on my face because he laughed. "Yeah, I heard y'all. So, you think I'm sexy?" He leaned forward and stared down at me, smiling.

My eyes rolled at him. "I already told you I thought you were sexy. So, overhearing it shouldn't surprise you." I shrugged.

"True, but it's nice to hear you talk about me." He returned my shrug as he picked up the left boot, looking at it. "Why you don't wanna go home?" Blaze glanced back to me, waiting on my response.

I pretended I didn't hear his first statement. "King's there and I don't want to be bothered with him right now. I'm actually surprised y'all not together. I mean, you two have been joined by the hip since you got out." Taking the boot from him, I pulled it on, then went to stand in the mirror. The boot was hella cute and for a hundred-fifty dollars it wasn't bad at all.

"If you need somewhere to stay then I can help you find a place." He offered.

Glancing over at Blaze, I laughed before my attention went back to the mirror. I stared at myself in the full length mirror, then slowly turned around. I looked at the boot trying to figure out if I had an outfit to go with them. The dark blue skinny jeans, black shirt and black leather jacket I wore wasn't gon' get it.

"What was that look about?" Blaze spoke bringing my focus back to him.

"You finding me a place, in turn means yours, right?" I asked while walking down a few spaces to pick up a pair of pretty, suede, peek toe, cream colored heels, with a rhinestone embedded bow trimmed in gold on top of the shoe.

"Shid, we can go there or to the hotel up the street." The seriousness in his voice made me laugh, which was short as I turned, bumping into him. "Why are you laughing? I'm being serious? And don't give me that King bullshit either. Like I said, fuck King. He ain't got shit to do with this."

His closeness caught me off guard, but his big, strong hands, that grabbed my ass and squeezed it, had me lost for words. He then pulled me close to him. The feel of his hard dick pressing into my stomach, had me frozen in place.

Blaze was straight forward and obviously didn't give two fucks about what King might have thought. That was the third, maybe fourth time he'd made that perfectly clear. If it wasn't for the fact I kind of knew his profession and that he was cool with King. Then just maybe the outcome would've been different.

"But he does, excuse me." Knocking his hands off my ass, I tried to push him back, but he didn't move. Instead, I was pushed back pretty hard, which caused me to stumble into the shoes hanging on the wall, making a few fall down. "Dude, what the fuck?" A gasp left my mouth as Blaze grabbed a handful of my hair and jerked my head back.

"You keep telling yoself that 'cause you damn sho' ain't convincing me. So, stop playing and come take this ride with me." With every word he spoke his face came closer to mine. Once he stopped talking, his lips stopped moving. I was so transfixed on his mouth and on kissing him again that I didn't realize it wasn't him moving closer to me, instead it was me moving closer to him.

The smile his lips formed into brought me to the realization of what I was doing.

I need to get the hell away from him.

"Let me go." He didn't, instead his grip tightened in my hair before he tilted my head back. "Blaze, let me the fuck go."

"N'all, I think I'mma chill with you today. What you think?" He licked his lips and smiled at me.

I'd be lying if I said his persistence wasn't a turn on, because it most definitely was. "I think you should let me go."

Blaze let my hair go but didn't move back. Not being able to hold my uninterested façade any longer, I bit into my bottom lip as I diverted my eyes away from his. He took hold of my chin and brought our gazes back together. Even so, he still didn't say anything.

I rolled my eyes at him as a small laugh slipped through my lips. "Fine, you can buy me dinner. Now can you move back?" He didn't budge. "Please, can you move back?"

"You got *me*?" He chuckled lightly. My brows furrowed in confusion at that. His eyes dropped down and mine followed only to see I did have him.

My hands had fisted the sides of his shirt, holding onto him tightly. "Oh, right. Um, yeah…" I trailed off but ended up letting out a laugh. I released my hold on him, then I pushed him back. "Just move, I'll be done in a minute." Blaze grabbed my ass as I walked around him. "Don't make me slap the shit outda you." He laughed while picking up the shoes that we dropped. "Excuse me, can I get these in a size six, please?" I asked, holding out the cream colored shoe.

The lady gave me a smile as she glanced over at Blaze. She looked as if she wanted to say something but decided to keep it to herself. "I'll be right back."

"You got people looking at me funny?" I said as I sat next to him and began to pull off the lavender boots.

"How the hell I got folks looking at you funny when you the one pulling on me?" He pointed out.

I wanted to hit him with the boot, but I thought better of it. "I wasn't pulling on you." His raised brow had me laughing and changing the subject. "What happened that you and King parted ways? Had a fight?" My leg crossed over my right thigh as I turned to face him.

Blaze reached into his pocket and pulled out a cigarette. He put it to his lips, then pulled out a lighter and lit it. Noticing me staring, his brow raised. "You want one?" He offered, holding out the box of Newports.

My eyes rolled at him. "No, I don't smoke. Besides, you can't smoke in here." I told him.

Blaze took a pull of the square, inhaled then blew out the smoke. "Where you see a sign that says I can't?" He asked trying to be smart as he took another drag of the cigarette.

I pointed toward the window and Blaze glanced over before shrugging. "I didn't see that."

"Put that out before you get us thrown out of here." I laughed at his uncaring attitude. Blaze took another hit of the square then put it out on the bottom of his shoes. My head shook at him. "Now back to you and King. Y'all have a fight?" I repeated my question.

He shook his head no. "King and I don't be together all the time. Shid, we both got jobs to do. What King do to piss you off? I'll beat his ass for you, just say the word." Blaze's offer was tempting as hell.

I laughed no less. If I thought it would get King off my ass, I would most definitely take him up on it. "I'll hold you to that one day. King is just being his overprotective self is all, it's nothing I can't handle." That was a lie. It wasn't nothing to handle, honestly. Hell, I had already let the thing that happened with Chase go. It wasn't like I really had a choice in the matter. "You know if King finds out I'm with you its gon' be a fight, right?"

Blaze didn't seem bothered about my revelation. "I ain't fuck'd up about King, I told you that. You shouldn't worry about that shit either because regardless of what he's saying, you're got."

That had a laugh slipping through my lips as well as a smile forming on my mouth. "I'm got? What does that even mean?" I asked, genuinely curious.

"You're got? Oh yeah, um, yo language, shit." He mumbled.

I started laughing at the thoughtful look that came to his face. *My language? What the hell is my language?*

"Taken, involved, spoken for, claimed, um... In a relationship. Either one of those words you wanna use is what you are." He explained to me.

My mouth formed into an *O* and I slowly nodded. "Right. Well, that's a problem because I don't date hoods."

With that, I picked up the shoe boxes and headed towards the register as I noticed the woman coming from the back.

"What you mean, baby girl? This fate." He assured as he followed me.

Glancing back at Blaze, I started laughing again. "Fate? Really? How so?"

Blaze took off his Pacer's snapback, then ran a hand over his deep ocean waves. "Shid, I don't know yet, but when I figure it out, I'll tell you."

Again, I found myself laughing. "You're funny as hell. I didn't peg you for the type to have a sense of humor." He was making me laugh, which was always a plus in my book. A hood with a sense of humor was the worst kind, but I could play his game for the time being.

"Your total is four hundred fifteen dollars." The salesclerk told me.

Damn! Mumbling to myself, I searched my wallet for my credit card. "I need to stop coming in here, y'all gon' break me." I joked with her.

"Girl, that's why I'm happy I work here. The shoes are so cute and with my thirty percent discount I go crazy. Given I just started here a few weeks ago, my closet is full." She told me with a laugh.

Laughing, I rolled my eyes as well as shook my head in understanding. "Just as mine is. It's so bad I have to use my guestroom closet, but that's almost full. My ass needs to go rent a storage room." My head shook at how true my statement was.

"Here, I got it." Blaze suddenly said, reaching over me. Seeing him holding out money, I grabbed his wrist

140

before the lady could take it. "What the hell are you doing?" He asked, snatching his wrist out of my grasp.

"I can pay for myself, but thanks anyway." I found my card, then slid it to her. Just like I had done him, Blaze did the same to me. He grabbed my wrist, trying to stop me from paying.

"It ain't shit, I got you." He offered once again as he held out his money.

I took it from him and put the four-hundred-twenty dollars into my pocket. "Thanks, you can charge my card." I smiled at the woman before I glanced at Blaze. "We can use this for dinner."

"You have ID?" Nodding, I grabbed my license, then handed it to her. "Peaches?" She said it as a question, looking up at me.

"Yep." I replied as she handed it back after looking at it.

"I'm Monica." She introduced herself with an edgy tone of voice. She spoke as if I was supposed to know her, but I didn't.

That was the first time I'd ever saw her. So, I ignored her tone of voice and grabbed my card back from her. "It was nice meeting you, Monica." I took my bags from the counter and turned around, almost running into Blaze. "Would you stop that? Damn." Blaze stood in my way as he stared down at me with a slight mug on his face. "Are you just going to stand there looking crazy, or move out the way?"

He stepped aside and let me walk past him. "I could've paid for yo shit."

"So, could I, which I did. I'm no leeching bitch, baby, I have my own—" I was in the middle of saying, until Blaze's laughter cut my words short. "What's funny?"

"You have your own or does King have you on an allowance." Blaze tone was mocking as if he really thought King was dishing out money to me.

My legs stopped moving and I looked at him. I felt hella insulted by what he asked. "N'all, daddy, King don't have me on shit, I work for mine."

"Fuckin' yo boss is considered working for yours? Huh? Well, I guess you do gotda put in some work, don't you?" He smirked cockily at me. The palm of my hand shot out so fast that I tried to slap his cheek from his face. But the son of a bitch caught my wrist. "N'all, sweetheart. I don't play that hittin' shit. Why you getting mad for? I'm just asking questions."

I snatched my wrist from his hold, then held my hand out towards him. "Give me my phone so I can go fuck my boss for a check. I'm pretty sure he can drop more than four-fifteen, and that's just to eat my pussy." That was a lie, Sly didn't have to pay. Hell, I didn't charge, but Blaze didn't have to know that.

Blaze glared down at me. "I'm gon' ignore that bullshit you spittin' because you mad." He said. "So now you don't wanna eat?" He asked as he pulled up his jeans

With my hand still held out, I shook my head. "Daddy, you don't have to ignore it. And I'm gon' eat regardless of the bullshit that comes out yo mouth. If you follow then you can join me, if not, oh well. Now can I have my phone?"

Blaze took my bags from my hands, turned around and started walking away.

"Blaze?" I called to him.

He turned to face me while walking backwards. "You want yo shit, get in the truck. I ain't gon' wait for yo ass, though. I'm hungry as hell." He told me as he shrugged. Why I laughed was beyond me. Blaze was most definitely persistent. "You gon' stand there smilin' at me or get yo ass in the truck? I told you I'm hungry."

His ass was most definitely going to be trouble for me. I felt it. A small chuckle left my mouth. "You know you're rude as hell, right?"

He tossed my bags in his trunk then closed it before he replied back.

"I never claimed I wasn't." He gave a nonchalant shrug before he started walking towards the driver's side.

I stood there and watched him for a short second. "So, you're not gon' open my door?"

Blaze stopped walking and looked at me with a raised brow. "What the fuck is wrong with yo hands?"

My eyes rolled hard at him, that was exactly why I didn't mess with hoods. They were some rude ass mothafuckas. Even so, Blaze's rudeness was sexy. That was the only reason I walked my ass to his truck and got in.

Chapter 9

Peaches

"We didn't live too far from here." Pointing out of the window of the Denny's, to 31st and Grant, I began giving Blaze instructions to where my parent's house used to be. "Then make a right on Mississippi. We lived in the third house from the corner." I explained as I took a bite out of my chicken and sausage quesadilla.

"Here I thought you were an uptown preppy type of girl." Blaze replied, making me shake my head.

"Nuh uh. I don't even know what that is." I laughed at him. "Why would you think that if King's my brother?"

He shrugged, then grabbed his cup and took a drink. "Shid, I figured y'all had different mommas. You just don't seem like you from this part of town. But, shid, y'all were basically in the heart of the hood, being right in the middle of Delaney and Dorie Miller." He explained to me.

144

My head nodded, showing my agreement. He was right, where we used to live was in the crossfire of everything that went on between the rivaling gangs from both sets. Delaney wasn't that close to where we lived, but the worst part of Dorie Miller was.

Delaney and Dorie Miller were one of the worse projects out there. The gangs from the two projects always found some dumb shit to beef about, and given police hardly came out to deal with crimes, killers, prostitutes, and drug dealers felt they had no rules and did what they wanted. As a result of there being less police, there were more dealers, pimps, and crack heads to have free reign to do as pleased, so the traffic was nonstop. Even though we were up the street from the projects, where we lived was still considered middle class.

Wiping my mouth, I glanced up at him, still nodding my head.

"Yep, it was bad, but it wasn't." I took a bite of my quesadilla, then pointed towards Blaze. "And how does someone from these parts of town act exactly?" Taking the quesadilla out of my hand, he ate it. My lips popped and I laughed at him.

"You laugh a lot, why is that?" Blaze asked as he placed his elbows on the table. He stared at me intensely, which caused my eyes to look away from him. "I know I ain't that gotdamn funny. Shid, let me in on what got those garage size dimples in yo cheeks."

Again, I laughed. "I'm always laughing about something, it's a disorder." I admitted and Blaze started laughing. "So, don't think it's you even though, you are kind of funny." I lied with an uncaring shrug. Mentally I rolled my eyes as my insides became jittery.

Blaze laughed, but his stare said he wasn't buying the lie I was telling. The slant to his eyes, as he licked his lips, while he gazed at me caused my body to become excited. I looked down at the table and rolled my eyes as I tried hard not to smile. I then grabbed my iced tea and took a drink, trying to rid myself of that feeling.

"So how old are you?" The giddiness wasn't leaving so I chose to change the subject instead.

"Thirty." He answered simply as his eyes followed some chick who walked past.

Mine rolled at him and I shook my head. *Typical nigga.* "And you from around here?"

Looking back at me, he nodded. "Yep, right up the block. What you laughing for?"

"No reason, up the block. If so, I guess the fate Gods didn't want us to meet until now, huh?" I questioned.

Licking his lips, Blaze laughed. "I was just thinkin' that shit. I mean I'm always around these parts, beside the two years I was locked up, and not nann time did we clash." He pointed out to me.

If it was up to my dad and King, I would never have met any niggas they dealt with. Mike and Leon didn't count because we all used to live on the same street.

"If it wasn't for that night at the club, I'm pretty sure we still wouldn't have met." I told him truthfully as I took another sip of my drink.

"That's why I'm saying its fate." Blaze looked so serious as he said that. "So, you need to stop playing and come on home with me. Sweetheart, this was meant to be so it's gon' happen regardless. Shid, that's fate."

My hand went to my mouth as I barked out a laugh. "You are too much. No, I'm not going home with you." I wiped my mouth, then took a drink of my tea. Looking at Blaze, my head shook as I pushed away from the table. "I have to go to the bathroom. Once I come back, I'll be ready. Here." I pulled his money from my pocket, then slid it to him before I reached into my wallet and grabbed a twenty. "This is for my food." I gave the money to him. "You can keep the change if you want. I'll be back." Blaze opened his mouth to say something, but I turned, walking away from him.

Once in the restroom, I went to the first stall, quickly handling my business and then leaving out to wash my hands.

"That sink doesn't work." A female that looked to be around my age stated as she pointed to the sink I was standing in front of.

"Oh, okay. Thanks." I gave her a small smile, then went to the sink next to hers.

"Lost your way, baby?" I heard her say.

My brows furrowed hearing that, because for a second, I thought she was talking to me. I looked at her only to find that she was staring in the opposite direction at Blaze.

"N'all, I didn't." He responded, staring at me.

Glancing my way, she rolled her eyes, like she had suddenly caught an attitude. "Well you do know this is the lady's bathroom, right?"

"Bitch, shut the fuck up and get out if you done. Yo ass do know the men's bathroom is next door, right?" Blaze snapped at her.

My mouth dropped wide open from his reply.

"Nigga, who in the fuck is you talking to?" She bucked, walking up to him like she was straight about to whoop his ass.

"Whoa, whoa, whoa, Blaze—" I tried to defuse the situation, but Blaze's deep loud voice raised over mine, which shut my ass up.

"Bitch, I'm talkin' to yo tack headed ass. Now get the fuck out!" Blaze pulled me out of the way, then he opened the door for her.

"Rude ass mothafuckin' nigga." She fussed while walking out the bathroom.

I couldn't blame her for walking away given she started it. But ain't no way that nigga would've spit that shit at me, and I walked off. When the word bitch left his mouth for the second time would had been a go for the fight to start.

Once the door was closed Blaze turned to face me.

My head shook at him because of the way he had snapped off. "You ain't even—" I was telling him, but he shut me up as his mouth came down on mine. My entire body stiffened, and that giddy feeling began to run through me. I was literally just stuck as my mind screamed at me to kiss him back.

Blaze sucked and nipped at my bottom lip until I started to respond. My hands gripped the front of his shirt and I tilted my head to the side, kissing him.

Blaze took hold of my thighs, picking me up. Instinctively my legs wrapped around his waist as my back hit the door.

The door locking sounded like a deadbolt clicking hard.

Oh Shit!

The feel of his hard man pushing against my sex had me moaning into his mouth, as I grinded my throbbing pussy more on it.

Dammit, I need to stop!

Blaze pelvis thrust up, causing his dick to press more into my rolling hips.

It feels so good.

He moved us from the door and went to the counter. Blaze sat me on top of it, then pushed me back. His hands made quick work with the buttons on my jeans. Once they were undone, he grabbed the side of my pants and started to tug them down.

"Blaze wait." Panting heavily, I grabbed his wrist, stopping him. "We can't—" My mouth snapped shut as he snatched away from me.

A look of frustration covered his face and he seemed irritated as hell. "Fuckin' bitch, damn!" He cussed while he glanced down at his waist.

My brows raised at him and I got pissed off. "Nigga, fuck you! I don't know why the fuck you getting mad for. You the stupid mothafucka if yo ass thought I was really gon' fuck you in this bathroom. You stupid sonofabitch."

The words flew from my mouth before I realized it, but I wasn't gon' take them back just because he was pissed.

"What the fuck is yo stupid ass talkin' about?" He asked, looking genuinely confused.

"I'm not stupid, you're the dumb mothafucka that's getting pissed because I made you stop." I glared at him before I rolled my eyes hard.

Blaze suddenly turned away from me and answered his ringing phone. "Yo?" He spoke with his phone to his ear.

This nigga is rude as fuck.

"What the fuck?" Blaze snapped into the line. His head shook and he rubbed a hand over his face before he sighed. "Give me about fifteen minutes and I'll be there. I'ight?" He ended the call then looked back at me with a crease in the middle of his forehead. "Now what the fuck is you goin' on about?"

Rolling my eyes at him, I hopped off the counter and fixed the buttons on my pants. "Nothing, nothing at all."

"Yo, kill that shit right there. What the fuck was you yelling about?" He grabbed my arm, then pulled me back towards him.

"You the one who got pissed about me telling you to wait." The attitude in my voice could be heard. He had really irritated me.

Blaze's hand soon came to the side of my head, his fingers pressed against my forehead and he muffed me. "Man, shut yo dumbass up."

"Keep yo damn hands out my face." I slapped his hand away from me.

150

"I didn't get pissed at you, but at the mothafucka who paged me." He pulled a black pager from his waist and showed it to me. I read the twenty-six on it and immediately I felt embarrassed about my reaction. "Before you start talkin' about my hoes, this is business. One of my niggas need me to come through real quick. So, lose that fuck ass attitude you got." Blaze exclaimed while walking past me to the first stall and using the bathroom. Once he finished, he came out then washed his hands. When he got done, he grabbed my arm and led us out the restroom. "Now you can't talk?"

"Whatever, I don't have an attitude. But I need to get my ass home anyway. I got homework I need to finish." I stated as I let out a heavy sigh.

In all honesty, I really just wanted to get as far away from him as possible. We needed space for the simple fact, that giddy feeling had returned once again. My body hadn't felt that way since I was fifteen and messing with Jerron. I knew what that excitement brought, and I wasn't ready to feel those emotions again.

"Don't think this over, we gon' finish this shit, believe that." Blaze said, getting in the truck. "I don't know why the fuck you smacking yo lips for, I'm dead ass serious."

I glanced at him and started laughing. Blaze was staring at me with a straight face showing his seriousness. "Nigga, whatever. This ain't that, I barely know you."

"That ain't got shit to do with nothing. We gon' finish this. What time yo class over with?" He questioned me and that serious look didn't leave his face.

I was not fuckin' him and if he thought otherwise, he was going to be very disappointed. I didn't save myself for twenty-four years only to lose my virginity to a damn hood, fuck that.

Even so, I answered his question. "My class is over with at nine-thirty, but I gotda be at work right after. Before you ask, I work from ten to five and then I have to be back at school for my class that starts at five-thirty. And I don't get out of there until eight."

Blaze hummed as he stopped at a red light, he looked at me. "I'll see you about nine, ten, somewhere around there." Again, I laughed. "Why the fuck you laughing, though, when I'm serious as fuck, yo?"

"That's why I'm laughing. Do you seriously think I'm going to stay up and wait for you to get there?" My brows raised questioningly at him before I continued. "Then have to explain to King, who comes over to my place every morning at six for breakfast, why his friend is at my apartment?" I let out a small laugh. "Nuh uh, baby. You cute and all, but yo looks ain't worth that fight. You can say fuck King all you want, but that's my brother, *I can't*." My head was shaking the entire time I spoke. That nigga was crazy if he thought I was going to go against King. "Plus, I can't go there with you. I'm kinda seeing someone right now." I quickly added as Sly suddenly popped into my head.

Thinking about Sly was both a good and bad feeling. Good, because I honestly did want to see where things could go. Bad, because I wasn't fully ready for a commitment. Even so, Sly and I had been going pretty heavy for seven years and whether I was ready to commit or not, I would drop all my head buddies just to see where things went.

Besides, I didn't want to be the cause of our relationship failing.

"Well, you need too gon' head and dead that shit now. Let that nigga know whatever y'all had is over." Blaze said, giving me a sideway glance. "You sittin' there rollin' yo eyes when I'm serious as fuck. I don't share." The look on his face was serious.

My eyes rolled and I shrugged. "That's good to know because I'm not something that can be shared. Which is why I'm letting you know now that us, this, can't go anywhere. We can be cool, though, but it can't go past that." I told him truthfully. I wasn't the type to lead a nigga on to think we could be more, when I knew we couldn't be, for the simple fact that I wouldn't want anyone to do me like that and hurt me in the end.

"Yeah, i'ight." Blaze said with a nod of his head before he turned up the radio, ending our conversation.

Okay... I shrugged uncaringly.

***

Blaze pulled into my apartment complex and parked next to my car. He still hadn't said a word to me after he turned up the radio. And I didn't necessarily like that.

I reached over and turned the stereo down, then I faced him. "Thanks for dinner and the ride. Maybe one day we'll do this again."

"Most definitely we will. I'll be over here one day this week to finish what we started." He rubbed a hand over his mouth, and he looked at me. "A nigga just got out; you can't be playing no pussy games with me."

I pushed my door open and got out as he was still talking. "You a rude ass nigga, I swear. Bye Blaze, as always it was nice running into you." Shaking my head, I closed the door, then got my bags out his hatchback.

"Why you rushing to get out, I can't bullshit with you now?" He stared at me from the front seat, with a sexy smile on his lips.

"No, because you weren't bullshittin'." My lips pursed together as I pointed out the obvious to him. I wasn't stupid, I was far from it. I knew he was serious.

"Hell n'all, I ain't, but still, you can invite me in." He suggested to me.

Laughing, I closed the door then walked around to the driver's side. Blaze pushed his door opened and got out, blocking me from passing. "So you not gon invite me in?" He asked.

"You don't seem like the type to wait for an invitation, so what's the point in me doing so? Plus, I thought you had somewhere to be?" I leaned against the truck smiling at him. I just couldn't help but smile, even, though he was rude as hell. Blaze was funny and I had actually enjoyed his company.

"I don't wait for shit. I take what I want. Why you think I'm telling you to get rid of this nigga? I'm being nice about the shit, but you think I'm bullshittin'. I'm not baby girl, I'm serious as fuck right now. You gon' see." Blaze tilted my chin, he lowered his head, then bit at my bottom lip before he pressed his lips into mine. He gave me a simple peck. "I'll catch you later." Backing away, he gave me a once over, then hopped in the truck. He turned up the stereo, then reversed out.

Oh, my Damn, what the hell am I getting myself into? Mentally shaking myself, I made my way up the concrete stairs to my apartment. Once inside, I tossed my keys and wrist wallet on the table next to the door, then sat the bags at the closet.

I shrugged off my black leather jacket and threw it on the arm of my sofa.

A laugh suddenly slipped through my lips. "That damn man is crazy as hell." I chuckled to myself as I thought about Blaze persistent ass.

Never in my life had I come across a nigga like that before. And for the life of me I couldn't shake the nagging feeling of Blaze being a problem. Even with those thoughts I still couldn't contain the stupid smile on my damn face or the light chuckles that left my mouth as I reflected on the time, I'd just spent with him.

Pussy games? Who says that to someone?

Still laughing to myself, I kicked off my black flats and then pulled off my jeans. That left me in my black boy-short panties and a black fitted polo shirt.

I glanced over at my book-bag and groaned out a sigh before I pulled it to me. I grabbed my purple glasses and put them on, then went into the kitchen. After I put on a pot of Folgers coffee, I walked back into the living room, then flopped down on the couch.

A heavy sigh left my mouth as I got my Biology book and started on my unfinished homework.

Chapter 10

Peaches

About an hour and a half later I pushed my glasses up on my head and rubbed my eyes. I was happy that I was almost finished, all I had left to do was Math and then I could take my ass to bed. But I was in a groove as a shuffle of Trey Songs, Pleasure P, and Beyoncé played softly from the iPod dock speakers.

I hummed to Beyoncé's *Drunk In Love* as I started on my homework once again. Before I could really get back into the flow, my buzzer rang, letting me know that someone was outside. With a sigh, I got up and walked to the door and pressed the intercom.

"Who is it?" I didn't get a response the first or second time I asked. I figured someone had pressed the wrong buzzer and they either got in or left. I went back to the couch and sat down. As soon as my butt touched the sofa there was a knock on the door. "Son of a bitch." I now knew it had to be one of my childish ass friends. I went to the door again, this time I snatched it open. "Why the hell you... Blaze. Oh. Nigga, why you playing at my damn door?" I asked him while folding my arms under my chest.

"You always answer the door like this?" He asked, letting his eyes slowly roam before looking past me into my living room. "You got company?" He must have heard the music playing.

"No, I'm doing homework like I told you. Come in." I stepped out of his way and let him inside. "What are you doing here and how did you get in?" I asked. Blaze looked around the living room. His eyes soon landed on my work. He picked up my notebook and started reading over what I had done so far. Walking over to him, I took my book, then sat it back down. "Homework, like I said. Do you wanna finish it for me?"

"Nah, you got it." He said, while reaching in his pocket. "I took yo phone, that mothafucka ring too gotdamn much. I was about to toss that bitch." Blaze answered instead.

"Oh, wow. I forgot you even had it, no wonder it was so damn quiet around here. Thanks." Taking my phone, I sat it on top of my notebook. I turned my attention back to Blaze and caught his eyes fixed on my bare thighs. "Let me go put on some clothes."

"You straight how you are. You can lose the shirt, though." His deep voice had my pussy muscles tightening. Blaze ran his fingers up and down my side. Him doing so didn't help the sexual ache that began to grow in the pit of my stomach.

Blaze's left hand slipped under the back of my shirt, coming to the clamps of my bra. He undid the hooks and pulled me to him. His free hand slowly moved across my pelvis, causing my eyes to close. Thoughts of his big, strong, callus hands grasping my breast, squeezing them while the rough calluses of his palms brushed against my nipples, making them erect, had my sex throbbing.

His hand slid into my panties and he pushed a finger through my pussy slit. Blaze rubbing my swollen clit caused my eyes to snap open and my body jumped back, away from him.

"You, you should go." I panted. My eyes closed once more and I took in a deep breath as I tried to calm my overheating body down. God, I could still feel his fingers playing with my throbbing pearl. Blaze ignored what I said and he tried to grab me. I slapped his hands away from me and I quickly moved back to the other side of the couch. I needed him to leave. I hurriedly made my way to the front door. "Blaze, I done already told you I'm not going there with you. Come on now, you gotda go." Waving my hand towards the open door, I urged him out.

"Damn, I fuck with you that bad, huh?" He chuckled as he stared me over.

He thinks this shit is funny.

My eyes rolled at him as I became irritated with myself. "No you don't—. You know what? It doesn't even matter, just get out. I told you I'm seeing someone, so you have to go." I through at him once again. I hated how my body was reacting to him. It just wasn't right.

Blaze laughed as he walked towards me. You still saying that shit? I'm tellin' you, lose that nigga. I got a car full, if I didn't, I wouldn't be going no damn where. Keep playin' yo little ass games with yoself, but you ain't fooling me, though. I know that you want me just as I do you. Once you quit this bullshit you can have me." Blaze saying that broke my tensed posture and I laughed.

"You right, I want you, ain't no denying it. But you're not my type." I pushed him the rest of the way out as I talked.

Once he was on the other side of the door, I bit into my lip, looking him over, slowly taking in his semi-baggy, dark blue Gucci jeans that hung low, just below his butt. My eyes made their way to his loose fitting yellow Gucci shirt that matched his pants, then to the Pacer's snapback that sat halfway on the right side of his head before meeting his eyes. Blaze was everything I didn't want in a man.

"Looks can only get you so far with me, which isn't really that far. Night, Blaze." I gave him another smile, then closed and locked the door.

"Oh, we gon' get far, baby." He laughed from the other side of the door. "You already mine, that's what you fail to realize. You gon' see, tho', believe that." Blaze said before he knocked on the door.

I bit into my bottom lip with a stupid smile on my face. That damn man knew he was persistent as hell. Still smiling, I turned to look out the peephole only to see his retreating back.

He was most definitely going to be a fuckin' problem.

After making myself another cup of coffee I went and sat back on the couch, my back rested against the arm of the sofa. I then brought my knees up and sat my biology book on my propped up legs as well as my notebook.

Halfway through the page I heard keys jingling, which caused me to glance up. I looked just in time to see my front door opening. My eyes locked with his beautiful light brown ones for a second before I turned my attention back to my book. It wasn't long after that my book was pulled from my lap.

I was never gon' get finished with this shit.

A sigh left my mouth as I stared at Sly. "What are you doing here? I thought you were pissed at me?"

"I was, I still am. Peaches, I know you a flirt, but kissing niggas that shit not right and you know it. You can't be doing that bullshit, then you go and do it in front of me. If you're not ready for this then tell me now." Sly said, looking me in the eyes.

Lifting up, I climbed into his lap. "Sly, you already know how I feel about relationships. But truthfully, I'm honestly not ready. Regardless of that, I'm willing to give us a try." I wrapped my arms around his neck and my fingers caressed the back of his head.

"So, I didn't see Blaze just leave here?" He questioned me.

I let out a heavy sigh, then got off his lap. "Sly, you're trying to start a fight."

"No, the fuck I'm not, Peaches. But if you gon' be fuckin' with that nigga, let me know now and I'll stop fuckin' trying." Sly snapped at me, pissed off. He got up and stood in front of me, the redness in his face showed he was angry.

That was the reason I didn't want a relationship. Besides King ruining shit, I wasn't up for the bullshit drama a relationship brought. I didn't want to stand around arguing with a nigga about shit.

"Yeah, he was here. So what? It ain't like we did shit, he brought me my fuckin' phone back—" I started to explain but Sly cut me off before I could finish.

"He brought yo phone back? Why the fuck did he have your damn phone in the first place, Peaches? How did he even get it, huh?" He yelled at me.

I threw my hands up and let out an irritated sigh. "If you shut the hell up and let me talk then yo dumbass would know why, damn!" I snapped at him.

"Okay, talk." He told me as his arms folded over his chest. "Talk!" He yelled at me to explain. This nigga had his fuckin' nerve. "You ain't saying shit, Peaches. Why the fuck was he here?" Sly continued to fuss at me. That time he got into my face.

I wasn't about to argue with that dumbass fool when he wasn't listening. "Sly, I'm not about to argue with you." In the middle of me talking, I turned away from him only to have Sly grab my arm and snatch me back to him.

"Hell no, don't walk away. We about to talk about this shit now." He barked out.

I jerked out of his hold, then turned around and punched him in his chest before I pushed him away from me. "Don't come in here snatching on me and shit! When I was trying to tell you, what happened yo ass wanted to cut me off." I yelled at him, pissed off.

161

I knew I needed to calm myself down because I wasn't necessarily innocent. But I didn't like the fact he had snatched on me. "If you want to stop trying then do so, that's your choice. I'm not gon' beg yo ass, Sly. You here in my shit because you wanna be, not once did I call you over. Blaze and I hung out, so fuckin' what? That's all we did, talked and ate, then he brought me home. He came back because he had my phone, that's it." I took a deep breath trying to calm myself down. I licked my lips, then rolled my eyes before I stared back at Sly.

"I already told him we couldn't be anything more than friends for the simple fact I was kinda seeing someone. I was talking about yo dumbass, but if you gon' stand here bitchin' with that jealousy bullshit, then we might as well not even fuckin' try." I told him more calmly now. "The door is right behind you, Sly and you can walk out that mothafucka at any time. We're still going to be cool. But I'm not about to kiss yo ass because you wanna be jealous all of a sudden." I told him truthfully.

Even, though, most of everything I said was true, except the part about nothing didn't happen. I couldn't tell him I kissed Blaze or that he had touched me, and I liked it. I couldn't do that to Sly. He already didn't like Blaze being around. So, to tell him the whole truth, was only going to prolong this stupid ass argument he wanted to have.

A part of me was hoping he would say fuck it and walk away, but there was also this very small part in me that wanted it to work. I had never been in a relationship before and I kind of wanted to experience being in one. And I would like it to be with him.

Sly was about the only decent guy out here that I knew and could trust not to be on bullshit with cheating behind my back. I wanted to have a normal relationship with a guy that was on his shit, that had a life outside of dealing. Sly was clean, he had a legit job and an actual career. That was what I wanted in my man. I didn't want to be no one's dependent.

Hearing Sly sigh, I rolled my eyes already knowing where his head was at.

"Nope, no. Don't touch me Sly, go on somewhere." I pushed myself out of his hold and moved away from him.

"I'm sorry, but aside from business, I don't trust him. Blaze has already made it clear that he wants you. He doesn't care who you're with and I know him, Peaches. He got his eyes set on you and I don't want you to fall for his bullshit. Baby, I don't want to lose you before I fully get you." He was so cheesy, but his cheesiness was what I liked about him.

Sly wasn't the hardest dude around, but he was hella sweet and corny as hell. How he got in the mix with King and his bullshit was beyond me.

Probably with a fuckin' proposition.

"If you lose me it won't be because of Blaze. Sly, I don't know how many times you want me to say it, but whether I'm ready or not, I want this to work. I don't want to be the reason it doesn't, so once we make things official my little friends are gone, I swear." I told him truthfully. If we weren't committed, then I wasn't going to pretend that we were. I was young and liked to have fun. "And Blaze is not one of those friends, I promise you that. When have I ever lied to you about anything? I've always been straight with you, haven't I?" Besides the thing with Blaze, I'd never lied to him about anything.

"You're right, I can't help my reaction when it comes to you though. I'm sorry." He mumbled the last bit while walking closer to me. "Am I forgiven?" His hands came to my hips, he gripped them tight, then picked me up.

"No, Sly. Stop, put me down. I'm mad at you." My eyes rolled in my head as I tried to put on a serious face. My façade quickly failed once we fell down on the couch and his fingers dug into my sides. "Sly, stop!" I laughed out loud while wiggling underneath him.

"First, say you forgive me." He told me. But I couldn't at that moment because I was laughing so hard. My stomach was tight from his fingers wreaking havoc on my sides. "Say it." He repeated.

"You're forgiven, Sly!" I hollered, bucking my hips, trying to throw him off of me.

Sly laughed before he stopped and looked down at me. "You just saying that so I can stop." His finger ran down the side of my face.

My lips twisted to the side in order to keep myself from smiling right away. I looked away from him then back, my eyes rolled. "So what—" He started tickling me again. "I'm playing, Sly, stop. You're forgiven, I swear. Gimme a kiss." After I said that, Sly broke out laughing. He pecked my lips before he got up. "Oh, you haven't seen me in how long? And that's how you gon' kiss me?" I asked jokingly.

"I'm sorry, baby." He stopped walking and came back to me for another kiss.

I pushed him away. "Nuh uh, don't try to kiss me good now." Even, though, those words left my mouth, I jumped on him, nonetheless. My arms wrapped around his neck and my legs locked at his waist. "Are you staying the night?"

Humming, Sly leaned in and pecked my lips once, then twice. "Yeah, I missed laying next to you." He confessed as he kissed me again.

My left hand ran over his silky black hair as I sucked on his bottom lip, then the top. Sighing, I gave his lips a lingering peck. I pulled back, then rested my forehead against his.

"You missed me too?" His hand ran through my hair as he walked us to my bedroom.

There wasn't a point in lying, I did miss sleeping with him. For the last four years I'd gotten used to him being next to me most nights since I had my apartment.

"Sabes que me hace falta tu a mi lado." (You know I missed the feel of you next to me.) I mumbled, puckering my lips. Humming, Sly lowered his head pressing his lips to mine. "Eep!" A squeak left my mouth from the unexpected fall. "Cabrón." (Asshole.) I said as Sly dropped me on the bed.

"I'm not eating yo pussy so don't try to run your little game on me." My mouth opened then closed, making him laugh. "That's what I thought, scoot your ass over." He waved me to my side of the bed.

Grabbing my pillow, I hit him. "I wasn't going to ask you to. I did miss you sleeping with me. Bae, I'm not running game on you, never with you. Now come on, get naked and lay with me." I moved over and patted the side of the bed he'd occupied for the past four years.

I took off my shirt and undid my bra, I tossed it to the side. "Give me your shirt."

Sly took off his shirt and gave it to me before he removed his jeans. He pulled the covers back, then got in the bed, making himself comfortable.

Once he was, I laid my body halfway on top of his. I placed my right leg between his as my head laid on his chest. Sly kissed my forehead as his fingers began drawing invisible circles on my thigh.

"When we tell King, I want you to marry me." A sleepy yawn left my mouth before I sighed. "What's that for?" Sly asked.

I traced my fingers over his toned chest, then placed a kiss on his left peck.

"I don't want to be a downer." Another sigh left my mouth.

"Then don't be. All you have to do is say yes when I ask. Time is nothing, Peaches. Until you're ready, I'll wait as long as you want me too. Just knowing your mine is all that matters." He explained as his arm held me tight.

Smiling, I kissed his chest then continued to kiss my way up to his throat, then chin. I move my body fully on top of Sly's and my mouth came to his.

"If you can give me a drama free year after we tell King, then I'll say yes. I mean no bullshit whatsoever." I bargained. I hoped within that year I would had actually fallen in love with Sly instead of having this heavy *like* I felt for him.

"What? I done gave you seven, almost eight years with no drama and now that I'm this close, I'm not going to fuck up." He finished saying with a hard slap to my thigh.

"Ouch, Sly, damn. That shit hurt." I whined. He chuckled as I popped his chest. "That shit not funny, you bastard. Sly, don't start playing. I'm tired and you know we have to get up at five before King shows up." I finished saying with a yawn at the same time he huffed out a breath.

He was irritated with sneaking around. I knew that, but King's reaction of the news was what I feared most. Sly's irritation didn't touch the fear I felt when it came to my brother. Even with these thoughts I still felt the need to reassure him.

"Bae, I promise I'll tell King soon. Even if he do go off, at least he'll know, and we won't have to sneak around no more." Another yawn left my mouth and my eyes closed. I buried my face into his neck and got comfortable.

"Alright Peaches." He sighed as his hand rubbed up and down my back.

I waited for sleep to take me, but it didn't come easy as my mind strangely went on Blaze. I began to wonder what he was doing at that moment. My stomach soon tightened as the feel of his rough callus hands touching me invaded my wandering thoughts.

"What you smiling about?" Sly's voice broke through my reverie.

I didn't answer, instead I pretended I was asleep as I tried clearing my mind of that cocky smile, persistent attitude, and rude personality that was Blaze.

But I couldn't.

That wasn't good, not at all.

I need to get him out of my head and fast.

Chapter 11

Peaches

One Month Later

I sat outside of Dr. Sliverio Rodriquez, MD office. I stared at the sign for a few more seconds before I got out of my car and fixed my scrubs. A sigh left my mouth as I ran a hand through my hair. I had just gotten out of school and I was tired. I really didn't feel like going to work, I wanted to go home.

A sigh left my mouth once more and I grabbed my purse, then locked my doors. I pressed the alarm button, securing my baby. That was a must when I worked at a Doctor's office that was in the hood. Niggas around there would steal yo shit without a care.

Going to that place could be so tiring at times. Especially when I had to deal with some of the most lying, ghetto ass folks that went in there. Bitches could have two different STI's and still be claiming they never had sex. Regardless of the nasty, dirty ass folks that went there, I still loved my job as a medical assistant, especially since it came with good pay.

"Hey Dane." I spoke, smiling as I waved at my co-worker.

Dane was a big, sexy, dark chocolate grizzly bear. He was big, cocky, I mean his whole body was full of muscles. One might have found it strange seeing such a big dude working as a MA, but Dane was harmless. He was just a big, chocolate teddy bear. Too bad he was married.

I would've had eyes for him if he wasn't, though. He was sexy, smart, had a bomb ass personality, and a legit job. What more could one ask for?

"Peaches!" Dane called, slapping his hands together in front of my face.

"Sorry, I was thinking about something. How's Jennifer and the baby?" I asked him as we made our way to the back to clock in.

"Good, Megan's little badass getting into any and everything she can get her hands on. Jen told me to invite you over for dinner like three weeks ago, but I forgot."

Laughing, I hit him in the arm. "Just like a nigga. Three weeks really, D? Damn that's messed up." He shrugged with a chuckle.

"You know I'm a forgetful mothafucka. So what yo tiny ass been into? And don't lie saying nothing, yo ass

170

always have a story." Dane said, making me laugh at his nosiness.

"Shit, same old same old. Hey, have you heard of some dude by the name of Blaze?" I asked him, he was from the hood and well known too. Dane used to play ball with King back in the day, sometimes they still played at the Rex when his nose wasn't up in Jennifer's ass.

I asked him about Blaze because I couldn't ask King without suspicion being raised, even though nothing was going on between us. But it had been well over a month since I'd seen his rude ass, which was a good thing. But at the same time, I couldn't keep my mind from wandering to him. Especially after he told me that I was, *got,* and he also promised we were going to finish what we started.

A part of me was kind of hoping we would.

What the hell am I saying? It's a good thing he's not coming around no more. The last thing I needed in my life right now was a fuckin' hood.

Sitting at my desk, I started up my computer, then turned back to Dane who had suddenly become quiet. I didn't mind talking to him about it at that moment because the clinic didn't open for another ten minutes and we were the only two at my desk.

"Dane?" I called his name questioningly.

He let out a loud sigh as he pulled out the chair next to me. "Shit, he ain't nothing nice is all I can really say. I ain't no scary dude, I'll drop a nigga in a minute. But shid, that's one mothafucka I wouldn't want to piss off, no lie. That nigga straight crazy, but he's smart as fuck." He pointed out.

I knew Blaze had a mouth on him, his damn words could be reckless as hell. I had witness that firsthand. But I didn't think he was scary. Regardless of what I've learned about him from Missy and Kim, I wanted to see what Dane knew about Blaze. "What you mean he crazy? How so?" I asked as if I didn't know anything about Blaze.

"Blaze ain't scared to up strap on no nigga. Remember Carl that used to play ball with us back in the day?" Dane asked.

Carl. Just thinking about him had a sigh leaving my mouth. I had the biggest crush on him when I was eighteen. But he was too deep in the streets, fucking anything with legs and I just couldn't deal with a nigga that can't be faithful. Even thinking about him at that moment still didn't change the fact I was head over heels for him.

He was the only hood I ever liked.

Carl was a caramel skinned brotha with pretty, green eyes that had specks of brown in them. He stood six feet, three, the height of a basketball player, but he was built like a football player. The fast life got to him, though, hoes and being a dope boy was all he knew. And just like most young dudes in the hood, he got hooked on the shit, crack and heroine. On top of that he was smoking woo. He smoked it with weed, cigarettes, hell, everything that could be smoked he had woo mixed in it. That shit was sad and crazy to me

His ass was so bad, he'd gotten so small, but I had a crush on the guy and with me wanting to be a nurse. I thought I could help him. We had made plans to meet, but we didn't because he never showed up. Two months had gone by when word got out that he was found dead and his body was burned. I never knew what really happened, but the night we were supposed to meet was the night he died.

"From the look on your face I know you remember." Dane said, and I nodded my head while playing with my fingers. "Blaze did that shit. My dude Tank used to fuck with Blaze back then, before he got with Tasha. Apparently, Carl stepped to him on some disrespectful type shit. Carl ass was high from what Tank told me, but to Blaze disrespect was just that, so he killed him. Said he beat his ass bad in front of everybody. Fuck'd up if you ask me. I mean everybody knew how Carl's ass got when he was gone on that shit. Apparently, Blaze didn't give a fuck and bodied his ass. I wasn't there but I still kind of think it's more to that story." He shook his head then shrugged.

Everything I'd been hearing about that nigga was reason enough for me to stay away from him. I didn't want a nigga that was in the streets. I refused to become like my momma was. Staying at home, all alone, worried about when I'mma get that call telling me my man's dead. Fuck that. I already had to deal with that shit because of King's ass.

"Damn. And King cool with this nigga?" I asked, not wanting to believe my brother could hang with someone like that. To my surprise, Dane's big black ass laughed like something was funny.

King wasn't good, I'd never claimed he was, but I didn't think he'd go that far. Yeah, shooting a nigga would be something normal to him, but to burn somebody for being disrespectful was just fuckin' psychotic.

"What's funny?" I asked him not seeing the humor in it.

"I know you want to think King's ass can't do shit wrong, but that mothafucka just as crazy as Blaze ass, if not crazier. Fuck you mean King cool with him? Those nigga's grow up in their line of work *together*." Dane stated.

"Yo lying ass. I've known King my whole life, he ain't shit like that." A part of me just didn't want to believe that King was like Blaze. I couldn't picture my brother being psychotic.

"Like I said, King shows you the shit he wants you to know. I used to hang with him back then, Peach. And wherever King was, Blaze ass wasn't too far behind and vice versa." Dane stated his expression was serious. I believed him. But I didn't want too.

I smacked my lips before turning away from him. "Don't yo ass got to work or something?" Yes, I was pissed because of what he said, I mean I wasn't saying my brother was a saint. Hell, he was far from it. He was hot headed and would pop a nigga in a minute but setting fiends on fire for some disrespectful type shit wasn't right.

It wasn't like folks on drugs were aware of the bullshit they were doing, hell, they were high ass fuck. King would've laugh at the mothafucka or probably hit his ass, but not kill 'em. Hell, crackheads made those damn streets funny and niggas needed a good laugh to deal with that life.

To be honest, I was mostly mad because Blaze killed Carl. Especially when I felt that I could've helped him if he would've made it to my apartment that night. That's what I wanted to believe anyway.

"Why you asking about him?" Dane questioned from behind me.

I shrugged before answering him. "I met him and his friend Sam at Voodoo like a month ago, almost cut his dick off. I just wanted some insight on him." I replied as an approaching figure caught my attention. Dr. Sliverio Rodriquez, walked down the hallway towards us. I turned to him and waved. "Good morning." A smile came to my lips as our eyes locked briefly.

"Morning." His lips seemed to move in slow motion and my eyes followed him as he continued down the hall.

A sharp pinch snapped me out of my little trance. "What the hell, Dane?" I snapped, grabbing my arm. "Did you just pinch me?" I asked him as I looked at the red mark right above my elbow.

"Stop eye fucking him." He laughed. "Don't make me tell King on that ass." He threatened.

My lips smacked hard and I rolled my eyes. "What the hell he gon' do? Shit, but threaten me. King's not my man and last I checked I'm grown." I told him before glancing back at Sly who I had plans on sneaking off with later on.

"Don't play, I'm still waiting on my invitation to the wedding." He laughed.

My head snapped towards him so fast I swear I heard my neck crack. Did he think King and I were... *Peaches and King?*

"What the hell are you thinking, Dane? That's nasty, ain't no incestuous shit going on up over here. We don't do that..." My words trailed off. I was a split second from going off on him. That was until I realized that he was one of those friends that King kept in the dark. He didn't know that King was actually my real brother and not my friend. King had a deep fear that if niggas knew we were family, they might try to hurt me to get at him. Which was why he told folks we were friends.

Instead of going off on him like I wanted too. I waved him off, no longer mad because he didn't know the truth. "King, is like my brother, I don't see him as nothing other than that. We've known each other since we were kids." I said calmly.

The nigga looked at me like I was lying or something. "That's how it always starts then the next thing you know y'all will be fucking." He shot back.

My lips pressed tight together in order to stop the smartass comment from leaving my mouth. I chose to ignore what he said, with a simple shake of my head as well as a hard roll of my eyes.

Dane simply laughed it off knowing what he said had likely pissed me off. "Let me get to work before you try throwing yo little fist at me." He stated with a nod towards the door.

My eyes followed the gesture, a sigh slipped through my lips as I watched the two front desk receptionists come in. Officially telling us the office was now opened.

I hope no bullshit starts today.

***

"Peaches, can you pull up Mr. Carter's file then call him to come in around one-thirty?" Dr. Rodriquez asked coming out of his office.

"Sure. Does Mr. Carter have a first name?" I questioned, getting ready to pull his name up on the computer.

He glanced up from the file in his hand and looked at me. Sly licked his lips, then shook his head before his eyes returned to the papers. "No, just Carter. And he's not in the computer." He told me before walking into room three where a patient waited.

God, that man is fine as hell. I bit into my bottom lip as my eyes followed his retrieving back, until the door closed behind him.

A long breath slipped through my lips as I stood from my chair to go to the file cabinet, but I stopped and glared at Dane.

He was leaning against the wall opposite me, grinning. "Peaches, got a little crush I see." He taunted, with his wide smile still intact, showing off his pearly whites.

"Don't yo nosy ass have work to do?" I laughed, going around him. I made my way to the file cabinets to pull Mr. Carter's folder. Once I found it, I turned back to Dane waiting on his response.

Not a word left his mouth, though, only a hum in the back of his throat, before he walked off.

***

"Trina Daniels!" I called out as I looked around the waiting room. "*Trina Daniels?*" I repeated, when I didn't see anyone get up, I turned to walk into the back.

"Hold up, that's me. I was in the bathroom." She yelled out to me. I looked over my shoulder and noticed it was the same Trina from Voodoo's.

I smiled at her. "I'm Peaches, come on to the back with me." I introduced myself while holding the door open for her. Once we were in the back, I led her to the scale. "Step on so I can get your weight." She seemed to have a slight attitude for some odd reason, but I paid it no mind. I was at work and didn't want to act stupid. After I wrote down her weight, I took her in room one. "You can sit on the bed or the chair if you like." I told her as she stood there.

Starting up the computer, I looked back at her only to notice she was still standing, looking at me. I Ignored her gaze and continued to do my job. After I pulled up her info, I grabbed my sphygmomanometer and stethoscope.

"I need to take your blood—"

"There ain't nobody else in here that can help me?" Tina asked snobbishly as her arms folded under her chest.

My brows rose at that before I rolled my eyes. "Nope, just me. Now you either let me do what I need to, or take yo ass back in the waiting room, your choice. To be honest I really don't give a fuck which one you choose." I finally snapped at her. I didn't know what her problem was but she wasn't about to take it out on me. Especially when I didn't do shit to her ass.

"You know whatever you got going on with Chase gon' stop. He got a baby, a family to take care of. He don't have time for no gold diggin' ass hoes like you comin' after him. Bitch, I'm baby momma, girlfriend, wifey, everything to that man. So, stay the fuck away from him." She snapped, taking a step towards me.

She was pissed over Chase. Someone I'm not even dating? That bitch had me fuck'd up to address some play, play bullshit at my job.

"First off, don't come at me with that bullshit! As you said, whatever *I* got going on with Chase is none of *your* concern. Now I don't know who you are to him and personally I don't give a fuck. You need to take that shit up with yo nigga, not me." I replied back as calmly as possible.

"N'all bitch I'm taking it up with you, right now. And this my first and only time warning yo ass." Her voice rose loudly as she moved back away from me.

I knew from her loud tone; she was going to be overheard and I didn't want to lose my job over this bitch. So, I tried to calm myself down. "Like I said, talk to yo nigga not me because I didn't know shit about you. Now, with that said, yo ass came in here for a reason and it wasn't for me. So, you can sit yo ass down, and shut the fuck up. Worry about that infected ass pussy of yours. That's what yo ass need to be worrying about because I can smell that shit from here." The more I talked I got pissed off. I couldn't believe that hoe came to my job trying to check me over a nigga that didn't seem to mind her ass.

"And apparently, he ain't to fuck'd up about you seeing us conversate because you were right there when we were talking and you ain't say shit." I stopped what I was saying and took a deep breath. "You know what? Get the fuck out before you make me lose my damn job for beatin' yo triflin' ass. Bitch, you got me fuck'd up." I snapped, opening the door. "Bye, take yo ass to the health department so they can treat yo triflin' ass." I told her, and the bitch just stood there mugging like she was about to do something.

"What's the problem?" Dr. Rodriquez asked as both he and Dane stopped at the door, before they entered the room. The both of them looked every bit of confused.

"Don't even worry about it, hold this." I told them as I took my chain with the brass knuckles on it, off. I gave it to Dane.

That bitch had me all the way fuck'd up. She ain't know me from shit to piss, but she gon' step to me like she knew. Oh, but she was going to learn Peaches was the right one to fuck with.

"Goes to show how I'm not fuck'd up about you, bitch. Come on, mama, fuck with me."

I never been one of those girls that just stood there and argued. What was the point when I didn't know how to argue, besides calling someone a bitch? That was as much of an argument anyone would get out of me. And I damn sho' wasn't gon let nobody hit me first, that's just not my thing.

My fist flew out towards her, but before I could hit Trina I was pulled back. *Why was it that whenever I was about to do some damage someone always grabbed me? Damn.*

"You better grab that bitch! Hoe, you don't know, I rock hoes like you all day. Bitch, you ain't scaring no mothafuckin body, step to me if you wanna, bet you get that ass handed to you. Stay the fuck away from Chase or you will be seeing me again." She yelled at me.

It's funny how the bitch got her voice when I was grabbed. I tried to get free from Dane's big ass, but that fucka wasn't letting up. Fuck'd up thing about ol' girl was if she really wanted to fight, she would've run up because nobody was holding her scary ass.

Dane continued to move backwards, further away from the scene as I fussed and thrust around in his arms.

"Fuck you, bitch. If you want it I go to lunch in a half hour, have yo triflin' ass outside." I yelled before a door was closed in my face.

Rude much!

"What the hell is wrong with you, Peaches?" Dane snapped at me.

My eyes rolled hard at him. "That bitch shouldn't have come at me like that. Especially when she doesn't even know me. You ain't hear her ass in that room. And I'm not about to let no nigga or bitch step to, talk to, or mug me any kind of way. Especially when I didn't do shit to them." If she had a problem with me talking to Chase, why not say something at the club that night? Why wait a month or so later to come at me with that bullshit?

"Peaches, I get that. But come on, man, you at work. Put that pride of yours to the side until you leave here. To make matters worse, yo ass packing in the office." Dane trailed off as the office door opened and Dr. Rodriquez walked in.

A heavy sigh left my mouth at Dane's ending sentence. I forgot to leave my damn gun in the car.

"Dane, you can take your lunch break, I've already sent everyone else out." Sly told him. Dane cast a glance at me before shaking his head, then leaving out, closing the door behind him.

"I—" I was about to explain.

"Shush." Sly said, cutting me off. He took off his white jacket, then loosened his tie. While he did that, not a word left his mouth. We sat there quiet for what felt like ten minutes and I couldn't take it no more.

"Look, I—" Again I was cut off as he suddenly jerked my body to his and his lips roughly came down on mine. A laugh left my mouth before I pulled back. "Sliverio, we can't—." My protest was ignored as he pulled me back against his body. "Sly, we can't do this here." I mumbled between kisses, but just like before, he ignored me. Instead his hands grabbed the hem of my shirt, pulling it over my head. Once it was off he pushed me on his desk.

Sly removed my shoes then pulled down my scrub bottoms with my panties while I worked on the buttons of his shirt. After the last button came undone, I made quick work with his belt, pulling his jeans and boxers down his hips.

"Vas a dejarme entrar?" (You're going to let me in?) Sly asked, pausing. I nodded my head and he looked at me a bit harder, longer, searching my expression for any doubt. "You're sure?" He asked, his Spanish accent thick with lust.

It was beyond sexy and made me hornier. I was already sexually frustrated, thinking and dreaming of Blaze's ass. Sly was just what I needed at the moment, a reliever.

I was tired of being a fuckin' virgin!

"Sí, papí. Quiero sentirte." (Yes, Daddy. I want to feel you.) I whispered; my tongue flicked over his lips as my arms locked around his neck.

Sly groaned in the back of his throat before his lips came back down on mine. He sucked on both my top and bottom lip before his tongue slid into my mouth. The thrust of his hips caused his hard dick to slide into my fold and rub against my swelling pearl.

A moan left my mouth as he pulled away, causing the sound to echo through the room.

Sly kissed his way down my neck, going to my breasts. He took hold of both my titties, he squeezed them, then sucked the right nipple into his mouth while he pinched and rolled the other.

"Sly, don't tease me, eat my pussy, baby." I moaned out. We only had an hour for lunch and if he kept at that pace. I wouldn't be able to cum, nor would he get to nut like I planned on us both doing.

"Beautiful, I plan on tasting every part of you." He said while kissing down my stomach to my pelvis.

My hand fisted into his hair and my hips rose off the desk as he ran his tongue down to my sex. Instinctively, my legs widen immediately.

"Eager, aren't we?" He didn't even know the half of it.

If only he knew this desperate ache wasn't because of him.

"Sly, *Por Favor*!" (Please!) I panted in an anxious tone.

With my words and his groan, Sly started to dive in.

His lips sucked on my swollen nub as his hands kept my thighs apart. My teeth sank into my bottom lip hard to keep from moaning out in pleasure as his mouth sucked on my clit.

As Sly nipped and sucked on my hardened pearl. His head pulled back as his fingers parted my lower lips, and he continued to wreak havocs on my swollen nub. He pinched, rubbed, then spanked my sensitive clit, causing my hips to raise off of the desk and more against his franticly moving fingers.

My head went back as my hand ran over his silky, smooth hair before grabbing the back of his head. I grind my pussy against his face to meet the strokes of his tongue. My legs soon began to shake, making Sly suck harder.

"Ah! Fuck! Sly, baby, harder! Chuparme más duro papí!" (Suck my pussy harder, daddy!) I moaned loudly, my hips bucked, muscles tightened, thighs shaking as my back arched.

"Coño, me encanta el sabor de tu crica. Te vienes para mí, mami." (Damn, I love the taste of your pussy, baby, cum for me mami) Sly mumbled against my sex, as his hand slapped hard against my throbbing pussy once, then twice before his mouth came back to my clit. My body shook violently and I came hard into his mouth.

Sly greedily licked, sucked up every drop of my sweet nectar.

Heavily panting, I fell against the desk while trying to come down from my orgasmic high.

"Sweet, but messy like always." Sly commented with a laugh.

"Fuck you. You started it so don't complain now." I chuckled as I took in the messy papers and scattered pens on his desk. I moved his name plate then reached over into his top drawer and grabbed a condom.

I was a virgin, but I loved the feel of his tip pushing inside of me. We didn't have sex fully, but what we did wasn't far from it. Plus, Sly was the only guy I did that with. I knew it was torture for him, but he never made a fuss about it, nor had he ever tried to go further when I did let him in.

"Baby, I'm not complaining, I love it and you know that. I just don't like the mess I have to clean up afterwards." He laughed again while sitting me up.

I hit him, laughing as well because it was true.

I opened the condom, then rolled it down on him. I then took hold of his dick and placed it at my sex. My lips came to his as my right arm wrapped around his neck, the other still holding his hardened dick as he slowly pushed forward.

Whenever we did that, a part of me would hope that would be the moment he goes further and push all the way inside of me. Only so, I could get it over with and no longer be a virgin.

Sly's tip pushed inside of my pussy and I sucked in a breath. It had been a year, if not longer, since I'd let him do that, but I needed it. Just getting head simply wasn't going to feed that aching need in the pit of my stomach.

"I love the feel of you." Sly mumbled. Pulling out, he pushed back in, going a bit deeper.

The pain added with the pleasurable pulse of my pussy, caused a muffled moan to leave my mouth and go into his. My nails dug into the nape of his neck as the kiss deepened. My eyes closed as I lifted myself up, then slowly began to come down on Sly's dick, trying to take more of him.

There was a slight rip on the door, then another three before the door creaked.

The sound had my eyes opening.

Only to have them lock with the man responsible for my sudden ache.

Blaze.

Oh, my God!

Chapter 12

Peaches

"*Shit!*" I said out loud, I was beyond embarrassed. *What the hell is he doing here?* I hadn't seen that nigga in a month and he just pop up at my job.

"Did I hurt you?" Sly must not have heard him come in. From the concerned look on his face, I knew he hadn't.

Blaze stood at the office door frozen, as his eyes jumped from me to Sly.

"Sly." I whispered his name, then nodded my head forward gesturing for him to look at Blaze.

Following my movement, he glanced back, doing a fast double take.

"Fuck." He said before quickly handing me my shirt. Sly then pulled up his boxers and slacks. making me roll my eyes.

He had already seen us, so why was he rushing?

"I think I may need a restraining order on you, if you're going to be following me like this." I told Blaze, playing it off as if I wasn't embarrassed as well as trying to get rid of the sudden tension that was forming in the room.

"Mr. Carter." Sly said his name then looked at me as if saying that, he was there for business, not me. "Blaze, come in." He gave him a slight smile, acting as if Blaze hadn't just walked in on us.

What he said finally dawned on me...

Carter? Mr. Carter? I called him here. Shit!

The smile that was on his lips soon disappeared as Blaze threw his fist into Sly's face.

To say I was shocked would've been the understatement of the freaking year.

What the hell is he doing? Why is he hitting him?

"Blaze, what the fuck! Get off of him!" I screamed at Blaze as I went to pull him off Sly. My attempt failed when Blaze push me back before his Timberland boot started coming down on the side of Sly's face. "Blaze, stop it!" He was literally stomping the shit out of him. "Blaze, Stop!" I yelled once more, trying to grab him, but again he pushed me off.

"Nigga, what the fuck is wrong with you? Didn't I warn yo ass to stay away from her? I told yo ass if I ever saw you touch her again, I'll kill yo punk ass!" Blaze threatened, punching Sly in the face.

"Damn it Blaze, Stop!" I screamed louder as he pulled a gun from under his shirt and started pistol whooping him. *This mothafucka is seriously fuckin' crazy.* "Oh My God, Sly." I mumbled in disbelief. My eyes were wide with shock and I pushed Blaze hard away from him. I then quickly went to Sly's side, seeing the blood run from his head, mouth and nose.

"If you touch him, I'll kill his ass. Now get yo shit on." Blaze snapped at me, looking pissed off.

"Fuck you, nigga. You can't come in here like you run shit. He ain't done nothing to you!" I snapped before jumping on him and swinging. "You fuckin' lunatic!" My fist hit harder with my ending words.

"Peaches, get the fuck off me before I knock yo ass out." Blaze yelled. He pushed me back hard, making me stumble into the desk.

"Try it with yo punk ass!" I screamed, about to start swinging on his ass again. But Sly stopped me.

"It's cool, Peach." Sly grabbed my hand. He then got up off the floor and leaned against his desk.

What Blaze had done to him wasn't cool and Sly didn't deserve that bullshit. "What the fuck you mean it's cool? He had no reason to come in here and put his fuckin' hands on you!" Pissed couldn't begin to describe how I was feeling at that moment. And with Sly willing to just let it go as if it was nothing, only added to the fire I felt.

"Keep talkin' that shit, Lil Bit. I'mma put you on yo ass and best believe I ain't worried about King. You got one more time to disrespect and put yo hands on me, I'mma fuck you up." Blaze warned and he looked every bit of serious.

But I wasn't scared of him. I went to push out of Sly's arms, but he held me tighter.

"You ain't gotda be worried about King, nigga. As I said before, I handle mine. I don't give a fuck who you think you are, but I'm none of these bitch ass niggas out here that's scared of you. I can promise yo ass that. Fuck with me Blaze if you want to." I threw my own threat back at him. No I didn't think I could beat his ass in real life. But I wasn't going to let him talk to me any kind of way either. My dad and brother didn't raise no damn punks.

To make my threat sound good, I started to struggle in Sly's arms. "Let me the fuck go, damn. Come on Blaze." My voice raised at him.

Blaze didn't look bothered with my attempt. "Do yo brother know you fuckin' this nigga? Huh?" A slight smirk came to his lips as he stared at me.

The rowdiness I had moments ago, left. My mouth quickly clamped shut and my body froze from the question. The realization that he was trying to punk me, had my lips pursing together and I glared harder at him. I was literally trying to kill him with my stare.

"That's none of yo fuckin' business, nor is it his." My words weren't as strong as before. Blaze found the nerve that scared the hell out of me and that was, King finding out about me and Sly.

"Fuck what you talkin' 'bout, but from the way you just tensed up, I'm guessing he don't. So how about this, which could actually help the three of us out. In order for me not to kill you, you fire her and to keep the both of you safe I won't tell King what I just walked in on." Blaze bargained.

Is he serious?

"Are you blackmailing me?" I asked dumbly. We were grown as hell, who in the fuck blackmailed anymore? That was high school shit.

Blaze picked up my bra from the floor, then pushed it into my chest. He then sat in a chair, leaning back, with his legs wide opened.

"Call it what you want—, if you hit me, I'm gon' beat yo ass. So un-ball those little fists of yours and move back." *This son of a bitch.* "As I was saying, Sly, she's putting in her two-week notice." Blaze said, and I got ready to pounce on him. But again, Sly grabbed me.

"No, the fuck I'm not! You can't do this! I fuck who I wanna. King don't have a say in that, period. So, I don't give a fuck if you do call him! He might yell, but he won't hurt me." My matter of fact tone of voice didn't seem to faze him. And the hand I put on my hip only made him laugh at me.

"Probably not you, but Sly though, I'm pretty sho' he'd put this nigga in a black bag without a second thought." He stated as his hand dug in his pocket and he pulled out a cigarette. He lit it.

"Fuck you!" I was so pissed at him. I just wanted to hit him.

"Soon, I promise." Blaze smiled at me then winked. He turned his attention back to Sly, glaring at him. "Nigga, didn't I tell you not to touch her. Peaches, put yo gotdamn shirt on." He snapped with such bass in his voice, I started to do it.

"Blaze, chill, damn. I agree with her, this don't have shit to do with you nor King, so cool it with them blank ass threats." Sly told him, causing Blaze to stare at him as if he was stupid.

"Blank? Nigga when have you ever known me to make a threat I never followed through with?" Blaze asked, sitting his gun in his lap and to my surprise Sly let me go.

He actually let me go. What the hell? *Why would he do that?*

"I'm not losing my job, nor is King gon' touch him, bet that. In fact, I'll call King my damn self. This that bullshit." I hoped King wouldn't flip out and kill Sly.

My eyes slanted, staring hard at Blaze. I snatched my shirt off of the desk, then forcefully yanked it on before I grabbed the office phone. I picked it up, only to have the phone snatched from my hand. My eyes snapped up to meet Sly's, who took the phone and placed it back on the hook.

"Don't call King, we'll work something out." He said, with a glance in Blaze direction.

"Sly, are you serious?" Our eyes locked as I whispered to him, hoping Blaze couldn't hear. Every other day he'd been working my fuckin' nerves about us having to sneak around. Now all of a sudden, he didn't want to say shit because of Blaze? "You don't want me to tell King about us?" I questioned him.

"Peaches." I heard it in his voice, he didn't. After arguing and fighting he wanted to change his mind. If anything, it was the perfect time to tell him.

"You know what? Fuck you *and* him! I can't believe this bullshit." I snatched my gun off the desk before walking out of the room. I made sure to slam that door behind me. Dane entered the back office just as I was walking out.

"What happened?" Shaking my head, I walked past him to my desk grabbing my purse and keys. "Peaches wait, tell me what's wrong." Dane said as he caught my arm, making me stop.

"Dane, it's nothing okay. I'll talk to you later." I pulled my arm from his hold, then left the office. Once I made it outside, I saw Sam leaning against the passenger door of a burgundy truck, smoking a Black & Mild.

"Hey, Peaches, you can't speak?" He called over to me.

My eyes rolled into my head, not wanting to take my attitude out on him. So, I ignored him and continued on to my car. I hit the unlock button on the remote then got in, starting it up. I glanced over at Sam and a smile soon came to my lips. I pulled up on him, then let the window down.

"You hungry?" I asked, making him laugh.

Sam pushed himself off the burgundy Ford Expedition XLT and walked to my car. "I can't get a hi, but instead an invitation?"

"Take your mind out the gutta, pretty boy. I'm talking about real food, my treat. I mean if you wanna stay out here and wait then…" I trailed off with a shrug.

Sam thought about it for a minute. "I'll ride with you. What we eating?" Sam asked, getting in.

"I want some tacos. Are you cool with that?" I asked while looking back at the truck.

"Sounds good to me—" He was in the middle of saying until I cut him off.

"Is this you?" I asked, pointing to the truck. I hoped it wasn't.

"That's Blaze truck, mine is at his place." He informed me.

Nodding my head, I smiled before I pulled the .9mm with the silencer from under my seat.

"Hold on, Peaches, what the hell—" Sam started saying.

I cut him off as I started shooting up the passenger side of the truck. I shot out all three windows, the doors and the front and back tires, then hurriedly pulled away.

"Oh, my God, I feel so much better." I laughed, turning up French Montana's Marble Floors.

"Pull the fuck over and let me out this fuckin' car. Bitch, you crazy!" Sam snapped, turning down the radio.

Coming to a stop light, I looked at him like he was stupid. "You gon' call me a bitch while I have a gun in my hand? Really? Do you not remember what happened last time?" I asked, waving the gun towards him.

"Fuck that. You just shot up that man's truck and he just got it today. That's a sixty-thousand-dollar truck, your little gun—" He said twinkling his fingers towards my 9. "–ain't gon be shit compared to what he has when he finds yo ass. Now let me the fuck out!" Sam fussed at me.

I couldn't help but burst out laughing as I pulled off.

"I'm not worried about Blaze. Fuck him, real talk. Plus, how would he know it was me if you don't open up yo big ass mouth and say shit?" Truly I wasn't worried, Blaze had me fuck'd up if he thought otherwise. Coming to another stop light, I securely slid my gun back into its holster under the seat. "What you want from PJ's, I'm hungry as hell?" I glanced at him and did a double take when I noticed his facial expression. He was clearly shocked. "What?"

"You acting like you just didn't do shit." He told me in disbelief.

"I didn't do anything. What are you talking about?" I questioned dumbly. When he didn't say anything, I pulled out my phone and called PJ's. When they answered I ordered myself seven tacos', some Mozzarella sticks, and a strawberry Icy. "What you want?"

"On everything King yo damn brother, I swear." He laughed before telling me what he wanted. "What Blaze do to you anyways?" He asked once I hung up.

"He walked in on me and Sly, then flipped the fuck out before telling Sly to fire me otherwise he was going to tell King. Who the fuck blackmails anymore? Shit's crazy." Sam burst out laughing, hitting my door. "What's funny?" I asked while pulling into PJ's parking lot.

"You just shot up that nigga truck because of that? Man, I could see if you said he broke into yo shit and stole something, then I'd understand. But you pissy over a blackmail Blaze ass ain't falling through on? Niggas not snitchin' over who you fuckin', Blaze was just messing with you. But shid, he gon' beat that ass for fuckin' with his truck. Shid, burn the nigga clothes or something, don't fuck with his ride." Sam explained in a serious tone. One that didn't faze me at all.

With a shrug, I got out the car to go get our food. Once I had it, I returned to see him on the phone.

"Nah, he had to go see Dr. Rodriquez. I guess they sent him the wrong type of pills and that shit had him getting sick." I heard him say, making me roll my eyes.

I'd been around King long enough to understand the code he was saying. I knew if it was King and they sent him the wrong type of pills he'd go crazy. Then again, it wasn't really code because they were talking about pills whether they were referring to the heavy shit or not.

"Nigga, I know you did not just light a blunt. Are you tryna kill me?" I looked at Sam like he'd grown a second head. Beside my bitches, wasn't nobody allowed to smoke in my ride, King's ass didn't even smoke in my damn car.

"Let the window down." He said before inhaling deeply.

"You know, you're a rude, disrespectful ass nigga for real. I don't like your kind at all." I told him truthfully, making him laugh. "You laughing but let me find one burn mark and I'mma fuck you up." I spoke honestly.

"Why yo ass so mean? Damn Peach, breathe. You need to hit this blunt." He held the blunt out towards me.

Rolling my eyes, I glanced at him, then smiled as I looked at his ear.

"Why you smiling? My niggas know I'm with you so if something happens to me that's yo ass." He informed me seriously.

I burst out laughing at him. I pulled into my apartment complex and parked in my section. "Boy, ain't nobody gon' do shit to yo scary ass. I was just looking at your ear, does it hurt?" I asked, flicking his ear, making him drop his blunt.

"What the fuck, Peaches?" He snapped at me.

"Dude, pick that shit up before you burn my damn floor." I snapped and he gave me a mean look. I turned away from him so that I wouldn't smile in his face.

"You gon' make me fuck you up, on my life. You ain't gon' keep talkin' to me like I'm some bitch. I'mma rock yo little ass, keep on." He threatened as I turned off the car.

My lips twisted and my eyes rolled up, showing him, I wasn't worried about it. With a glance in his direction, a laugh slipped through my lips at his hard stare.

"I'm not worried about you, Pretty Boy. Now get the food and come on." I told him while closing the door.

Sam soon followed. The hard slam of my car door had my head turning his way. My mouth opened and I was ready to snap at him.

"Don't say shit." He warned me.

His pissed off expression had my hands going up and a laugh ready to leave my mouth.

"Stop whining. But for real, does your ear hurt?" I asked seriously, looking at the red tip where the bullet grazed him.

"Like yo ass care." He replied, staring at me.

"I don't, but I'm being nice, tryna make a truce. You know, hold up the white flag." I said with a wave of my finger.

"I know what the hell a truce is, but I don't trust yo little ass." Sam's head shook at me.

Again, I laughed out loudly at that. "Wow, way to realize it after getting in my car and now walking into my house. If I ain't trust a person there's no way in hell I'm leaving with them." I told him while dropping my keys on the side table. I then kicked off my white Nikes. "Wait, wasn't it about a month ago you were ready to marry me?"

"You talk a lot of shit, and that was before your brother told me to step the fuck off." He laughed at that.

My eyes rolled up in my head because I knew he was telling the truth.

"And you say a lot of dumb shit, *and* you're dumb as hell for listening to King. But you're not my type anyway." I turned on the TV, then glanced back at Sam before heading towards my room. "You can sit in the living room or kitchen, I'll be back." I said, walking to my room and then closing the door.

Once inside, I went to my dresser, grabbing a pair of light blue shorts that stopped at the top of my thighs. I matched it with a hot pink, spaghetti strapped tank top. Along with my pink, knee high socks, laying them on the bed. I stripped off my clothes then went and hopped in the shower.

***

Twenty minutes later I was out, drying myself off. With the towel wrapped tight around myself, I opened my door with a scream.

Sam quickly pulled out his gun, looking towards my room door.

What the hell?

"Why the hell you screaming?" He asked, looking back at me as I put my hand over my racing heart.

Once I calmed myself down, I picked up the hair brush and threw it at him. I had forgotten all about him being there. Which was how he literally scared the hell out of me.

"What you mean why am I screaming? You scared the shit outda me. Why are you even in here? And put that gun away."

Sam started laughing as he picked up the brush, sitting it on the bed. "Yo scary ass, I was going to the bathroom and opened the wrong door. I had just walked in when you came out. Shid, you scared me too. You lucky I ain't shoot yo ass." He laughed, walking past me and into my bathroom.

"Lift up the seat." I yelled while walking to my bed about to slip my clothes on until I realized I didn't get any panties or a bra out.

After a few short seconds Sam returned as I found my underclothes.

"You gon' quit tryin' to play me, I ain't no nasty nigga. I grew up in a house with females, so kill that dumb shit. Don't compare me to none of these triflin' ass niggas you be messing with." Sam said, drying his hands on my towel.

"I don't mess with nasty niggas and not once did I say you were a triflin' dude. I simply told you to lift the seat just as I tell King when he uses my bathroom." I pointed out to him.

"You talk too damn much." Sam said while grabbing the nape of my neck, kissing me.

Well damn.

That was all I thought as I began kissing him back, dropping my panties and bra in the process.

My hands gripped the front of his shirt tightly as I stood on my tiptoes.

"Short ass." He mumbled against my lips, picking me up.

"Fuck— eep!" A squeak left my mouth as he dropped me on the bed. "I'mma beat yo ass, keep playing."

Sam ignored what I said instead, he pulled his shirt off, causing me to bite into my bottom lip at that V on his pelvis. *My God! He was sexy.*

His hands soon came to my towel, and he pulled it open. Sam's eyes began to roam over my naked body for a few seconds before he leaned forward.

My stomach sank in instinctively as his lips came to the spot just above my naval. He kissed his way up to my breast, my breathing picked up as that infamous knot started to form in the pit of my stomach.

Taking hold of my breasts, Sam's tongue flicked over one nipple, blowing. Once the small chocolate nub became erect. He repeated the action on the other before pulling it into his warm mouth, sucking on the small pebble.

One of his hands soon found its way between my legs, covering my mount.

My pelvis thrust forward and a moan slipped through my lips when his finger pushed through my wet fold. His finger moved from my throbbing clit to my contracting opening.

A groan sounded in the back of his throat once his finger felt the pulse of my pussy trying to catch and pull it inside my wet core. Pushing my legs further apart, he ran his finger over my clit, rubbing until my pearl swelled. Then he moved back to my opening.

My mouth parted as he slipped a finger into my throbbing sex. He began to massage my inner walls, causing a moan to leave my mouth. "Aah, God!"

Sam brought it to his mouth and sucked my nectar off of his finger. "Whatever we do, it stays between us. And if you're about that jealous type shit then we need to stop this here." Sam said as he looked down at me. His hand went back to my pussy. That time he pushed two fingers inside my throbbing sex. A slight hiss left my mouth as he grabbed my pubic bone and pressed down.

My head nodded in understanding at the same time my hips raised. "You're not my man, I'm not yo woman. I got it." Which I did. I wasn't looking for a relationship with him, I just wanted head, simple as that. After the bullshit with Blaze and Sly's punk ass, I needed what he was about to give me.

He smiled at me, then moved down to my pussy, kissing my second pair of lips.

His fingers expertly worked along my pubic muscles, massaging my inner walls, as his mouth sucked on my clit. My eyes grew wide from the instant pleasure that rushed to my lower stomach and pussy. The work of his fingers immediately had my ass muscles tightening, causing my thighs to shake.

Looking down at him with a raised brow and meeting his gaze, I receive a wicked but sexy smile. The look Sam gave me had something inside of me wanting to stop.

And I should've gone with that feeling.

***

Torture is what Sam was putting me through. His lips and tongue continued to suck and lick up every ounce of juice that leaked from my sex.

"Sam!" I called, tangling my hands in his dreads, tryna push him away. But the fucker wouldn't let up as he brought me to my third orgasm. "Ooh! Fuck! Ahh, Sam!" I was a moaning mess as my thighs violently shook and hips bucked off the bed.

"Damn, you sweet as fuck." Sam groaned out before he sucked my sensitive clit into his mouth once more. He then licked down my slit, teasing my opening. He moved back to my clit, sucking it into his mouth while sticking a finger into my pussy.

"Oh my God!" My hips bucked as his finger moved inside of me. He sucked even harder on my clit. I was sure I was going to die from… From… Shit, I didn't know what the hell he was doing to me, but I was gon' die because that was a damn orgasm I'd never felt before. And to have three back to back, Sam was going to kill me. "Sam, *please!*" I begged. Even though I wanted him to stop, I was enjoying it, enjoying the constant torture his lips and tongue were putting me through.

"You want me to stop?" I didn't know the answer as he began to kiss my inner thigh, sucking, licking, and biting at the skin. I wanted him to stop, but I was loving every bit of the torture he was putting my body through.

"No, don't stop!" With that Sam kissed his way back to my pussy, sucking on my labia then my clit once more before making his way up my body. I was so high on lust, on him, I wasn't thinking.

His lips touched mine, kissing me deeply as he grabbed my right leg, putting it on his shoulder.

Sam leaned on his forearm, grabbing a condom. Once it was open, he rolled it down his dick. It was then that I came slamming back to reality and my body went still. Sam must have felt me because he didn't move.

"You okay?" He asked, pulling back slightly.

"No, I can't have sex with you." I was not about to lose my virginity to a fuckin' hood. Getting head was one thing, but to actually have sex with one, I couldn't do that.

"Peaches!"

My eyes widened and I quickly pushed Sam off of me. "Shit, shit, shit, hide." I whispered, yelled at him. "Hold on King, here I come!" I yelled as I quickly pulled on my sports bra and top, my shorts fell on the floor in the process.

"Where I'mma hide at?" Sam asked, the laughter in his voice could be heard with the question.

"I don't know, jump out the window or something." King could not find him in my bedroom. I was freakin' the fuck out.

"You're on the third floor." Sam pointed out.

203

At that moment I didn't care. He just needed to go. "So what?" Sam started laughing at me. "Shut up before he hears you!"

"Peaches, what you got to eat?" King yelled back to me.

My eyes rolled at him. Typical King, I swear. *How the hell did he even know I was home*? My fuckin' car, shit.

"What's up, King?" I heard Sam's voice say.

I turned around to see my room door open and him gone. *What the fuck is he doing*? Quickly, I pulled on my socks and combed my hair into a messy bun, then I left out my room.

"What the fuck you doing here, nigga? We been calling yo ass for over an hour." King asked Sam just as I walked into the living room.

"I jumped in the car with Peaches when she left the office. I wasn't about to wait on Blaze ass, you know how long they could be. I wasn't trying to spend my off day in a truck." Sam shrugged while grabbing the PJ's bag off the table and pulling out his tacos.

"Where you get PJ's from?" King asked hungrily, forgetting all about Sam being alone with me.

"PJ's, nigga. Get yo hungry ass from over here." Sam laughed before taking a big bite out of his taco.

I stared at King's posture for a good minute. Once he was relaxed, I shrugged and entered the living room, where they sat.

Once I went over, Sam handed me the food bag.

"Peaches, you ain't get me nothing?" King asked glancing from mine to Sam's food.

I looked at Sam and he winked at me. His action caused my eyes to roll. I laughed with a shake of my head.

"Nope!" I told King, popping the P as I looked around the table then to Sam. "Where my drink?" I asked.

"In the freezer." He stated, taking another bite of his taco. "Man, this shit good as hell." He boosted, picking with King.

I laughed. "Everything taste a lot better when you still have Peaches lingering in your mouth." Sam immediately started choking on his food and I burst out laughing. "I'm kidding, damn, chill. PJ's always have good taco's, you should taste their Gyro, shit's crazy good." I said, still laughing.

King clearing his throat reminded me that he was there. He gave me a weird look then glanced at Sam. But he had started back stuffing his mouth to notice.

"What?" I couldn't help the stupid big smile that came to my lips.

Damn Sam's head game was like a drug.

My insides were flying with butterflies, while my cheeks were damn near pushed into my eyes.

Damn!

"Keep smiling like that I'mma slap the fuck outda yo dumbass." King snapped at me.

Even that didn't wipe the smile from my mouth. If anything, it made me laugh once again. "Fuck you, King. You just mad because I didn't bring you nothing to eat."

"This shit good as fuck too, King." Sam added and we just started laughing.

"Fuck y'all!" He snapped at us.

"I love you, King. Gimme kisses." My lips puckered up as I leaned towards him. King muffed my head back, causing me to fall back on the couch and I glared at him. "See, I did get yo triflin' ass tacos and some Mozzarella sticks, but since it's like that—" He reached for me. "Nope, nigga, get off me!" I yelled as he tried kissing me. "Move, King!" I laughed out as he kissed my cheek then pushed my face into the pillow. "Stop, yo ass too damn old to be acting like that." Laughing, he snatched the bag. Shaking my head, I got up to get my drink. "Sam, you want your drink?" I called out to him.

"Yeah!" Grabbing his Coke, I walked back into the living room and sat next to him. I handed him his drink before I turned on the T.V. "The game on, turn to it. I missed last night's game." Sam told me with his mouth full of food, causing my face to scrunch up in disgust.

"Ain't nobody about to watch a rerun of a basketball game." I replied, snatching the remote from him, only to have King take it from me.

"Hell yeah, the Bulls playing. I missed that game too. Aye, Peaches, where my drink?" King questioned, trying to find the basketball game.

"You ain't got one and I'm not watching the game—" My words were cut off by the loud banging on my door. The sound had both King and Sam pulling out their guns. "Put that away, you asses. Who the hell you gon' need a gun for at this time of day? Don't nobody know y'all asses even here." I snapped at them. I swear, those niggas there.

As soon as I clicked the lock, the door came flying open and it wasn't long before I was hemmed up against the wall by a murderous looking Blaze.

Chapter 13

Peaches

After screaming from the initial shock, I calmed myself down then glared at him. "Blaze, what the fuck is wrong with you? I could've had a heart attack, you jackass!" I snapped at him, trying to get free. "Let me go!"

"Why the fuck you shoot my truck up?" He snapped at me, gripping my shirt tighter.

My attitude quickly left, and my brows furrowed. "Wait, I did *what*?" I asked as if I was shocked, getting into character.

Blaze pushed me more into the wall as his glare hardened. "Don't play stupid."

"I'm not, someone shot up your truck? Wait! You think it was *me*? Why the hell would I do that with yo boy outside?" I asked seriously, staring into his eyes.

"Don't fuckin' play with me, Peaches." He snapped at me once again.

"Blaze, what damage could my little Ruger do to your truck? Besides, just ask Sam if you don't believe me." I said as I pointed towards the living room.

"Sam's here?" His brows furrowed in confusion.

Rolling my eyes, I nodded. "Didn't I just say that? Look straight ahead if you don't believe me." I repeated, trying not to laugh. "Now, let me go." I yanked my arms free then pushed past him, going back into the living room.

I sat back in my seat. Grabbing a drink from the table, I started to drink a little before it was ripped from my hands. "What the hell, Sam?" I looked at him like he was crazy as some of the drink wasted on me, making both him and King laugh.

"Baby, this is mine. You better look at yo brother." Sam said nodding towards King.

I looked at my brother and notice my drink by him. He glanced my way then back at the tv. I glared hard at him. But before I could say anything, Sam started talking.

"Who was at the door?" He asked, his eyes glued to the basketball game.

I looked up to see Blaze still standing where I left him, looking from me to Sam. I glared at him hard. Blaze face was contorted into a mugging scowl. It was the same look he had when he went off on Sly's ass.

"Don't start that shit in my house." I said, but he ignored me.

"Nigga, what the fuck yo ass been doing you couldn't answer the fuckin' phone when I called?" Blaze asked, pissed as he walked fully into the living room. But him asking that got King's attention and he looked our way with a thoughtful expression on his face.

"My phone ain't rung…" He trailed off, feeling his pockets then checking the couch.

"Don't tell me you lost yo phone? You had it in the car, you ain't been anywhere but in here, the kitchen, my bathroom. Call it." Quickly, I got up to get the cordless phone from the kitchen, then came back.

I glared at Blaze to see that he had taken my seat.

What the fuck was his problem?

"Here." Ignoring Blaze, I gave Sam the phone.

"Don't be tryna see my number. I don't do late nights." Sam said, glancing down towards my covered sex.

Clearing my throat, I shook my head as I sat on the long couch, tryna see if I heard it. "You probably left it in the car."

"Why the fuck y'all together anyways?" Blaze asked angrily before looking me dead in the eyes, forgetting all about his truck. "Haven't yo ass had enough for a day?" He threw at me.

My mouth dropped open as my eyes widen at his implication. Especially in front of King.

"G, don't come at my—" King started, but I stopped him.

"No King, it's cool. What you mad for? Last I checked we were all grown in here. So who the fuck is you to ask someone for an explanation? But one thing you ain't gon' do is disrespect me in my own shit. That, baby, you're not going to do. I done told yo ass I'm not none of these little dumb, mindless ass hoes you be fucking with. So don't come at me like I am." I checked his ass. Blaze had life all messed up.

"As for what you referring to, daddy, best believe it's never enough. I get it when I want it, fuck you mean?" I was pissed off, that nigga hardly knew me and he was actin' like he was my dude. I stood up from my seat and went to the door. I could literally feel their eyes burning a hole into my back, they were watching me hard. "What y'all staring at?" I asked with an attitude.

Sam was the first one to answer my question. "Shid, I'm watching just in case I gotda run. Yo ass seem to always have a gun somewhere." He sounded so serious.

I tried not to laugh, I really did, but once King agreed and started laughing, I couldn't help it.

Leave it to Sam to break the tension by being the dummy he is.

"You stupid, I don't always have a gun." I said as I grabbed my keys. I held my keys out so they could see what I went to get.

"Shid, could've fool me." Sam told me with a shrug.

Rolling my eyes, I threw him my keys. "Go check my car for your phone. King will call it, and don't scratch my baby."

"I'll come with you, I'm about to light this blunt. You coming?" King asked Blaze as he stood up.

"Yeah, I'll be out there." Blaze replied but he didn't get up.

With a roll of my eyes, I grabbed the remote and flopped down on the couch. I then began to flip through the channels just as the door closed.

"Why you gotda talk to a nigga like he ain't shit?" Blaze asked me.

Glancing at him, I rolled my eyes again. "Says the nigga that practically just called me a hoe, but it is what it is. You're entitled to think what you want, it ain't like I give a fuck." I shrugged at him. "Just like I can think whatever I want. And for the record, I never said you wasn't shit. Hell, I don't even talk about you. But you're not going to be disrespecting me either. If it's gon' be like that then its best you stay away from me as I will you." I explained truthfully. Blaze was crazy as hell, which I could see. I wasn't used to a dude like that and I didn't plan on getting used to that type.

He chuckled before he gave me a slight smile. "We too much alike. I can see it now, we ain't gon' get along. But we can make it work." Blaze said, making me laugh.

"If we don't get along that's because of you. I'm cool with everybody. Just as long as you stop acting like King, then we're not going to have a problem." I told him truthfully.

"I get you grown, but if you gon' be mine then these nigga's you fuckin' with, you got to let them go. Believe I don't mind poppin' no nigga." Blaze warned in a serious tone of voice.

I couldn't help but laugh at that. "You're funny." I left it at that, there wasn't a point in going back and forth with him. Then I had a second thought. "Who said I was yours, or going to be for that matter? I'm enjoying my single, drama free life."

"So you don't want me to be yo man? Huh?" He asked me and I didn't say anything. "Come here?" Blaze called to me.

My eyebrows rose at that. Shaking my head, I turned back to the TV. That nigga was bipolar as hell and I didn't have time for no crazy mothafuckas.

"Peaches, you gon' ignore me?" He continued to ask me questions. "Peaches." He said my name once more.

I bit into my bottom lip to keep myself from laughing. I still didn't say anything to him, I continued to focus on the TV. It wasn't long after the spot next to my feet dipped.

"What if I said you still got yo job?" He asked.

I laughed at that while looking at him. "I could've told you that. Sly's not stupid. He wouldn't want King on his ass for firing me for no reason. We've been knowing each other far too long for that bullshit you was tryna pull." I looked at him and shook my head. I then smiled at him before laughing. "You were wrong for walking in there the way you did."

"Shid, I was shocked to see Sly's ass getting some, but then when I saw it was you, I couldn't help it. You're too beautiful to be letting that nigga—"

"If it was you, would you be thinking that same thing?" I asked, turning to face him fully.

Blaze licked his lips as he watched me. "The beautiful part, yeah. The fuckin', hell n'all, but since it wasn't, I don't think you should be fuckin' these niggas."

"Why are you so quick to judge when you don't know the first thing about me?" I moved closer to him until I was straddling his hips, placing myself right on his dick.

"I don't judge, sweetheart. I call it how I see it." He explained.

"My point exactly. Whether you fail to realize it or not, that's judging, daddy. How you think you see me isn't how it is, not in the least." I trailed my hands up his chest, then over his shoulders. My arms wrapped around his neck and I pressed my chest to his, closing the space between us.

Blaze moved his hands up my thighs, slowly bringing them to my waist. Just that simple movement set my body ablaze and I found myself letting out a slow, shaky breath.

"Yes, I enjoy sex more than a little bit, but its oral sex only. Believe it or not, I'm still a virgin in all my holes. What you walked in on was Sly pushing his tip inside me, it wouldn't have gon' no farther than that. Sly is the only person I've ever let get that close to fuckin' me. Daddy, I didn't lie when I said I don't return the favor, I just get head nothing more. I don't fuck or suck no nigga and if you ever hear that I have, it's a lie. The only parts on a man you'll catch me sucking is here…"

My mouth went to his neck and I began to suck on the skin lightly, causing Blaze's hands on my waist to tighten. That had me sucking harder as my hips started a slow but hard grind. "Here…" I whispered in his ear as I pulled the lobe into my mouth, giving it a hard suck. I then bit into his lobe and pulled back, kissing my way to his mouth. Once there, my tongue traced over his bottom lip.

Blaze's mouth automatically parted. "Here..." I mumbled softly against his bottom lip, sucking on it lightly before moving back slightly. "And here..." My tongue flicked his top lip before catching it between my teeth, causing Blaze's eyes to snap to mine. My eyes stayed locked with his as my mouth moved to his bottom lip.

Pecking his lips lightly, my arms tightened around his neck, so did his hold on my waist. As I began to kiss him, Blaze let out a groan. His left hand left my rocking hips and came to the side of my face as he deepened the kiss.

My head tilted sideways, and I caught his tongue between my teeth, then sucked it into my mouth. I gave his tongue a few sensual sucks, then pulled away with a smile.

"And there. Those are the only five places you'll ever hear that I sucked. I'm far from a hoe. My cherry is still intact, and I plan on it staying that way." I whispered, kissing him once more before I climbed off his lap.

My smile was wide as I slid back into my spot on the couch. And I once again started my search to find something to watch. "I have some lotion in the bathroom in case you wanna take care of that." I nodded toward the tent in his pants.

"Are you fuckin' serious?" Blaze snapped, he looked like he wanted to say more, but at that moment King and Sam walked in. They both stopped in their tracks and looked at us. The pair stared between me and Blaze like they expected to find us doing something. Especially King's ass.

"The fuck wrong with you, Nigga? Folks, lookin' like somebody done ate his babies." I burst out laughing at King's dumbass as he looked down at Blaze. I swear that nigga did not need to smoke. "Peaches, what he do? Tryna spit game, wasn't he?" King asked, glaring at Blaze. "Nigga yo dick ain't getting wet with this one, boss. Don't fall for her, I'm telling you." King suddenly said, making me laugh.

"King shut yo dumbass up. Why would you tell him that?" I asked but didn't really want the answer. But seeing that, King was so high he didn't realize it.

"Shid, I'm being honest, yo ass be playing with niggas hearts. How you think I be knowing what yo ass be doing?" He shook his head while letting out a depressed sigh. "Niggas that don't know you my sister be talking about you, like grown ass niggas. Sometimes I have to do a double look at these mothafuckas, like ain't you the same mothafucka that just popped off Smoke ass an hour ago. Boss, I'm telling you man, yo ass gon' get my ass locked up for killing one of these mothafuckas. What the fuck you be doing to these niggas?" He asked.

I glanced at Sam who looked curious, like he really wanted to know. The wondering expression on his face had me laughing out loudly.

"King, shut up." I was feeling hella embarrassed with King asking those questions.

"N'all, I'm being real. Shid, half my hoes don't be whining like that and ain't none of them bitches killas, you know what I'm saying?" King continued to explain. He was high as hell.

Looking at Blaze, I licked my lips. My eyes locked with his and I smiled. "Just give them a taste of my sweet, juicy peach. It's the best drug around, wanna taste?" I asked Blaze.

Immediately King started to fuss. "Get fuck'd up. Take yo ass to bed or something."

"King, I was playing, dang. Calm down." I laughed, clapping my hands together before what happened at work today came to mind. "Oh, King, why this ol' busted ass bitch, Trina, come to my job? You know what? I gotda call my bitches for this shit." I told them as I got up to get my phone.

***

"And you didn't beat her ass?" Angel asked me later that night as she jumped out her seat, making us laugh.

After calling Kimmy, Angel, Ebony and Missy over to tell them what happened with Trina. We all sat in my living room laughing at Angel's ass because she was ready to fight.

"Girl, sit yo small ass down. All that fuckin' girl gotda do is flick yo ass and you falling' over." King told her and I burst out laughing.

"Fuck you, King. Small or not I can fuck some shit up, best believe that. In fact, nigga try me, run up, King." She playfully snapped before jumping on King and started swinging. King pushed her off and got up, making Angel run across the room. "Nah, for real though, go on King, ain't nobody playing with yo ass." Angel yelled out a laugh from the other side of the room.

"Nah, nah bitch. Don't run now!" I told her, laughing.

"For real, King, stop!" Angel laughed out loudly as King yanked her up and then threw her over his shoulder. "Peaches, get yo brother." King slapped her on the ass hard and Angel let out a moan, making King freeze. "You know I like that rough shit. Keep playing, daddy, you gon' forget all about Ebony's ass." She spoke seriously, making King laugh.

"Get yo nasty ass outda here, you won't be able to handle me, boss. I'll have yo ass like her. Screaming, saying you feel me in yo stomach." King joked as he put Angel down.

All eyes seemed to turn towards Ebony whose eyes were wide with disbelief, causing us all to burst out laughing.

"Damn, E, you can't take the dick?" Missy asked her.

"Fuck y'all and King shut the fuck up. Ugh, you get on my fuckin' nerves." Ebony snapped at him before changing the subject. "Anyways, back to Trina. So, she's Chase's baby momma. I wouldn't want to fuck with nobody that's been in her." Ebony replied, scrunching her nose up as if she smelled something funky.

"I ain't fuckin' him, he just gave me head. Shid, good head at that. You know me, though, I can always find a new head buddy." I told them truthfully as I thought about Chase. "It just be that clingy part that fucks me up. Niggas be starting to think we're dating after a while. All because he starts to get a taste regularly and we sometimes lay back and watch a movie or some shit. I'm not ready for all that, though, I love being single." I said while looking directly at Blaze.

He gave me a funky look which had me rolling my eyes as I looked at the others. Even, though, I had Sly, I was really starting to rethink us even being together. For him to punk out the way he did with Blaze, I couldn't deal with a soft man. I knew he wasn't tough, but I at least thought he'd put up a fight for us to be together.

"Plus, having King for a brother, it's not gon' end well, not at all." I told them truthfully, letting out a depressed sigh.

"Man, if you serious about a nigga then I ain't gon' trip on him. But if he hurts you, then hell yeah I'mma beat his ass or kill him, depending on what he does." He let out a laugh. "I ain't crazy, Peaches. I just be tryna look out for you." King said with a shrug.

I believed him. King seemed so calm when he said that I couldn't help but too. I stared at him for a while longer trying to see if his calm demeanor would fade. It didn't. A thought came to me and a sigh left my mouth. I was nervous as hell.

"You're serious about that? If I really like a guy, you wouldn't trip? You'd support me and the relationship one hundred percent?" I asked, feeling slightly sketchy about his relaxed posture.

"Yeah." He replied with a nod.

"Okay well…" I trailed off, not knowing how or if I should say something to him about Sly. Especially since what happened earlier that day. A part of me just wanted to say forget about the relationship Sly and I had. But then it had been seven, almost eight years of me constantly dealing with him.

"You like somebody?" King asked, leaning forward, resting his arms on his knees.

I noticed everyone looking at me and I glanced at Blaze. "I do but... I don't know how you're going to react about who it is." The tightness in my stomach had me feeling like I was going to get sick. I don't know why but that whole conversation started to feel like a setup.

"Oh, it's somebody I know?" He questioned. His tone of voice was one of curiosity.

Nodding my head, I looked at Sam.

"Oh shit, I already know!" The four of my bitches said in unison, making Sam and King look at them. But not Blaze, his eyes were burning a hole in the side of my face.

"Who is it?" King asked me.

I felt like I was about to get sick. "Umm...Sly..." I trailed off, watching confusion cover King's facial expression.

"Who?" King repeated dumbly.

"Sly." I watched his face contort in recognition and my leg automatically started bouncing up and down.

"The fuck you mean, Sly? Dude I work with?" King snapped as he hopped up off the couch, looking pissed.

I quickly jumped out my seat once he stood. I opened my mouth to say something, but he cut me off. And I knew I was in trouble then.

Chapter 14

Peaches

"**B**itch, you done lost yo fuckin' mind." He went off on my ass. King suddenly got quiet as if something came to mind. He looked murderous.

He moved so fast that; I didn't even realize he had grabbed me until I was slammed into the wall with his hand around my throat. "You fuckin' that nigga, Peaches? Huh?" He yelled at me.

"What!" I yelled shocked that he would even ask me that and especially in front of everybody. "King, no! Now let me go!" I was far from a crier, I hardly ever cried. It wasn't until King ass pulled some bullshit like that.

King's reaction just proved the reason as to why I didn't date. The stinging to my cheek had my eyes widening as tears slipped from my eyes.

"Peaches, I swear on everything, if you're lying, I'mma beat yo ass and kill that mothafucka. Now, is you fuckin' him?" He continued to scream at me.

I roughly wiped the tears from my eyes as I glared up at King.

"King, don't start that shit. Let her go." Missy snapped, getting up until Ebony shook her head, telling her not to get involved.

"No! I ain't fuckin' him. I was just saying I like him, that's it!" I yelled at him and his hand seemed to tighten. "King, let go—" My words got cut short as King was pushed from me.

Blaze had rocked King hard in the jaw making him stumble. "What the fuck wrong with you, nigga, hitting on her because she like a nigga? I don't give a fuck if you her brother, put yo hands on her again." Blaze snapped as he pulled his .9mm from his pants and dropped it on the table. "I'll beat yo ass, my nigga, boss!" He then pulled up his jeans while continuing to mug King hard. "You cool?" Blaze asked, looking at me. "Fuck wrong with you? Got her crying." Blaze went to step up to King again.

I pushed myself off the wall, getting in front of him. "Don't, okay, it's cool." I told Blaze while pushing him away from King. But I was soon pushed out the way once King got up.

"Nigga, this me all mothafuckin' day. I take care of her ass when these fuck ass niggas don't give a fuck, including Sly! Niggas don't give a fuck about her, all they ass want to do is claim they busted her first! Nigga, if yo ass ever jump in our shit again I'll... Nah, fuck that!" King punched Blaze in the face. Shit got crazy from there on as he started laying it to Blaze, making him fall into my flat screen TV.

"Oh, my God! King! Stop!" I screamed at him. "Sam, stop them!" He made a grab for King, but King ducked sideways, causing Blaze to hit Sam hard as fuck in the face. "Oh shit, King, Blaze, stop!"

"King, get off him!" Ebony yelled with me, but King wasn't paying either of us no mind

Blaze blocked King's last two punches that were aimed for his face. He tangled their arms together before he head-butted the shit out of King, twice. Blaze's fist soon followed, connecting to his jaw. Which caused King to stumble into Sam, making them both fall down.

Blaze didn't miss a beat as he got up and started throwing punch after punch to Kings face and ribs.

I didn't care what King might have done to me; at the end of the day he was still my brother. He was all I had.

I jerked Blaze back as hard as I could, pulling him off of King. I then jumped on his back, catching one of his arms, I locked it with mine as I held him tightly around his neck.

"Sam, get King!" I yelled at him and he quickly grabbed him before he could come back at Blaze.

"Peaches, let me the fuck go before I beat *yo* ass!" Blaze yelled at me, trying to get loose, but I wasn't letting up. I had a good lock on him, or so I thought.

"Blaze calm down and I will. Sam, get King out of here!" Sam looked like he was having problems keeping his hold on King.

Weak ass nigga, man, I swear.

"Angel, Kimmy, Missy, help him! Oh, shit!" I screamed out as Blaze pried my arms apart and he pushed me off of him. "Get him out, Blaze stop!" I yelled, jumping in front of him. I was trying to push him back, but Blaze simply flung my little ass on the couch. "Would y'all stop, damn, I have people that live under me! King! Fuck this!" I let out a frustrated growl and stomped to my dining room table. I grabbed the Taser gun that was taped underneath.

"Nah, fuck that, let him go. Nigga, you wanna pop stupid like you don't know!" Blaze snapped and pulled his shirt off. He then dropped a second gun on the couch just as King broke loose. He knocked Angel, Kimmy and Missy on the floor.

These niggas were really going at it. I mean seriously rocking the shit out of each other in the face. Let it have been me, I would've been knocked the fuck out.

"Ah No! My table!" A scream left my mouth as King sent Blaze into my living room table, breaking it. Pointing the Taser gun, I shot.

"Ahh!" King growled as it shot into his back, but the mothafucka still ain't fall.

What the fuck is he on?

"Y'all breaking my shit! Stop!" They asses were still rolling around on my broken table. "Fuck this, I'm calling the police!" As if I said the magic word, they both stopped, looking around stupidly.

"Who called the police?" Both those idiots asked in unison. They looked at each other and started laughing.

Okay, what the fuck?

"Man, get the fuck off of me." Blaze pushed King off him then stood up. He wiped at his bottom lip then spit the blood from his mouth onto my carpet. Once up, King's ass turned around and did the same shit.

"Yo ass always got to start some shit, I swear, dumbass." Ebony snapped at King for the first time since the fight started. Grabbing her stuff, she continued to shake her head. "Peach, I'm gone, these nigga's stupid. Call me tomorrow, boo." The other girls agreed and left as well.

After my eyes roamed around my destroyed living room, I just sat on the couch putting my hands on my head.

"Damn, Peaches I'm sorry—" King started, and I just shook my head.

"Don't even. Look at my fucking living room, King. Y'all busted my fuckin TV! Do you know how long it took me to save just to buy that?" I stated in a calm voice when on the inside I was anything but that as I looked at my table.

"Peaches, I can get you another one." He said.

That pissed me off more. If I wanted him to buy me one. I wouldn't have worked so hard to get it on my own. Hell, if I wanted it to be that simple, I could've used the money my parents left me when they died. But I wanted to work for what I got.

"King, I don't want yo fuckin money!" I screamed at him. I was so fuckin' mad, that my body shook. "This bullshit could've been avoided, but you always got to do this. And for what? Huh? To show how fuckin' controlling you are? I'm grown, I pay for my own shit. I'm working and going to school for the second time." I pointed out as I walked closer to him. "I'm not a fuckin' kid!" I once again yelled at him, hoping my words would embed themselves inside his damn head. "When are you going to realize that? Then you wanna put yo hands on me! You know what? Just get out! In fact, all y'all get yo disrespectful asses out my shit! Bye! Get the fuck out!" I yelled, pushing Sam and King towards the door.

"Peaches—" King said my name.

My fist went back, and I socked King in his mouth. I didn't want to hear a gotdamn thing he had to say. "No, fuck you, King! You gon' put yo fuckin' hands on me, you a bitch ass nigga! I swear, you are. Fuck you! Then you break my table, Mommy's table, 'cause you wanna act like a bitch!" I went to swing on him again but was grabbed from behind. "No, let me go, damn! You gon' break my fuckin' table, Mommy's table, King! I fuckin' hate you! Let me the fuck go!" I was trying my hardest not to cry, I just wanted to keep hitting him. But Blaze tight hold on my waist prevented me from doing so. And that only made the urge to cry even stronger.

"Y'all gon' head. I'll catch up with you niggas later." Blaze said, pushing me behind him.

Surprisingly, King listened. He didn't even put up a fight when Blaze closed the door.

Who the fuck he think he is?

"No, you take yo black ass with them!" I snapped as I pushed him towards the door.

"What I tell yo ass about putting yo hands on me?" Blaze asked, pushing my hands off of him. "Now go take yo ass in the room somewhere and calm the fuck down!"

Who was he talking to?

"No, get the fuck out!" I pushed him again towards the door.

A mug suddenly covered his face. "What the hell I just tell you? Go sit yo ass down, Peaches." He snapped, pushing me towards the living room.

You know what? I don't have time to be arguing with this man.

"You lucky I got a headache, otherwise I'd beat yo ass." I said, jumping at him. I *was* getting a headache, but it wasn't the real reason I walked away. I knew getting his ass out was going to be an even bigger fight. If I didn't live in an apartment, that fight I wouldn't mind having. But the old folks that lived above and under me were probably already freakin' the hell out with the commotion that had just taken place.

Turning away from Blaze, I went to the bathroom in my room. I got the Aleve and took two pills. A heavy sigh left my mouth and I leaned against the counter while shaking my head.

I was so happy I didn't call King at the office and let him know about Sly. Sure enough, he would of probably beat his ass worse than what Blaze did.

The slight knock on the door had me looking up. A groan left my mouth as my eyes locked with Blaze. "Why are you still here?" I asked annoyed.

He gave me a mean look. "Man, what I tell you about that attitude?" He asked, not sounding mad.

I looked away from him for a second to get myself together so that I wouldn't smile.

Does he really think it's cool to talk to folks the way he do?

I then wondered, why would I be smiling at his words if I really had a problem with it? I didn't have an answer.

How was it possible for me to barely know a person for a month and have it felt as if it had been years that we'd known one another?

"What the fuck you smiling for?" Blaze asked.

"I'm not." Shaking my head, I looked over at him. My eyes landed on his busted lip and I sighed. I grabbed a towel from the cabinet as well as the alcohol and some cotton rounds. "Come here." My head jerked sideways, beckoning him to me, while I wet the towel.

"We're playing doctor?" He questioned as he pushed himself off the wall, then came to where I sat on the counter.

"Blaze, shut up." With a laugh, I let my eyes roam over his face for a second. "King got you good under your right eye." I told him while pressing the alcohol pad to the cut under his eye. Immediately, Blaze hissed. "This makes you hiss, seriously?"

"That shit burns." He complained.

I laughed at that as I cleaned the cut and then put a Band-Aid on it. "Here I thought you're all tough and shit. When truly you're a soft—" He cut me off by muffing my head back. "Stop!" I laughed, smacking his arm.

"I dare yo ass to call me a bitch." He moved closer to me as his eyes roamed over my face.

Biting into my bottom lip, I looked away from him. "Then stop whining…" I trailed off as his fingers brushed against my cheek.

"It's a little red." He started rubbing the spot King hit and I jerked my head back. "Man, stop with that bullshit and let me look at it." He took hold of my chin once more.

"Its fine." I tried to reassure him. Even, though, the side of my face was stinging. I could actually feel it swelling.

"Man, chill with that. So, you can doctor my wounds, but I can't look at yours?" He asked and I chose to ignore him. I once again wiped the blood from his lip. "Huh?" He mumbled while lifting my chin, so I was looking at him. Averting my eyes from his, I didn't answer, just continued to wipe at his lip.

"I'm finished." I tossed the towel in the sink, then looked back at him. "It's getting late so…" I left it at that figuring he'd get the hint that it was time for him to go.

He laughed, shaking his head. "So, you puttin' me out?" He asked.

"Yeah, I am." I shrugged, then tried to push him back.

"You gon' make me fuck you up, Peaches. Boss you are. I can't spend the night with you?" He blocked me on the counter so that I couldn't get down.

That nigga had lost his mind if he thought he was staying a night. "Hell no!" I shook my head. "No, you got to go." In the middle of my protest, I was pulled to the edge of the counter. Blaze head went into the crook of my neck as his hands slid up my thighs. "Blaze—" I grabbed his wrists, stopping his moving hands.

The two sexual encounters I had throughout that day. I thought that was more than enough fun for me. Even so, my treacherous body wouldn't agree as lust soon consumed me. That throbbing ache immediately started in the pit of my stomach. But even with those feelings I couldn't do it because I knew I would give in fully to him.

Damn, I had to stop, even though deep down I really didn't want to.

Blaze grabbed the hem of my shirt, pulling it off. My hands went to the sides of his face, guiding his mouth to mine. I gave him a simple peck, then pulled away.

"You should go, it's late." My hands went to his chest and I gave him a slight push back, then hopped off the counter. I walked into my room and went to the door. Looking back at Blaze, I watched as he walked over to my bed. He sat down and took off his shoes, before he stood and began removing his jeans. "What are you doing?" I asked dumbly.

"Going to bed. What the fuck it look like?" He stared at me like I asked the stupidest question ever. "Turn off the lights, I'm tired as hell." He let out a heavy sigh then rubbed a hand over his head.

This fuckin' dude.

Did he really think we were that good to the point he could spend the night?

"Blaze, you're not staying here, I don't have time to be fighting with King again over a nigga. Nuh uh, come on now." My head shook at him. Fighting King over Sly was more than enough for me, I wasn't trying to have a repeat of that.

"I'll handle King so don't worry about him. Now stop looking crazy and turn off the damn lights." Blaze told me while he got under the covers. As if to tell me the conversation was over, he grabbed the remote and turned on the TV.

Blaze confused the hell out of me. Did he really think it was cool to invade a person's life, like he had done mine? "Blaze, you're not sleeping in—"

"Man, get yo ass in this bed before I get up and drag yo ass over here by your fuckin hair. Don't nobody wanna hear that shit you spittin' for real." He stated, cutting me off rudely.

"Fuck you mean? Nigga, you in my place." I stared at him like he was crazy.

"What the fuck I just say?" He looked up at me. "Peaches, get yo ass in this damn bed."

Who talked to people like that? Especially the ones you just met.

"Make me tell you again." From the way he said that I knew nothing good was going to come to me if he got out of that bed. Letting out a frustrated groan, I slammed my door. "Don't be slammin' the fuckin' door either."

I'mma suffocate his ass when he goes to sleep. Stupid sonofabitch. Turning off the lights, I made my way to the bed and got in.

"Gon' Blaze, damn." I said as his arms went around my waist and he pulled me into his chest.

"Man, shut up. Yo ass might as well get used to this because this is how its gon' be from now on. And fuck what

King might say, you mine." He stated seriously as he kissed my neck.

I didn't say anything back to him. I simply shook my head as I made myself comfortable. If I thought arguing with Blaze would've made him leave, I would've kept on. But I knew it wouldn't and truth be told, I was tired as hell. I just wanted to go to sleep.

"Blaze, get yo damn hand off my tittie." I snapped at him as he suddenly started massaging my left breast.

He then pinched my nipple. "Night, Peaches." Blaze laughed without moving his hand, if anything he pushed my bra up more so both my breasts were bare.

"Blaze—"

"Take this thing off." He was already pulling my sports bra over my arms and head. He had done it with such ease you couldn't even tell I was trying to resist.

Once it was off, his palm was back to fondling my breast. After having my hands slapped hard for the sixth time, I stopped trying to push his hand away.

I soon felt his lips press into my neck, then my shoulder as he lightly bit at the skin, causing a heavy sigh to leave my mouth. "Blaze—"

"Peaches, shut the fuck up and take yo ass to sleep." He mumbled against my skin as he continued to lightly bite into my shoulder.

A soft laugh left my mouth as my treacherous body began to relax into his. Blaze's hand left my breast for a few seconds so his fingers could dance along my stomach, down to the hem of my shorts, then back to my breast. I couldn't complain anymore because for some strange reason it was comforting, relaxing.

"Night, Peaches." He told me once more.

A small smile came to my lips and I had to give him his props, he had that touch I didn't mind getting used to, as well as the feel of his body being molded to mine at night. His thick, long, muscular frame fit perfectly with mine.

"Night, Blaze." I mumbled, moving closer to his body so that every part of my back, butt, and legs were touching his.

Chapter 15

Peaches

S trong arms held me tight around my waist as my pussy started to throb from the hardness that poked at it. My hips wiggled as I tried to move away from the hard thing that was turning me on. My body soon froze once I heard a groan and a snap.

Snap...

The sound took my mind off the poking to my core as I began to hear dialing, then whispering.

My hand slid under the mattress, gripping the gun that rested at the edge. I laid there for a little while longer, playing sleep until I heard...

"No bitch, Peaches in bed with that dude, Blaze, from last night. And she's naked. Ahh!" Missy screamed as I quickly sat up with my .9mm pointed towards her. Hearing the scream must have woke Blaze, because he did the same thing as me.

He pulled his gun from his pillow, pointing it towards the door before looking at me.

Wait.

Realizing I was lying on top of Blaze shirtless, with no bra on, had me pointing my gun at him. "Why the fuck is you still in my bed?"

Blaze looked at me then back to the door waving his gun towards Missy.

"Don't yo ass know how to make noise when you enter somebodies' shit? I could've shot yo stupid ass and if you scream like that again I will." He told her, before laying back down and then looking up at me. "Get that gotdamn gun out my face before I slap yo ass." He said, then snatched the gun out my hand.

"Don't be taking my damn gun. What are you doing here? Get your hands off my ass. And Missy, what I tell you about just walking in here, huh? One day I'mma shoot you for real. Blaze, stop." I slapped his hand away from my right tittie. I made a move to get off him, but his ass pulled me down, rolling us over. "Blaze, stop. Move, damn."

"Bitch, she got on shorts. No, they ain't fuck. Bye y'all, we'll meet later." Missy said, then ended her call.

My mouth dropped opened and Blaze started laughing. "No, we didn't fuck, I don't know him! And who the hell you on the phone with?" I asked, already knowing she was on the phone with our girls. Then again, that was Missy's ol' nosy ass.

"No one, dang, but I see you're busy." She said, nodding towards Blaze. "I was only coming to check on you is all, but I see you're straight with Mr. Sexy Caramel over there, so I'll be going now. Your coffee and breakfast is on the table, bye babe. Call me later." With that she closed my door and walked out.

"Missy, don't leave me with him! He's crazy!" I yelled after her, not hearing anything other than my front door slamming closed. "That bitch! Blaze—" His mouth covered mine, cutting me off. Groaning, I put my hands on his chest and pushed him back. "Laying with you was fun, believe me or not, but you have to go. I have school in a few hours. Now get off me." I said with an attitude as last night came back to my mind.

Everything happened because of him. If his black ass hadn't tried to blackmail me, then I wouldn't have opened up about Sly and got the shit slapped out of me.

Oh, my God, Sly.

"Move!" I pushed him harder this time and he got up. Quickly I jumped out my bed, running to get my cell phone from the living room.

Once I had it in my hand I pressed and held the number three until it started ringing.

"Buen día, hermoso." (Good morning, beautiful.) I let out a relieved sigh as I heard his voice. "Hello? Peaches?"

"I'm here, sorry. Have you talked to my brother?" I questioned nervously.

"No, why?" Sly asked sounding curious.

"Well, last night I may have told him I like you…" I trailed off. It was quiet for a second before I heard him sigh. I could just picture him shaking his head.

"Peaches, after yesterday I thought we were going to wait and tell him?" Sly saying that had me instantly catching an attitude.

"Sly, you've been working my nerves about us hiding and now that I finally said something to him, you saying I should've kept my mouth shut? What kind of shit is that?" Now that King had his little outburst, I was hoping he would had calmed down. That way Sly and I didn't have to hide the relationship we had going on.

"Don't try to make it seem like you told King because you were ready. You said something so Blaze wouldn't beat you to it, Peaches. Don't try to pull that bullshit with me when you know your ass don't even want a relationship." He snapped at me and I could hear the irritation in his voice.

Is this mothafucka serious?

"You knew from jump I wasn't ready, but I was willing to give us a try. Sly, are you really that scared of this nigga that you're about to talk shit just to fuck this up? If so, tell me now and we can skip this bullshit ass argument you're trying to start and be done."

How do you go from wanting me to marry you one minute, to turning shit around all because another nigga comes along and threaten you? If he allowed Blaze to scare him then it was never meant to be.

"I'm not scared of shit. You should've just waited to tell King is all I'm saying." Sly let out a heavy sigh into the phone. "Look, Peaches…" He trailed off. I could hear the hesitation in his voice, so I knew he was nervous, hell, probably even scared.

"You are such a fuckin' bitch, Sly, I swear to God, ugh. You made your choice, I'm done. Fuck you, I got slapped for telling King that I liked you and yo ass gon' punk out now?" I snapped at him pissed off. "What happened to you not caring about him beating yo ass? So, the shit you been talkin' since day one was what exactly?" He didn't reply. "You going to ignore me now, for real Sly? When you finally find yo fuckin' balls and realize your mistake, don't come knocking on my door."

"Peaches, don't do this. You have to understand, look its complicated. Just know everything I've said to you wasn't a lie, I honestly do—" He started saying.

I hung up the phone, not wanting to hear the bullshit excuse he was about give. Not even two seconds of me hanging up the phone, it was ringing again.

Seeing Sly's name pop up on the screen, I answered. "What do you want?"

"You're trying to get me killed, huh? Now why would you tell King that?" He asked with a laugh before sighing.

Now he wanted to lighten the mood? Fuck Sly, I was so done with his scary ass.

"It doesn't even matter no more, you don't have to worry about him trying to kill you or none of that bullshit. I'll let him know he's successfully ran you away." I didn't know what happened, but I just felt so tired all of a sudden. I seriously thought Sly would've been the guy to not back

238

down from King's bullshit. And maybe when King saw that, he probably would've respected him and just let us be.

"Peaches, please don't be like this. I'm not trying to hurt you and I really do want to be with you. Like I said, though, it's complicated as hell right now. I just need for you to give me time, please? Peach, I've given you plenty of mine, all I'm asking is that you do the same for me, please." He pleaded with me before he sighed once more.

I did like Sly; he was the only guy I'd been messing around with constantly for seven years. He *had* given me time, a lot of it, but I just couldn't.

"Sly, I can't. Do you not understand that I got my ass slapped for telling him I liked you? It's already out there and I'm not about to take it back only to turn around and tell him again. No, I'm not doing that. I wanted to see where this thing we have would go when we turned it into something serious. You can either step up or leave me alone for good—"

My phone was suddenly ripped from my hands before it went crashing into the wall. My eyes went wide as I looked at a murderous looking Blaze, then to my phone that laid on the floor with the back off and the battery out.

"What the fuck is your problem?" I snapped at him as I jumped up, going to my phone to see my screen busted.

"Yo ass disrespectful as fuck. How the hell you gon be on the phone with that nigga like I ain't even here?" Turning towards him, I threw my broken phone at his head. "*What The fuck!*" He yelled, dodging the phone.

"You're not my fuckin' dude so it shouldn't even matter who I'm talkin' to, who I'm fuckin', none of that should matter to you for that reason alone. You are not my fuckin' man!" I snapped as my finger jabbed in his direction. "Now *you're* disrespectful for breaking my shit. Get the fuck out, Blaze! I told yo ass yesterday if this was how you were going to be, then stay the fuck away from me. I'm not gon' be fuck'd up about you not being in my life—" My words were cut off as my back hit the wall.

"What the fuck I tell you about talkin' to me like I'm one of those little fuck ass boys you be messing' with, Peaches? Boss, I will fuck you up." He bit out as his hold on my arms tightened. "This shit you spittin' to that nigga Sly is a wrap. Keep playin', I swear to you his ass will come up missing by the end of lunch time today. I'm not bullshittin', Peaches." Blaze voice held promise as his eyes slanted and he mugged me hard.

The look in his eyes told me he wasn't playing.

God, what is up with this dude?

"Fuck you and get out! I mess with who I wanna. Yo threats don't scare me, Blaze. Just like you said, I'm telling you I'm none of these fuck ass, dumbass bitches or niggas you be messin' with. Yo ass don't run me nor do you scare me, so you can get on with that shit *you* spittin', nigga. *Boss that!*" My index and middle finger pressed to his forehead and I pushed his head back just to get my point across that I wasn't scared of him.

Blaze suddenly grabbed me by my throat, pulled me from the wall then slammed me hard against the wall.

A gasp left my mouth from the unexpected action.

"You gon' make me fuck you up." Blaze grabbed a handful of my hair, then yanked my head back. "Yo fuckin' mouth gon' get you hurt." He spoke in a deep baritone voice that caused my pussy to clench together.

"You keep saying that— eep!" A squeak left my mouth as he suddenly picked me up.

Blaze pressed his lips to mine, as he walked us to the couch. He sat down with me in his lap. His hands grasped the nape of my neck and he kissed me harder.

What am I doing? I don't even know him and here we are fighting like we're a couple and kissing as if we're making up. This isn't right, not at all. Wasn't I just messed up about Sly? Knowing this, knowing it isn't right, why in the hell aren't I stopping it?

Truth be told, I liked the feel of him, the caress of his lips against mine, the way his large, callused hands moved along my back. The feel of his teeth biting into my bottom lip, the suction of his mouth when he pulled my top lip into his hot waiting mouth. And the slithering of his tongue as it slid through my parted lips to tangle with mine. I simply like the way he felt, I couldn't help but want more, feel more of him.

I loved it. And I couldn't stop it because deep down I wanted it. Right or wrong, I needed it. And it was fuck'd up to feel that way when I didn't even know him like that.

His possessiveness, persistence, his I don't give a fuck attitude, I wanted that, craved it. Him standing up to King only made me want him more. Everyone else wanted to sneak around and hide, not Blaze. He didn't care and I loved that.

Why did he have to be a fuckin' hood, though?

My hips started a slow but hard wind and grind on his dick. My arms tightened around his neck, bringing our bare chests together. Blaze pulled my shorts to the side, then slowly pushed a finger into my throbbing pussy. getting it wet. He then pulled out, bringing it to my swollen clit and playing with my pearl.

He rubbed, causing me to moan in the back of my throat. Pulling my mouth from Blaze's, I moaned louder as his finger pushed inside my sex once more, rubbing my sweet spot repeatedly.

Kissing up my neck, Blaze found my spot behind my ear and started sucking hard. Doing so had my inner muscles milking his finger, squeezing it tightly, making him groan as I became wetter. That caused his finger to move faster hitting my barrier, the thin skin that kept my virginity intact.

"Blaze." I began saying while grabbing his wrist to stop him.

"Shush, I know." Even though he said that, I didn't think he did as he brought his mouth back to mine. Blaze started jerking on the thin material, until he'd successfully ripped the crouch part of my shorts. He lifted my hips up off him for a few seconds.

Blaze pulled the front part of his boxers down, releasing his dick. Slowly he began to sit me down on him.

My eyes widened and I screamed into his mouth.

Oh, Hell No!

"Blaze—"

"Shut up we're not about to fuck right now." He told me.

What the hell he means right now? His dick was literally at my opening. Blaze's dick was bigger than Sly's. Don't get me wrong, Sly was thick, he wasn't little at all with his eight and a half inches. But Blaze was thicker than Sly, and from the feel of it, he was at least two to three inches thicker. *Fuck No!* My pussy wasn't about to be stretched that wide.

"Ah, shit! Blaze! Stop!" His tip wasn't even in and that shit was hurting.

"Damn, you tight." He groaned out as he managed to push his head in.

Once in, he just held still until I got used to his size. My inner muscles started to suck on his thick, hard, mushroom tip. Blaze let out a grunt, feeling that, he began to slowly move my hips up and down on him. He pulled out, then rubbed his dick against my swollen pearl, playing with my clit. He then brought his head back to my opening and pushed inside my tender, soaking wet pussy.

"Oh my, ah, ah shit! Fuck Blaze!" My moaning was a mixture of both pleasure and pain. The pain outweighed the pleasure, even so, the mixture of the both felt so good.

Blaze took hold of my thighs and lifted me up.

My hands held tight on his shoulders as he began to push his tip in and out of me, going a little deeper. My lips parted as I gasped out heavy pants.

The feel of him had me forgetting everything I had with Sly.

Fuck he feels so good.

"My dick gon' be the *only* niggas dick this pussy feel. This mine! Let me find out you letting a nigga taste or touch my shit, boss, his death gon' be on you. You hear me, Peaches?"

I could give two fucks about what he was saying, I was enjoying the feel of him too much to care. That was until he stopped. "Do you hear me?" He asked again.

"Yes, I hear you!" My orgasm was right there, I was so close all I needed was a few more minutes and I was cummin' all on his dick.

"Good, now that we got this established let's go get something to eat, a nigga hungry as fuck." He said, sitting me beside him. He then put his dick back into his boxers and got up. "I'm about to hop in the shower, then we can head to my crib before we go get something to eat." He walked off, disappearing from my line of view.

Did I just get played?

Oh my...

That bastard just played me.

I couldn't even be mad because Karma was a bitch and she'd just fuck'd me raw. Damn! I'd played many dudes, especially Blaze when we first met. So, I couldn't really do anything but laugh at what had happened. With a smile and a shake of my head I got up and headed to my room to see Blaze sitting on my bed, talking on his phone. Not saying anything, I walked right past him to my bathroom to shower.

***

Once I finished in the shower, I walked back into my room with a towel around my body. Seeing Blaze, I stopped in my tracks as I got stuck by the sight of him. Blaze's body was damped, and he had a towel wrapped around his hips. My God, that was a sexy man, everything was just muscle and tattoos. *My damn!*

Peaches, calm yo ass down. You're acting like a horny teenager. But damn, he looks so…

"I'mma have to take a rain check on lunch because I have school in an hour. Then I have to be at work so…" I trailed off as I slipped on a purple, lace bra and panties set before grabbing my lavender scrubs.

"All that purple ain't that serious ma." Blaze laughed at me.

"Yo ass don't have to wear it and my name's Peaches, not ma, or shorty. Nor is it little mama." I told him as I pulled my shirt on.

"Make me slap yo ass." Blaze said from across the room.

"You keep saying that, yet I haven't got slapped once." Looking at him over my shoulder, I pursed my lips together while rolling my eyes at him, faking an attitude. "Ouch! Did you just throw the remote at me?"

"You see the remote by yo feet, don't you?" He pulled his shirt on.

"Bitch." I mumbled to myself as I pulled my hair in a high ponytail.

"I'mma slap the shit outda you. Damn, shut yo fuckin' mouth sometimes. Its gon' get yo itty bitty ass whooped." He snapped at me.

A scream left my mouth as Blaze suddenly picked me up and slammed me on the bed. "Blaze, stop! Damn! Ahh!" I yelled at him, laughing.

Grabbing the pillow, he slapped me with it before pressing it to my face, shaking it. "Eh, yo ass drooling. You too damn old for that shit." Blaze laughed, getting off the bed.

"Fuck you! I wasn't, lying ass!" I rolled my eyes but still couldn't help the laugh that left my mouth. "You get on my nerves, messing up my damn hair." I feigned an attitude while taking my ponytail out.

"That shit was already fuck'd up. Yo ass need a perm." He shot back. My mouth dropped open and I grabbed my shoe off the floor and threw it at him. I then went to the mirror and began to fix my hair. "I was playing, man, damn." He said, walking up behind me and wrapping his arms around my waist with his head laying on my shoulder.

"I can't put my hair in a ponytail with you on me like this." I told him, standing up straight as Blaze pulled the band from my hair and sat it on the vanity.

He ruffled a hand through my hair before his fingers ran through it, moving it over my right shoulder. "Better, don't you think?"

Laughing, I shook my head while staring at him through the mirror. "Didn't your mother teach you never to put your hands in a woman's head?"

"That's my sister, but she's a little bitch. I never listen to her." He joked making me laugh. I ran the brush through my hair as Blaze continued to stand behind me staring.

"It's rude to stare, if you got something to say, say it." Swiping my lips with some strawberry lip gloss, I rubbed my lips together while rolling my eyes at Blaze.

What the fuck am I doing? I don't even like this dude.

"What's that look about?" He suddenly asked.

I hadn't even realized I was giving him a look until he said something. "I don't have a look."

"Don't start that bullshit, Peaches. What time you get out of school?" Blaze turned me towards him then picked me up and sat me on the dresser, stepping between my legs.

"I get out at one." A sigh left my mouth as I stared at him. Blaze ass was no good and I could seriously see myself getting into trouble with him. And with the giddy feeling he cause inside my body, I wouldn't even mind it. For that particular reason alone, told me I shouldn't take things with him too far. "Blaze, don't get to use to this because whatever this may be doesn't leave this apartment." I told him truthfully, making him chuckle.

"So, this is something, huh?" He questioned, pressing himself into me.

Shrugging, I looked away from him as I bit into my bottom lip. I let out a breath and composed myself, I looked back at Blaze as I got serious. "Whether this is or isn't, I'm not taking it there with you for the simple fact I don't want to fight with King. You saw how he reacted when I told him I like Sly."

"So, you like me, huh?" After I gave him a blank stare, he simply laughed me off before getting serious as well. "I ain't Sly, so how he reacted about you and dude won't be the same with me. I ain't no fuck boy that's scared

247

of King, he don't run me. I do what I want when I wanna and I get what I want when I want it. And right now, what I want is you." He explained with a nonchalant shrug.

The *nigga please* look I gave Blaze had him pushing my head back. "How many chicks have you spit that same line to?" I didn't know if it was game, he was trying to spit or not, the whole thing I was new to. It was new grounds for me, the feeling I felt at that moment I'd only felt once and it wasn't with Sly, but with Jerron. And he moved away before I could act on them, even with the times he did come back to visit, the feelings weren't ones I actually pursued.

Now that I was having them for Blaze, I didn't know how to act on them. And they were honestly clouding some of my judgment on him fully.

He's probably a hoe ass nigga just like every other hood I've met.

"Man, I'm being serious as fuck right now. Why you wanna play me?" He asked, licking his lips.

"I'm not trying to play you, I'm just not looking to get into anything serious with you, or no one else for that matter. Sorry if that's not what you wanna hear but—"

Blaze pressed his body more into mine, cutting me off. "Bullshit. So, you just let any nigga get close to fuckin' you, huh? From what you told me it was only Sly. If you weren't feeling me you wouldn't have let my dick inside yo pussy, would you? If I hadn't stopped, you would've let me bust yo ass wide open and you know it. So why fight it?" He pointed out with his question.

Is he serious? Who the fuck talks to people like this?

"I ain't fighting shit, I don't even know you—"

"Then get to know me. Look, Peaches, I'm not gon' beg yo ass because one way or another you gon' be mine regardless of that fuck shit you talkin'." He stated with a shrug. "Those words that's coming from yo mouth don't mean nothing to me, for real. I know what you really want, while you keep on pretending that I'm not what you need. Yo actions done already told me everything. You want us to be something, so don't fight it." He stated, swiping his thick, pink tongue across his lips. Catching my stare, Blaze smiled as he leaned towards me. I went to pull back, but he grabbed my chin. "Stop playing, man. Damn, so you not gon' kiss me, Peaches?"

"No, so stop trying, Blaze. And move yo hand off my ass." I tried to move his hand, but that only made him squeeze harder before he leaned down once more, catching my bottom lip between his teeth and pulling it into his mouth.

My neck stretched up and my tongue ran over his top lip as I fisted his shirt. Blaze tilted his head sideways as my tongue slipped into his mouth.

I have no fuckin' willpower whatsoever when it comes to this dude!

Just because I was kissing him didn't mean I was pretending I didn't like him.

Okay, I liked Blaze. I just didn't want a relationship with him, for the simple fact that the dude was fuckin crazy.

Blaze's hand slid under my shirt before slowly moving up my left side, cupping my breast.

"Peaches..." The voice trailed off and I quickly moved back from Blaze, looking over his shoulder.

249

"Sly?" Gotdamn! Did these niggas not know how to knock or make their selves known before walking into somebody's room?

"It's cool, I didn't know you had company." He said, glaring at Blaze before looking at me and shaking his head.

"Nigga, did you knock?" Blaze asked, turning towards Sly.

To my upmost surprise, Sly got smart. Hell, from the way he was acting in his office yesterday and on the phone, I thought he was scared of Blaze.

"Why the hell I need to knock for when I got a key?" Sly held up his key for Blaze to see. He then turned to me with a hard scowl on his face. "Peaches, you wrong as fuck. You wanna see where shit goes with me, but you're kissing this nigga. What type of shit is that?" He fussed at me.

Quickly pushing Blaze out my way, I jumped off the dresser. "Sly, it ain't even like that."

"Yes, the fuck it is! It's exactly like that, Peaches! Don't play me like I'm dumb when I know how you are. What is it like then, Peaches? Huh? What? You just let him taste you? Is that what it is?" Sly was pissed off. "Was she good, Blaze?" Sly went off as he glared from me to Blaze.

He had his fuckin' nerve to come in there, pissed and yelling at me after that shit he said over the phone.

"Sly, don't you try to turn this shit around on me, okay? You made your choice over the phone, so why are you even here?" I couldn't hide the attitude I had towards him. "I'm not trying to hide from King anymore. When I told you that, Sly, you snapped on me for doing so. When you've been nagging me to tell him all this time. But now it's suddenly complicated?" I fussed as my face contorted into a look of confusion.

"You threw the reason why I didn't want a relationship back in my face. You didn't even have the balls to stand up for what you wanted us to have." I pointed out to him. "You fell the fuck back because of a threat, if you did that so quickly it's obvious that I wasn't what you wanted to begin with. You made that obvious yesterday, then today. Sly, us being together was gone when you did that." I explained to him truthfully. "Even so, I still told King I liked you. And do you see my face? I got the shit slapped outda me and choked up. And for what? Only to have you snap at me for telling him?" I questioned in disbelief of his actions. "It's cool, though, there's no hard feelings on my part, I swear it's not." My lips pursed together, and my head shook at him in disappointment.

The look Sly gave me told me he didn't like what I said, and he was pissed.

"So, you're dropping me for this nigga, Peaches? After all these years, I fuck up once and you're done? One time? How many niggas have you been through since we been messing around? How many times have I complained?" He snapped at me.

No, he was not pulling that? He was trying to guilt me.

"You going there, Sly, really? We weren't together and you knew what it was when we started this thing. So, don't stand here and pretend like I'm the only person you've been with. Seven years without sex, Sly? I'm not a fool ass bitch, I'm not stupid. So, don't try to guilt me because it's not gon' work." I snapped at him. I was far from a gotdamn fool and I knew he was fuckin' someone that I didn't know about.

This man done lost his fuckin' mind.

"Nah, baby girl, you ain't the only thing Sly been hittin'. You a low as nigga for that bullshit right there. I told you at the party to step the fuck off, then at yo office. My man you got big fuckin' balls to come over to her crib, though." Blaze replied, pushing me behind him.

When he pulled up his jeans, I stepped in the middle of them. "Not in here you don't—" I started saying, but Blaze cut me off.

"You straight walked in here like I ain't told you shit?" Blaze snapped before looking down at me. "Why the fuck this nigga got a key?"

"Blaze, chill. He been had that key." I tried to explain, but it only enraged him more. His eyes slanted as he glared down at me before he shoved me out of his way. Blaze showed no warning as he rushed Sly. "*Blaze*! No! Stop!" I screamed at him.

Blaze's fist slammed into Sly's face, causing him to stumble back into the hallway. Sly didn't get a chance to react before Blaze rocked his ass again in the jaw. Sly wobbled then went down on one knee. Blaze foot came up and he booted him in the face with his Timbs. Sly fell on his back, causing a groan to leave his mouth. Even, though, Sly was down, Blaze didn't care. He didn't miss a beat as he lifted his foot and began to violently stomp Sly.

"Blaze!" I screamed.

Ignoring me, he glared down at Sly. "I told yo bitch ass to stay away from her, nigga. You thought I was playin'!" Blaze asked, kicking him once more across the face before he pulled his 9 from his jeans and cocked it back. Sly tried to lift up, but Blaze kicked his ass again. "Bitch ass nigga." He aimed the gun down at Sly. He shot him in his right leg, then the other.

"No! Blaze, what the fuck!" I screamed at him, but Blaze's psychotic ass wasn't paying me no attention. Blaze shot him remorselessly and as bad as I wanted to help Sly, I was kind of scared. A part of me was hesitant to move towards him.

Blaze pointed the gun at Sly once again and squeezed the trigger, sending a bullet in his right then left shoulder.

"Blaze, Oh, my God!" I gasped. When I tried to push past him to comfort Sly, his hand quickly shot out and he roughly pushed me into the wall.

"Peaches, if you try to help that nigga I'mma kill his bitch ass. Now, go get some towels and shit so he won't bleed out on the carpet."

"Are you fuckin' serious!" I yelled.

"Man, go get the damn towels, this nigga bleeding all over the carpet. Do you know how hard it's gon' be to get that shit out?" Blaze snapped.

I quickly ran to get some towels, but I had no plans to use them for the damn floor. That man was seriously fuckin' crazy! Now I saw the side of him folks were telling me about.

I returned back to the living room with an armful of towels. "Blaze, we have to get him to a hospital, or he'll bleed to death." I told him. My hands shook frantically as I tried to tie the towel around his leg.

"Blaze, are you fuckin' crazy, man! We have to get him to a hospital." I repeated anxiously.

"Fuck that! Let his ass drive himself to the hospital!" He exclaimed as he leaned against the wall with his arms crossed over his chest. "And didn't I tell you not to touch him. Let him do that shit himself."

My brows furrowed in confusion. *How did he expect him to do that exactly?* "Blaze, how can he do it himself." I snapped at him, but I really wanted to hear his response.

"He's a fuckin' doctor ain't he? That nigga can clean himself up." Blaze stated as if that was the simplest thing for Sly to do at that moment.

"Blaze, you fuckin' shot him! Oh, my God!" That nigga was fuckin' psycho! "I'm so sorry. I didn't think he would do this. I'll call the ambulance." I told him sincerely as I tried my best to stop his bleeding.

"No, the fuck you won't call no damn ambulance! Yo, clean this nigga up then put his ass out. He can drive his self to the fuckin' hospital." Blaze stupidly implied.

"Blaze, he can't drive! What the fuck?" I screamed at him. The more he talked, I found myself feeling stupid for even being attracted to his dumbass.

"Ah shit!" Sly groaned out in pain.

"I'm sorry." I tried to comfort him.

"The mothafucka drove over here, didn't he?" Blaze continued to rant.

Just as I felt him move to the side of me, we heard the front door open. I looked over in that direction.

"Peaches, what the fuck happened?" King asked, stopping in his tracks with Mike right behind him.

"Damn, what the fuck we miss?" Mike chimed in with a raised brow.

I let out a huge breath, relieved that my brother was here. "Blaze fuckin' shot him, he's fucking crazy. Get his ass out my shit. Now King!" My hand raised as I pointed towards Blaze.

"N'all, fuck that. Get his ass up out of here so we can go. A nigga hungry as fuck." Blaze said, leaning against the wall, rubbing his stomach as if he just didn't shoot Sly.

"Like for real, King, get yo boy out my place before I shoot his ass. I'm not playing, this was some stupid shit. I live in a fuckin' apartment! Nigga, this not a fuckin hood, you can't be shooting mothafuckas just because you feel like it! Who does this shit? Bye, Blaze." I snapped at him as I pointed towards the door.

"Why the fuck you getting mad for?" He asked the question like he was genuinely curious. "I told his ass already and that nigga didn't listen. So, this bullshit is his fault!" He snapped at me. "Sly ass knew what was up. And he tried to be on some slick shit and got his ass shot. His fuckin' fault, next time I'mma kill his ass. He know better." Blaze spat out, then turned his glare on Sly who looked like he was about to pass out. "So, keep playin', nigga you know me. Don't ever go behind my back again unless you got a death wish. And Peaches, stay yo ass away from him otherwise that's blood on yo hands." He finished saying with an uncaring shrug.

Once again, I found myself looking at him like he was crazy. "You don't tell me who I can and can't see. You know what? Stay the fuck away from me. King, get him to a hospital, I can't stay here." I needed to get as far away from Blaze as possible.

I grabbed my keys, purse and my broken phone, then walked to the table by the front door. I opened the drawer and got my Desert Eagle out. After checking the magazine, I slammed it back in place. I cocked the gun, putting a bullet in the chamber. A heavy breath left my mouth as I felt the stress of the morning building up.

A body brushed past me and my eyes slid towards the door only to find Blaze standing there. It wasn't until his lips twisted up into a smirk that I got pissed off again. It was at that moment I realized he had been the recent stress factor in my life.

"Blaze, stay the fuck away from me." My eyes slanted and I glared at him as hard as I could.

His smirk never left as he licked his lips. "Baby girl, what part of mine don't you get? Shorty, I ain't going nowhere and neither are you." He exclaimed.

A sickening ache started in the pit of my stomach because a part of me knew his words were true. And to know that pissed me off, causing my hand to grip the gun tight.

Seeing that, Blaze stood up straight with a mean mug on his face. "I wish the fuck you would." He said through clench teeth.

My teeth bit hard into my bottom lip as I tried to control the anger I was feeling. But I couldn't, I was just so mad. Who the hell did Blaze think he was? I had one King in my fuckin' life, I didn't need another.

His uncaring demeanor, pushed me to the edge and I snapped. "You stupid mothafucka!"

My hand shot out grabbing the front of his shirt. With a hard yank I pulled Blaze to me, with my gun gripped tight I hit him over the head with it.

Blaze's reaction was instant, before I could hit him a second time. His left hand shot out and locked around my wrist tightly, he twisted my wrist, causing me to drop the gun. Blaze right hand came to my throat and he jerked me to him, as he choked the shit out of me.

"What the fuck is wrong with you?" He yelled at me as his hand tightened around my neck.

"Let go of me!" I groaned as I tried to claw at his face. My feet left the ground as I was roughly picked up by my throat. The unexpected action caused a gasp to leave my mouth.

Blaze had yoked my ass up so quick, then slammed me into the wooden table by the front door, knocking the air from my lungs. He straddled my body and stared down at me, the look he was giving scared the shit out of me. "You gon' fuck around and make me hurt yo stupid ass!" He snapped at me.

"Nigga, you done lost yo fuckin' mind!" King's deep loud voice barked. Before Blaze could react, King had lifted his foot and violently booted him in the head, knocking him off of me.

King looked down at Blaze and tried to stomp him in the face, but Blaze grabbed his foot, then flipped him to the floor. His fist came up and he started to punch King in the face. "Boss, fuck you nigga." He spat out while throwing another blow to King's jaw.

Blaze went to hit him again, but King blocked the hit and pushed Blaze off of him. King jumped to his feet before Blaze could and kneed him in the face, his fist followed the blow with a two piece. One caught Blaze on the side of his head while he managed to dodge the other. He pushed King back than got up off the floor.

Blaze spat a wad of blood from his mouth, he then smiled at King. "Come on bitch." He beckoned him on.

This mothafucka was psychotic! "Would y'all fuckin' stop!" I yelled at them.

But King wasn't one to just walk away from a fight, he always had to run to it. Him and Blaze started throwing blows once again.

"Oh, my God! Stop!" I screamed at them, then looked at Mike. "Mike, stop them, please."

Mike shook his head at me. "Hell n'all, that ain't got shit to do with me." He said simply as he leaned against the wall and continued to watch them fight.

Pissed off with the whole situation. I jumped in the middle of them trying to break up the fight. As soon as I did, Blaze swung, his fist connected to my jaw, knocking me down.

"Oh hell n'all!" King snapped pissed off even more that I got hit. He slammed Blaze to the floor, he then grabbed his gun from his waist and started hitting Blaze over the head.

Mike came to me and helped me up off the floor, just as Blaze managed to knock King off of him. He grabbed the Desert Eagle I had dropped minutes prior to the fight.

Blaze aimed the gun at King.

"Fuck you gon' do with that, bitch?" King bit out as he too pointed his gun at Blaze.

"Y'all please stop! We have to take Sly to the hospital." I reminded them about Sly, but they didn't seem to care. "Y'all put the fuckin' guns down, please!" I pleaded with them.

Both of those mothafuckas were crazy as hell. Why wouldn't they just stop?

Those two crazy possessive mothafuckas were trying to take each other's heads off while Sly was laying just a few feet away from us, possibly dying. That mere thought scared me. But I also just wanted them to put their guns down. They were starting to scare the hell out of me.

"Stop!" I pleaded with them.

Blaze walked up to King. "Do what you gotda."

I saw King's hand tighten around the gun's handle and I had no doubt that he was about to squeeze the trigger.

"King, don't!" I screamed at him while grabbing his arm. King pushed me hard off of him, making me fall down.

Blaze eyes landed on me, and a murderous glare covered his facial expression.

"No!" I screamed at him.

POW!

To Be Continued...

A Dangerous Love 2: Can't Let Go
Available On Amazon

Made in the USA
Columbia, SC
14 December 2020

28044079R00146